The Ballad of Carson Creek
-Class of '61-

by
James Russell

For all the cool cats and kittens.

Chapter 1

"Toby, time to get up!" Elaine LaRue's voice bounced up the wooden stairway, through a solid oak door, and into Toby's consciousness with all of the softness of a fire alarm. He jerked to life.

"Unghmmm…" he groaned, squeezing his eyes shut against the golden glow that edged the thick linen curtains. He felt like a brick cemented in place.

"Toby!" Minutes passed.

Eventually, he began toying with the idea of actually getting up the first time his mother called, but then, siding with his weary inner voice, he rolled over in bed and covered his head with a heavy feather pillow. "Mmm…mm…m…" The soft cooing of a roof-perched mourning dove, drifting in through the open window, quickly lulled him back to sleep. He began dreaming that he was hearing faint footsteps ascend the wooden stairs outside his door.

"Up!" His mother said, poking her head in the room. Apparently, it hadn't been a dream. Her sea green eyes flashed in surprise. "Oh- Toby! This room looks like, like a…" She struggled to find an accurately descriptive noun. "Toby, it's an absolute atrocity!"

"Come on Mom-" Toby's muffled complaint was interrupted by the shrill ringing of his alarm clock. "Ahh, come on! It's Saturday!" he said, dragging the pillow off of his head. He tried to grab the clock, but accidentally knocked it behind his nightstand. "Son of a…"

"You watch your language." Elaine's eyebrow rose. "And get up. Today's a big day, remember?"

"I didn't get in 'till three this morning. Dean and me

were working on the-"

"I don't care, Toby. You are eighteen years of age. It's time you started acting like a responsible adult." Brilliant sunlight set the room aglow as she vigorously threw open the cream-colored linens. Coughing slightly at the cloud of dust they created, Elaine promptly set to work gathering dirty clothes that had been conveniently strewn all over the room. "You haven't worn this since last week…"

Toby fished the still-ringing clock out from behind the nightstand. His mother was already dressed and made-up, and he could hardly see straight enough to switch off the alarm.

"Oh, your father forgot his lunch again; I need you to drop it off on your way to the airport… what's this?" Elaine held up a glass bottle half filled with some sort of honey-colored liquid.

"Creamed soda."

She sniffed it. "*Cream* soda. Why is it in a Coca-Cola bottle? And you know you aren't supposed to have food in your room." She made her way toward the door with a load of dirty laundry on her arm. "Come on, your eggs are getting cold."

Toby let out a lungful of morning breath. "Alright…" He kicked the tangled sheets off and made his way across the sunlit room to a small corner chair, upon which rested a pile of neatly folded clothes. Rummaging through them yielded a plain white t-shirt and a pair of faded, grease-spotted blue jeans; the Toby LaRue Special. Donning these, he grabbed his pair of All-Stars, and, after blowing a kiss to Grace Kelly's wall-hung portrait, left his personal war zone behind.

The melodic sweetness of the Glenn Miller Orchestra, drifting lazily from the old family room Victrola below, accompanied his descent of the creaky wooden stairs. As he stepped into the rarely used dining area, he took a moment to revel in the heavenly balance of 'Moonlight Serenade' and the aroma of scrambled eggs and bacon. Unfortunately, this wondrous moment in time was short lived. It shattered when the voice of his twelve-year-old sister, Tracy, floated in from the kitchen.

"...don't know if Lindsey will be there or not, but I still don't think it's fair that Toby gets to end school earlier than me. They should make him go longer his last year, you know, like one to grow on. Why'd I ever start playing the stupid old flute in the first place? Anyway, the white one or the red one...?"

Blah, blah, blah. Pointless gabbing. If talking was an Olympic sport, Tracy would take gold, silver *and* bronze, Toby was sure of that. She never ran out of things to say, so he knew that something was amiss as he entered the small kitchen and her voice began to trail off. Her impish little face twisted into an amused smile. As the middle child, Toby didn't know which was worse: open pounding from his older brother, or Tracy's evil visage peering out from behind his mother's skirt. She stared on.

"What?" Toby asked impatiently.

"Oh, nothing," she sniveled, poking aimlessly at her eggs without looking down. Of the three children, Tracy was the only one who had inherited their father's dark features: russet colored hair and chocolate drop eyes, the latter of which now gleamed mischievously.

"Mother..." Toby said in a 'one-of-these-days' tone. Elaine pulled a sheet of steaming sugar cookies from the oven, and then turned and looked at Toby, using her thumb to brush a strand of dark blonde hair away from her eye.

"Your zipper is down sweetheart," she said impassively, turning back to the cookies.

Tracy let her laughter fly. "*Sweetheart*," she mimicked, batting her lashes, "your zipper's down *sweetheart.*" More giggles ensued.

Toby ignored her, and, squeezing between his mother and the small porcelain-topped table, passed out of the kitchen, through a short hallway, and into the tiny, sky-colored bathroom. He sat his shoes down and examined himself in the mirror. The face that stared back bore his father's strong jaw and sharp nose, but everything else was his mother; he had her eyes, her hair, even her ears. The only thing of hers that he didn't inherit, often to his chagrin, was her complete lack of facial hair. He scratched his lightly stubble-covered chin, and then began preparing his toothbrush for use. "What time do I have to be there again?" he asked, yelling back toward the kitchen.

"Where?" Elaine's voice answered.

"Uh air-ort." He spoke through a mouthful of foaming toothpaste. "Ut time does uh pwane wand?"

"Somewhere between ten-thirty and eleven. But make sure you're a little early."

Toby spit in the sink. "It'll take me almost an hour to get there." He rinsed his mouth out with a handful of water. "She's not going to be in some sort of disguise or anything, is she?"

"I talked to her on the phone last night. She said that she didn't think any word about her coming here had gotten out, but she wasn't taking any chances and will be wearing a white headscarf and sunglasses."

"Scarf and glasses…" Toby mumbled, applying a little dab of Brylcreem to his hair. After a quick, water-only shave, he shut the bathroom door.

"Hey, Mom?" Tracy's muffled voice came through.

"Yes, dear?"

"Do you think it'd be wrong to sell Aunt Shelly's autograph to all the kids at school for ten bucks apiece?"

Toby rolled his eyes. "Judas Priest…" he said quietly, putting up the toilet seat. He tried to unzip his pants. "Oh… right," he mumbled to himself.

"Tracy," Elaine softly chided, "It would be wrong to

sell them at any price. Your Aunt Shelly doesn't even charge for them."

"Yeah, well she doesn't have to. She's a *movie star*. I, on the other hand, could use a little pocket change… I should get *something* for being related to her!"

"Tracy," more harshly this time, "Ten dollars is hardly pocket change! Besides, you do get something: her as an aunt. And that's something that all of the 'pocket change' in the world couldn't buy. You know she loves all of you to death…"

With a flush of the toilet, Toby opened the door, shoes in hand, and made his way back through the hall to a plate piled high with steamy scrambled eggs. He began to inhale them. "Where's she going to crash?" he finally asked over a crunchy strip of bacon.

"She's staying at your Grandpa and Grandma Rainesburg's. Please don't talk with your mouth full." Elaine was bobbing a teabag around in a small china cup.

"Is she just coming for Toby's graduation?" Tracy asked, slightly disgusted.

"No, she's coming to see everyone, and because Monday is grandpa's birthday. Sixty-five, remember?" She took a sip.

"Sixty-five! Do people get so old?"

"Finish your breakfast dear." Elaine sat a large metal lunchbox on the table in front of Toby. "Your father was digging around in the barn this morning and never came back inside. Do you want to take my car?"

"*Your* car?" Toby remarked defensively, putting his fork down. "I'm taking my truck!"

"I… think your Aunt Shelly was expecting something a little less… conspicuous."

"Conspicuous?" Toby dabbed at his mouth with a napkin. "Well, they would never suspect that Shelly Rosegarner, Silver Screen Queen, would be riding around in a beat up, tricked out, '34 Ford pickup now would they?"

"I guess not," Elaine relinquished, "But is she in for a surprise."

"A pleasant one," Toby added.

"We'll see. Tracy has band practice at eight-thirty this morning. Then she has to help set up for the graduation ceremony."

Toby wiped his mouth again and glanced up at the wall clock. "Hey, that sounds like fun, Trace! I'm sure you'll have a super-duper time!"

Elaine cleared her throat. "If you could be so kind as to drop her off on your way."

"You should have done that twelve years ago; in a garbage dump somewhere…" He tossed the napkin on his empty plate. "Come on squirt, we wouldn't want you to be late for any extracurricular school activities, now would we?"

"I hate school! And I hate the stupid old flute!"

"Tracy!" Elaine scolded. "Go get your things."

"Arrggh… fine… I'll be right back," Tracy said with reluctance, standing up and disappearing into the dining room.

Toby scooted back and began to put on his shoes, Toby LaRue style: no unlacing or tying, just pushing and pulling until they finally slipped on; quite a feat in high-top Converse.

"I wish you wouldn't do that," Elaine said, rinsing her teacup out in the sink. "You ruin them that way."

Toby stole a hot cookie off of the tray while her back was turned, and then stood and grabbed his dad's lunch box. "Bye, Mom."

"Bye." Elaine turned and kissed him on his cheek, "Drive safe. Aunt Shelly said something about wanting to stop for a malt at The Strawberry on your way back, but remember, you have to be back here no later than two 'o clock; commencement starts at four, but they want you there an hour early, and we'll eat early too."

"Alright, see you later." Toby pulled his keys off the wooden key hanger by the door. "Come on, Tracy, or we'll sign you up for summer school!"

"I'm coming, I'm coming," Tracy said, reentering with an instrument case and a stack of sheet music under her arm. She gave Elaine a half-hug with her free hand. "Bye, Mom."

"Here." Elaine handed Tracy a cookie, "Your brother stole his. Have a good day, sweetie. Love you." She kissed Tracy on top of the head.

"You too."

Outside, the morning air was tinged with a crisp, cool sweetness. The wooden screen door creaked and slammed behind them, its echo bouncing between the large white house and matching block garage. As they crossed the dew-sprinkled lawn, Tracy, munching on her cookie, stopped to pet her Saint Bernard, Samantha. The massive mound of brown and white fur was tied to a large, shade-casting maple tree in the backyard.

"Be a good girl, Sam…" Tracy said, keeping her distance. However, with amazing speed for her size, Samantha changed from a cowering ground-hugger to a battering ram that sent Tracy and her loose-leaf sheet music all over the wet yard. "*Samantha!*" she yelled in dismay as the huge dog began a face-licking spree. Her arms flailed desperately, trying to keep the remainder of her cookie as far away from the dog as possible. "*Arrggh! Stop it!*"

Toby laughed as he continued on to the garage, briefly glancing out through the morning mist at the rolling, tree-dappled hills that surrounded the LaRue property. It was a beautiful morning. With that thought behind him, he threw open the bay door next to his mother's mirror-black station wagon. Inside sat his most precious possession: a battered 1934 Ford pickup that he had purchased and partially restored with two hundred of his own hard-earned dollars. He had transformed it from a flaking, faded old farm truck into the flat black and chrome hot rod that it now was. Of course, it still had a few nicks and dents and scratches, but that's what gave it so much more character, he always said. Stepping over a broken transmission, he climbed into the tiny, leather-lined cab and inserted a key into the ignition. He had not limited his modifications to the exterior alone. The un-muffled, definitely-not-stock engine rumbled to life like an irate lion. Thanks to him, this little truck was now capable of doing things that its designers had never dreamed of, especially in the speed and acceleration departments. He put it into reverse and eased its low-slung nose out of the garage. The gravel driveway crunched beneath the racing slicks that he had seen fit to wrap around the chrome rear wheels.

"Let's go Trace!" he yelled, getting out to shut the garage door. "Stop screwin' around with the dog!"

Elaine had come out to help Tracy pick up her flute music and now she walked over to the truck as Toby got back in. She coughed at the fumes wafting from the open headers. "Do you need anything special for later? I have to go into town in a little while."

A flustered Tracy finally clambered in next to Toby, sliding the lunchbox and her flute in between the two of them. Elaine shut the truck door for her.

"I'm running a little low on my Camels," Toby mumbled, avoiding her pitiless stare.

"I'm not buying you cigarettes," she said, squinting in the low shafting morning sunlight. "If you want to make yourself sick, then you'll have to do it with your own money."

"Then no, I don't." Toby revved the engine.

"Okay… I'll see you later."

"Bye," they said in chorus.

Toby let out the clutch and rolled onto Briggle Avenue, quickly picking up speed as he ran through the gears, and for sure waking up any still-sleeping neighbors.

The undulating, tree-shrouded road was paved with a very dry dirt and gravel mixture that sent a jet stream of dust out behind the truck, pinging in the fender wells and rendering the rear view mirror completely useless.

Tracy brushed the few remaining dewdrops off of her flute case. "Stupid dog. Are you taking Jenna with you?"

Toby switched on the radio; *'Runaround Sue'* filled the cab.

After listening for a while, Tracy asked again, "Are you?"

"Am I what?"

"Taking Jenna."

"Maybe I am, maybe I'm not. It's none of your beeswax."

Tracy laughed. "I knew it! You *are* taking her, and I'll bet you guys kiss all the way there and back! I bet you don't even come up for air! I'll bet-"

"I'll bet it'd take them a long time to find your hacked-up body way out here."

"Very funny. Ha, ha. Then you'd have to wash all the dishes by yourself."

Toby turned up the radio. He came to the end of Briggle and traded its potholed, paint-chipping surface for the smooth blacktop of Webber Road. Shady tree lines were replaced with fields of newly planted corn that rolled out for acres on either side of the hilly road.

"Do you really think we'll make it to the moon in nine years?" Tracy asked over the music. "Like President Kennedy said the other night?"

"Why don't you shut up for two seconds?"

"What do you think we'll find when we get there? I mean on the moon?"

"They'll probably find your real parents."

"Ha, ha… Wow! Look at that huge hawk over there!" Tracy exclaimed, pointing out Toby's window.

Toby searched the sky. "Where?… I don't see-" He heard a clatter come from Tracy's direction.

"Ha! Looky what I got!"

Toby turned to see his sister waving a pack of cigarettes in his face; the makeshift glove compartment, little more than a small toolbox welded sideways under the dash, hung open in front of her.

"Hey!"

"You lied to Mom! This pack is full!" She dangled it out the window, laughing all the while.

"Hey, give those back!"

"Oh look! We're coming up to the creek!"

"Trace, I swear- give me the goddamn cigarettes."

"Hmm… why don't you talk like that in front of Mom?"

"Why don't you give me the cigarettes or Mom will find out what happened to the *radio* in her *car…*"

Tracy stared straight ahead, taking into account this new inversion of upper hands. They passed the creek. Her eyes narrowed in defeat. "Fine…" Rolling her head, she slapped the pack into his hand.

"That's better."

The fields began to give way to houses, and soon the large brick forms of Carson Valley Middle and High School filled the windshield. Tracy grumbled to herself as Toby turned into the sparsely populated parking lot. He drove up to the front doors of the middle school and stopped.

"Have fun."

"Hardly anyone's here! It's too early!"

"But you need lots of extra practice, so get out."

She grabbed her flute and shoved the door open. "I'll get you for this…"

"So long, Trace; behave, get good grades, and maybe someday, far from now, you can graduate too. Now, off you go; remember- Monday's just around the corner!"

"Shut up," Tracy said, slamming the door.

"Bye, bye!"

Chapter 2

Toby waited for Tracy to disappear through the front doors before pulling away. He was elated that he would soon be completely free from the vile clutches of Carson Valley High School, and just to make sure that the few teachers who were mingling in the parking lot knew how he felt, he laid a long stretch of burning rubber as he pulled back onto Webber. The remainder of his trip into town would be much more pleasant without Tracy's childish, immature behavior, he thought, drawing a celebratory cigarette from the recently rescued pack and, steering with his knees, struck a match and brought it to the tip in cupped hands. When it lit, he flicked the match out the window. Smoking was not really as enjoyable to him as he led people to believe; this particular pack had sat untouched for nearly a week. He coughed slightly as the tobacco smoke burnt his tender throat, but continued to puff away regardless.

The countryside was soon rolling by at a comfortable seventy miles-per-hour and Toby was forced to turn the radio all the way up to hear over the cacophony of engine and wind. He tried to sing along with Frankie Lymon, but *'Goody, Goody'* wasn't quite so good when he pitched in. The song was soon finished, and the husky-voiced, fast-talking DJ began to read the weather report. Toby slowed so that he could hear more clearly.

"…Looks like we're going to have plenty of sunshine today, with a temperature high near seventy-five. And for all the farmers out there that have been praying for a little rain, tonight you're going to get your wish, and then some. Looks like we've a good chance that some possibly severe thundershowers may roll in late tonight 'round midnight, with a low near fifty-five. That's the weather; now it's time to play a little *'Peek-a-Boo'* with The Cadillacs…"

"Great…" Toby muttered at the mention of rain. That might put a damper on their racing tomorrow. He slowed the truck to a more legal speed as he passed into city limits, where his entrance was marked by a large white and silver sign reading: 'Welcome to Carson Creek, Ohio - A Nice Place To Live. Please Drive Safely!'

Soon he was rolling past houses, then small businesses. Carson Creek was a quaint little town; clean and pleasant were two words often spoken in conjunction with it, and, upon entering, you couldn't shake the uncanny sense that you were stepping into the past. Most of the residents were on a first name basis with each other, were friendly toward strangers, and would give you the shirt off of their back even if you didn't need it.

Toby downshifted as he came to a modestly sized, white block garage sitting on the corner of Webber and Main. 'A&L Automotive' was spelled out in thin metal letters above three gaping bay doors, through which could be seen several vehicles under repair. He pulled onto the asphalt lot and the truck coughed to a halt between his father's powder blue pickup and his best friend, Dean Krindle's, souped-up, lemon yellow '57 Chevy. Grabbing the lunchbox, Toby got out and made his way across the blacktop lot, shielding his eyes against the sun's glare on the brilliant white building. He flicked his spent cigarette away and walked through one of the big doors.

Inside, the spacious garage was relatively clean, save for a few dark puddles on the gray concrete floor. A perfume of automotive fluids filled his nostrils as he entered, married with the sound of a clicking ratchet.

"Hey…" he called out.

"Hey, Tobe," Dean Krindle answered from beneath a car. He continued to ratchet away until Toby heard a loud clang, followed by the clatter of a falling wrench. "*Ahh!* …goddamn it! Son of a…" Dean yelled through a clenched jaw.

"What? What happened?" Toby asked, now crouching down in search of his swearing friend.

"The frickin' ratchet slipped! Jammed my knuckles into the cross member!"

"Are you alright?" Toby peered under the car. Dean was on his back holding an oily rag to his bleeding fist. He rolled out from beneath the car and stood to his full six feet.

"Ahh…" he winced, gingerly pulling back the rag to reveal three split knuckles that resembled smashed strawberries. "I think I'll live. Just… get me a clean rag."

Toby walked over to a large steel workbench where he sat his father's lunchbox down and grabbed a relatively unstained, blue cotton rag. He balled it up and threw it across the garage to Dean, but it fluttered open and fell just short of Dean's grasping hand, right into a pan of fresh, glistening oil.

"What the hell'd you do that for?" Dean exclaimed, "Good luck finding another clean one!"

"So where's Dad and Ace?" Toby asked, ignoring his friend's complaint.

"Jeeze." Dean stooped to pick up another rag, still dirty, but cleaner than the other two. "Your dad's out front and Ace had to drive up to Mapleton."

"Yeah, I'm headed up that way."

"You picking up your aunt?"

"Yeah, but don't tell anyone, okay? I'd rather avoid a riot." Toby started to walk towards the front of the building. "What's Dad doing out there?"

"Writing up Mrs. Brecker's bill... probably with a huge discount."

Toby stopped with his hand on the knob-less door that separated the garage area from the sales counter. "Mrs. Brecker? Is she out there?"

"Yeah. Why?"

"My *Mother* told her that I'd help paint her garage and fence."

"And?"

"I'm waiting for her to die."

"What? Toby! Jeeze, the woman's like a hundred years old!"

"I know- it won't be long."

"How could you be like that?"

"I hate to paint!"

Dean just shook his head and slowly walked back to his work. "Oh, hey, I've got something I want to show you when you're done."

"Alright." Toby waited until he heard the front entrance bells jingle with Mrs. Brecker's exit, and then pushed the door open and made his way to the front counter, where his father stood scribbling something on a yellow pad of paper. A wooden cane lay on the desk beside him. "Hey, Dad?" Toby said softly.

Jack LaRue glanced up, or, since at five feet-eleven he was about three inches taller than Toby, merely averted his gaze from the notepad. A distant looking, almost vacant expression was presently registering on his lean, bearded face.

"Uh," Toby stuttered after a few moments of his father's characteristic silence. "I brought your lunch. It's on the blue workbench." His eyes scanned the small, mostly glass front room for a moment and eventually came to rest on the copper truck key he had been unconsciously flipping through his fingers. "I'm just on my way to pick up Aunt Shelly, and, uh, Mom wanted me to drop it off."

"Okay," Jack said, sounding congested. He took a drag from an ashtray-cradled cigarette, and then returned to his writing. Toby started to leave. "Toby…" Jack cleared his throat.

"Yes?"

"Mrs. Brecker is expecting you next Saturday."

Toby blinked, then sighed as he turned away, slowly bobbing his head up and down. "Alright…" He pushed back through the door and into the garage.

Dean had returned to his spot under the car, humming along with a battered, old, wall-hung radio that was about ten years overdue for the garbage can.

"Hey, Toby!" he yelled as Toby was about to exit through one of the garage doors. "I said I wanted you to see this." Once again, he rolled out from beneath the car, and then started walking towards the back of the garage. The soggy paper stick of a Dum-Dum pop protruded from his lips, bobbing up and down as he spoke. "Over here… come here." Toby sighed, followed, and soon joined Dean in front of a beautiful, black, highly polished dragster sitting atop a wood plank trailer. Its long, rocket-like body of glossy paint and its massive chrome engine glistened under the florescent shop lights. The name 'Jolly Roger' was painted on the side in white script beneath a red skull and crossbones.

"You washed it," Toby said flatly. "I gotta go."

"No, no wait…" Dean said, kicking the pieces of a broken cinder block aside as he moved towards the tiny, tire-flanked cockpit. "Look at that." He pointed to a metal pail full of coarse black sand sitting on the concrete floor.

"Where'd you get that?"

"Outta the frame! I was readjusting the seat like you said, and when I pulled the bolts out, that shit just started pouring out all over the place! It was all the way up to the motor mounts… Who knows how long you've been riding around with all that!" Dean ran his fingers through his thick, greased-back hair, shaking his head.

"Well, where the hell did it come from?!" Toby asked, eyes wide.

"Probably some jealous bastard who got tired of us winning all the time. Look at that! Try and pick it up! There must be close to twenty pounds there! Wait'll I tell Smoosh… And all this time I thought it was just your cheeseburger addiction slowing us down."

"Holy Moses…" Toby said, putting his hands in his pockets. "Who? Novello?"

"I don't know. But that'd be my guess… At least now that it's out though, we should start kicking kiester again. Oh, and I, uh… found this under the seat cushion." He reached through the roll cage and into the cockpit, pulling out a small, black and white portrait of a young woman. The once blank white border had been singed away, leaving a jagged brown line that encircled the girl's beautiful face. "Looks like Jenna went through the fire with you."

"The fire…" Toby felt his leg through his pocket. The surface skin was hard and tight; mostly scar tissue. Carefully, he took the photo. "But… Oh, yeah; this seat came out of the old dragster, didn't it? I lost this that day… I'd just taped in there…" He put the picture in his back pocket and coughed. "You know Cal told me that Peterson still can't get any grass to grow back. And no corn came in where the field caught on fire."

Dean snorted in amusement.

"Well, I'll see you later," Toby said, walking back towards the bay doors after one last glance at the bucket of sand.

"I'm gonna find out who did that… my way," Dean

said.

"Yeah, well don't say anything to anyone just yet, okay? Just play it cool. It's better for us if whoever did it doesn't know that we know, you know?"

"I know… Hey, you're still coming tonight, right? Even with your aunt here?"

"Yeah, I'll be there." Toby stepped into the bright sunlight.

Dean followed him, squinting. "I see you never cleaned out that scrape last night. Oh, don't forget the chips and dip. And I got the pool all heated, so bring your trunks. And Jenna can bring her, uh…" Dean made a funny shape with his fingers and winked.

"Yes, sir," Toby said with a mock salute, then turned away. "Take it easy."

"You sure you don't want a Band-Aid or something?"

"What?"

"Never mind." Dean threw a wave over his shoulder. "I'll see you later."

"Yeah, stay cool."

The last traces of morning mist had burned away as Toby drove across the lot and onto a moderately populated Main Street. Carson Creek was finally beginning to wake up. Several shop front windows were being graced with 'Now Open' signs as Toby rumbled past; his crisp, sunlit reflection joined the signs, jerkily dancing along from window to window. The truck's highly polished chrome rims were gleaming with brilliant flecks of mirrored sun. It was a happy morning, he thought, a perfect day for a short road trip, and a perfect day to graduate, though he would gladly do the latter during a hurricane, earthquake or typhoid epidemic if necessary.

Before long, he had passed through and out of the city limits, over another several miles of field-flanked road, and into Willowgrove, Carson Creek's northern neighbor on the maps. Willowgrove was generally looked upon as 'The Prettiest Little Town You Ever Did See.' It was larger than Carson Creek, but its residents were, for the most part, less hospitable, it being mainly an upper-class community. However, it did have a few bright spots in its populace, as Toby had come to find out.

Soon he was rolling through the lovely tree-lined streets of a high-class residential area. Every time he drove through here, he laughed mischievously to himself, imagining dainty old ladies or snobbish old men wondering what the devil was rattling the windows off of their houses. Sometimes he would catch one of them peeking out from behind a lacy curtain, face registering a faint or more often not-so-faint disgust. This was his statement, his expression, thundering past cars that cost more money than he'd ever made, past ancient Victorian-style homes half a block long, that someday his generation would rule the world, so 'ah, ah, ah!'- be nice.

His musings came to an end as he arrived at a large, olive green house with several red-leafed Japanese maples in the front yard. Fourteen-Twenty Pembrook Drive; the Gibson residence. Remembering that Jenna's ailing grandmother was staying with them, and since it had never worked anyway, he decided against blowing the horn. He shut off the truck. Before opening the door, he pulled the picture of Jenna from his back pocket and slid its singed edge under one of the gauge rims on the dash board, then got out and made his way up the cobblestone driveway, ascended the wraparound porch's sturdy white steps, and walked to the massive oak door, where he politely rang the buzzer. In a moment, wooden floor footsteps could be heard approaching from within. The door cracked open noiselessly.

"Oh, hello, Toby!" It was Sylvia, Jenna's mother.

"Hello, Mrs. Gibson."

"Come in, come in," she said, pulling the door open wider. "Jennalyn will be down shortly." Her accent and skin color proved her Brazilian birthplace.

"Thank you." Toby stepped into the huge, mostly hardwood foyer. A sizable staircase with maroon carpeted steps started its rise about ten feet from the door.

Sylvia shut the door behind him. "Make yourself at home." She gestured to a gold-colored, oak-legged loveseat to his right. "Can I get you anything?"

"No, no thanks. I'm alright." Toby wiped his feet on the doormat that he'd been standing on. He liked Sylvia. Her personality was very much akin to his own mother's, though her appearance was much more cosmopolitan. She reminded him of the First Lady.

"Well, I'll be in the kitchen if you need anything."

"Okay." He sat down on the loveseat.

She disappeared through a short hallway, footsteps echoing behind.

Toby leaned forward, resting his elbows on his knees and his chin on his fists. The heavy, yet familiar citrus smell of the Gibson house filled his nostrils. He was not a stranger to this wait. Jenna was his first and only girlfriend, and he'd been dating her for over two years now. Two wonderful years. With her at his side, he was the envy of every guy in school, not to mention a lot of guys long out of school. But while, at first, he had been attracted to her purely by her beauty, two years had shown him many different aspects of her person, and he had come to genuinely love the whole package. He didn't really know why she loved him back, but he was inexpressibly glad that she did. He wasn't even aware that he'd drifted off into sleep until a soft whisper breathed into his ear.

"Toby…?"

Toby's eyes fluttered open. "Hmm?" He inhaled sharply through his nose and turned to see Jenna's sky-hued eyes smiling at him. She could convey a complex feeling solely with her eyes better than anyone else he knew, and this one was a cross between amusement and mock offense.

"I've been sitting here for five minutes… What time did you go home last night?"

"Oh, uh… I didn't go home last night," he yawned, "I went home this morning." He yawned again, this time rubbing his eyes.

"Toby… you promised that you'd only be another hour. That was at ten."

"I know…"

Jenna stood. She was tall for a girl of seventeen going on twenty-five: about five-foot-five. "How are you going to stay awake for your graduation this afternoon?"

"I'll manage…hopefully. That a new dress?"

"I told Callie you'd notice." She flashed him a pearly white smile that contrasted against her lightly tanned, part Brazilian skin. "But, actually, no; it's a skirt." She pulled at the lace-edged hem.

"Oh, sorry." Yawn.

She stretched out her hand. "I don't expect a boy to know the difference between a dress and a skirt, but I do expect him to be awake when he comes to pick me up."

Toby took her hand and stood up, embracing her. "Sorry…" He kissed her on the cheek, catching the scent of lilacs on her long, chestnut-colored hair.

"That's what you said last time."

"Sorry." He was about to kiss her on the lips, but she put her hands on his chest and ever so lightly pushed him back.

"We'd better get going," she said, looking away. "I'll be out in a minute; let me say 'bye to Mom."

"Alright…"

She walked off towards the kitchen, leaving Toby standing alone, wondering for a moment about her slight, yet sudden, change in behavior. He forgot about it when he heard a sound on the steps - Jenna's equally beautiful, but not identical, twin sister, Callie.

"Hello, Callabria," he said with a smile.

"Hello, Tobias," she answered coolly, not slowing her stride. She began walking towards the kitchen as well.

"Just 'hello'? No kiss?" he asked with his arms spread wide.

"Drop dead," she said without looking back.

"Well, everyone's so loving today!" he exclaimed, turning to let himself out. Halfway back to the truck, Jenna followed him out of the house, a light sweater and a purse slung over her arm. He went to the passenger door and opened it for her. "Vere to, Fraulein Gibson?" he asked in his best nazi soldier voice as she slipped in.

"To ze zeppelin field, Fritz."

"Ya mein general!" Toby said, clicking his heels.

Chapter 3

"And avay ve go," Toby muttered, shoving the tall floor shifter into first gear after backing out of the Gibson's driveway.

"I thought you'd be driving your mom's car," Jenna said. She patted the eight-inch patch of bare seat between them. "Where do you plan on putting your aunt?"

"You can sit on my lap," Toby said matter-of-factly.

"Uh-huh… Why didn't you drive something that more than one-and-a-half people could fit in?"

"Look, there'll be plenty of room, alright? She can put her stuff in the back."

"I'm not talking about her luggage, Toby; I'm talking about her body."

"You and everyone else…"

"Well?"

"Crash awhile, alright? Everything'll be juuust fine."

She smiled and cocked her shaking head towards him, "Toby, Toby, Toby…"

"What?" His palms remained on the steering wheel, but his fingers flared out slightly in a show of innocent ignorance.

Jenna held his gaze for a moment, and then turned away with a weary smile. "Nothing." She began to rummage through her small purse.

"What'd your dad say about tonight?"

"You mean Dean's party? Dang it…" Jenna tucked a straying lock of hair behind her ear and began removing things from her purse one by one.

"Yeah. What's wrong?"

"I still haven't found my keys. I've looked everywhere… mint?" She held up a cellophane-wrapped starburst mint.

"Do I need one?"

"My house keys, car keys… the keys to the store; God help me if dad finds out that I lost *those*."

Toby slid his left hand to twelve 'o clock on the steering wheel while the right one worked in conjunction with his teeth to twist open the mint. "I'm surprised he hasn't found out already." He spit a small bit of cellophane out the window.

"Callie and I've been sharing hers. I might just have to go downtown to Fleischer's and have- *Toby!*"

"What?!" He jolted to attention.

"What on Earth did you do to your arm?"

"Huh?" Toby began a slightly alarmed examination of his upper limbs.

"Your left one; right there." Jenna pointed to a ragged-looking, purple-black scab about the size of an egg that marred Toby's forearm just above the elbow. A quick glance established that it had not yet been cleaned- a generous amount of what appeared to be axle grease had worked itself into the semi-raw abrasion.

"Holy-… I don't know…!" He twisted his arm for a better look. "I wonder if… no, I don't, uh… know…"

"Watch where you're going!"

Toby looked up just in time to avoid a mailbox with a casual swerve. "Looks like burnt hamburger…"

"It certainly needs dressed."

"What?"

"Cleaned."

"Right. Uh, well, we need gas anyway… I was just going to stop at- right there…" He nodded towards a Shell station that was slipping by to join the quivering rearview landscape, "But I'll just swing by the strip. I'm sure Willie's got a first aid kit."

"Will he be there this early on a Saturday?"

"Oh yeah, he'll be there bright and early after that mess the Royce-Magnum car made all over the track last night… damn it… now it's starting to sting."

They continued on their northward course through Willowgrove, soon coming to a bustling downtown square, where diagonally parked cars and package-wielding pedestrians kept the Ford's clutch from getting cold. A ruby traffic light brought them to a halt between the courthouse and a long line of swanky department stores.

"It looks like Dad's busy this morning," Jenna said, eyes fixed on the gilded facade of Gibson's Fine Fashions. "I wonder if Claire's working today."

"Well, it's a bummer we don't have time to stop and find out. Darn, I was looking forward to seeing your old man."

"I'm sure the feeling was mutual."

Toby was having a difficult time finding a comfortable spot to rest his arm. "Ahh… why'd you have to go and tell me my arm was about ready to fall off?"

The light turned green and they eased onward.

"So, why were you out so late last night?" Jenna asked.

"Me and Dean were putting a new manifold on the dragster."

"Oh… does that take a long time?"

"Well, it does after about two-thirty when your brain starts to crash. I don't know what time Dean went home; he wouldn't tell me."

"He probably slept there."

"Do you blame him? Jeeze, I wouldn't want to see my parents either if all they ever did was plan my future and think of new and exciting ways to spoon feed me."

"Yes, but on the other hand, they probably paid for half of the dragster, if not more."

"A few sweet grapes…"

Before long, they had passed through downtown Willowgrove, overtaken several more blocks of high class living, and were rolling along on yet another dusty road bordered by various types of field vegetation. The sun, now in full shine, was casting a blinding glare across the chrome-trimmed windshield.

"Dang, I should have brought my shades," Toby said, squinting.

"I don't think mine would fit you." Jenna pulled a pair of black sunglasses from her purse and slid them on.

"Oh, trying to say I've got a big head, huh?"

Jenna laughed. "*Trying* to say? Did I stutter?"

They crested a hill and the shiny black line of Blossom County Dragway spread out before them. The fielded area directly around the drag strip was fairly flat, save for a few trees, a pair of ten-foot bleachers, an undersized announcer's booth on stilts, and a small red and yellow filling station marked by a pole-topped sign that read: *B.C.D. Racing Fluids*.

Toby hung a left and pulled onto the dusty lot after passing through an open gate in the freshly planted chain link parameter fence. The only other vehicle in sight, a rusty old Chevy pick-up, sat beside the station. A figure rose behind the grimy windows of the building as Toby stopped next to one of the two gas pumps, both of which sat in a square of shade cast by a dilapidated tin awning. He killed the engine.

"Well, hey!" A voice rumbled from the station. Toby turned to see a burly Negro in his mid-fifties standing in the doorway, displaying the biggest gap-toothed smile he'd ever known.

"Hay's for horses, Willie," Toby quipped with a smile, getting out of the truck.

"Well, if it ain't the Cool Cat hisself." Willie laughed as he wiped his hands on the front of his grease stained, hole-worn coveralls. An equally well-kept Cleveland Indians cap sat skewered on his head. He walked toward them with a slight limp. "An' it looks like he brought his little kitten with 'im." He bent down and fluttered a massive hand at Jenna through the open truck door.

"Hi, Mr. Crissman." She waved back.

"*Mista* Crissman?" Willie exclaimed. "Honey, you makin' me soun' like a old man! My poppa named me 'Willie' fo' a reason: so's I be a chile foreva."

"Do you have a first aid kit Mr. *Willie* Crissman?" Toby asked.

"Uh-huh, yessuh; in a case of emergency, *Mista* Toby LaRue."

"Well, I've been wounded." Toby held up his arm.

"Well, well…" Willie examined the large scrape for a moment then leaned down to flash Jenna another jack 'o lantern smile. "You been bitin' him agin?"

"Don't ever let a Gibson girl give you a hickey, Willie," Toby said with an arched brow, "They'll suck out all your blood and sell it in their dad's store for ten percent over retail."

"What?" Jenna chirped.

"Well, I don't suspect I'll evah face the situation, long as they kin control they flutterin' hearts roun' me, handsome as I is." Willie snapped his coverall straps.

"You know you're the keenest cat around, Willie. Don't rub it in."

"Heh, heh. Well, come on; I'll patch you up." Willie turned and ambled toward the building. "How'd you do it?"

"Uh… I don't know. I'll be right back, Jenna," Toby said, slamming the door shut.

"You best bring 'er along, so's she kin hold yo' hand."

"I'll be right back," he repeated.

The small interior of B.C.D. Racing Fluids was only slightly cleaner then the exterior. The wall to the left of the doorway was covered with a modest inventory of shelf-cradled automotive fluids. Metal fuel cans of all shapes and sizes littered the floor, and the right side of the building was occupied by a distressed looking teacher's desk, behind which Willie was easing into a creaky wooden chair.

"Well, let's see…" One of the desk drawers squeaked open and after a moment of rustling, Willie produced a small, metal Red Cross kit. He unlatched it and pulled out some handkerchiefs and a bottle of rubbing alcohol. "All outa peroxide."

"Oh, Willie…" Toby moaned in dread.

Willie slapped the battle scarred desktop. "Park it, boy."

Toby eased into a half sitting-half standing position as Willie unscrewed the cap and tipped the bottle over into one of the hankies. A strong antiseptic odor filled the room. When satisfied with the amount of saturation, Willie gripped Toby's arm and pulled it closer.

"You won't feel a thing…" He grinned.

"Oh, God…" Toby prayed in a quivering voice. He just about put a human-sized skylight in the roof as the alcohol-soaked cloth was eased onto the gaping abrasion. A loud hiss escaped through his gritted teeth.

"Hol' still, boy…"

Toby pulled futilely against Willie's clamp-like grip. The hankie was soon sporting black spots as the alcohol cleaned the grease away.

"What in the worl' was you tryin' to do, oil it off?"

"I didn't even see it… *ahh!*… Jenna did. Must've done it last night or- *ahh!* Jesus, Willie! Why don't you just amputate?"

"Aww… You want me to call yo' momma?" Willie wiped away the last of the dirt, revealing that the scrape wasn't quite as bad as it had first looked, and then he pulled a long scrap of white gauze from the kit. "Don't really need this, but I 'spect it'll make you a good conversation piece," he said as he wound it around Toby's arm and tied it in place. "There, gooder'n new."

"Yeah, thanks." Toby loosened the bandage slightly. "You'd better check and make sure there's no more. I don't know how I do that; it happens all the time. Just the other day-" Toby was interrupted by the sound of pinging gravel that floated in through the open door. He watched through the grimy windows as a car pulled up next to his truck. Occupied only by a young male driver, it was an immaculate '60 Chevrolet Impala convertible dressed in white with aquamarine accents.

"Oh, just great…" Toby growled.

"I think I jes' gonna set in here; he ain't come for gas."

"Yeah…" Toby stood and exited the building. "Thanks again, Willie," he said before passing through the doorway.

"Yup."

Toby's black Converse kicked up clouds of dust as he made his way across the small lot, sandy hair fluttering in a light breeze. He hopped into the truck in silence.

"No, I don't think so, Stuart." Jenna was speaking through the open window to the young man sitting in the convertible. He was clean cut, had slicked, curly black hair, and was vigorously puffing on a cigarette.

"Ahh, come on Jen… celebrate in style. It's going to be a real cherry bash." He pulled the cigarette from his mouth. "There's no one else I'd rather spend the evening with…"

"No, Stuart. I already have plans."

"What, with candyass here? Come on, Jenny, you're worth more."

The truck rumbled to life. Toby hated Stuart Novello almost as much as he hated school, heavy labor and the flu, maybe even more.

"What's the matter LaRue?" Stuart spoke over the engine. "In a hurry to be somewhere?"

"Yeah, your funeral. Flake off, Novello, will ya?"

"No, actually I was just telling Jenna here about the superbitchin' grad party I'm throwing tonight for all my friends. Too bad you're not one of them."

"Yeah, well, go tell the mayor, ditz. Or is he too busy cheating on your mom?" Toby produced a cigarette of his own and lit it.

Stuart's face reddened slightly.

"Hey, I heard you're going to Harvard or somewhere." Toby blew out a puff of smoke. "That's great. It ought to be a real lesson in humility."

"Why?" Stuart tried to sound cool, but his inner hatred caused his voice to waver.

"'Cause when you get there, you're just gonna be a little punk from the sticks. No one to boss around, no one to protect you. You really think they're gonna give a rat's ass who you are? Gimme a break." He put the truck in gear and began to inch away.

"Go to hell, LaRue!"

"Ladies first." Toby punched the gas and left Stuart Novello to spit out the plume of dust that rose from the spinning rear wheels.

Toby's eyes danced back and forth between the road and the rapidly disappearing reflection in the rearview mirror.

"Toby…" Jenna chided.

He remained silent.

"Just be careful… remember what happened to Don Hauldman? They never proved it, but I know what-"

A smile crossed Toby's face and he slammed on the brakes, bringing the truck to a screeching, jolting halt that left them sideways in the center of the road, at the head of two long trails of hot rubber.

"What in the world are you doing?!" Jenna shouted, one hand on the dashboard and the other brushing her hair out of her eyes. "Toby!"

He maneuvered the truck around and started back towards the filling station. "I didn't get any gas."

Jenna readjusted the sunglasses that had slipped down her nose. She still looked stunned. "Forgetting gas is no reason to do that!"

"I didn't forget the gas."

"What?"

"I couldn't let a golden opportunity like that just slip away! It was perfect… you should have seen his face when he pulled out!" They reached the gate and pulled through again. "And I wasn't about to sit here and chat with him either."

"Well, could you at least warn me next time?"

Toby drove to the exact spot that he had just vacated a minute ago and shut the truck off. "You'll just have to wait and see… hey, Willie!"

Willie emerged from the station with an even bigger smile than the first time. "Ha, ha! Boy, you never hea' cussin' like that agin! Not in the best bar in town!"

"Did you like that?"

"Sonny, you jes' made my day!"

"Mine too…" Jenna pitched in.

"Fill 'er up, Willie." Toby leaned forward and pulled out his wallet. "With your special recipe…"

"Yessuh!" Willie removed the gas cap and stuck the fuel hose in, then began cranking the pump. "How low is she?"

"'Bout an eighth left."

Willie continued to crank for a few minutes, then hung the hose up and disappeared into the station. He returned a moment later with a galvanized steel fuel can in his arms. "Boy, you betta' put that cigarette out…" After emptying the can's contents into the tank, he screwed the cap back on and patted the side of the truck. "Ahh… jes' what the docta ordered…"

"Thanks, Willie."

"Yup. That'll be…" Willie leaned back to read the pump, then muttered to himself, mentally adding up the price, "…hmm… 'bout four-eighty."

Toby handed him a five-dollar bill. "Perfect. Give me a couple'a Cokes too."

"Comin' right up…" Willie limped over to a weathered Coca-Cola chest that sat in front of the building, pulled out two frosty bottles, then shuffled back.

"Thanks," Toby said, taking one and giving one to Jenna. He fired up the engine. "I'll see you around. Maybe later."

"Okie-doke." Willie waved goodbye.

Chapter 4

Toby pried the Coke top off using his own personal, dash-mounted bottle opener. Jenna, slowly recovering from her boyfriend's brake pedal antics, did likewise. The twisted metal caps clattered to the floor.

"Mmm…" Toby held the bottle up after taking a sip. "Slushy."

Jenna wiped the condensation off of hers. "Thank you."

"Well, I guess you're worth ten cents."

"You sure?"

"Hmm… maybe nine. But I'll give you a chance to make up the difference." He tapped his cheek. When Jenna didn't respond, he leaned towards her. "Come on, pay up."

She gave him a quick kiss. "There, happy?"

Toby shifted the truck into a non-factory fourth gear. "Happi*er*." He put his arm around her. After taking another drink, Jenna removed her sunglasses and eased her head onto his shoulder.

"So my kisses are only worth a penny?"

"Jenna, if you charged me a penny a kiss, I'd be living in a debtor's cell."

They rode in silence for several miles, just enjoying each other's presence, the fresh country air whipping through the truck cab.

"What on Earth did you do to my picture?" Jenna broke the silence, pointing to the singed portrait hanging on the dash.

"Dean found that in the dragster, under the seat. You went through the fire with me, and you didn't even know it. Doesn't that make you feel special?"

"Oh… No, it doesn't. What time does your aunt's plane land?"

"Uh, ten-thirty or eleven. What time is it?"

She glanced at her tiny wristwatch. "Ten-fourteen. You'd better speed up."

"Speed up?"

"Mmm-hmm."

"Sweetheart, you just said the magic words." Toby handed her his Coke and brought the truck to a complete stop in the middle of the deserted road.

"Okay, maybe we're not understanding each other's definition of 'speed up'…" Jenna said, sitting up straight, as the fumes of Willie's 'special recipe' began to filter into the warm cab.

"Final round eliminations…" Toby began in a storyteller's voice, revving the engine, "…on a steamy summer afternoon."

"Toby…"

"Sitting in the opposite lane: scum of the earth, Stuart Novello. I roll onto the strip and the crowd goes wild. *'Toby, Toby!'*" he imitated the cheers in a hushed tone. With an earsplitting roar of the engine, the entire truck began to shudder as the rear wheels spun out a steady cloud of billowy, cotton-like smoke that floated past them on a stern-ward breeze. The noise slowly receded and the truck lurched forward a few yards. The sweet aroma of burning rubber washed over them.

"Toby!" Jenna was clinging to the window sill.

Toby continued his impromptu narrative. "More cheers: *'Yay Toby! Boo on Novello!… Novello's a bottle of piss!'* We both roll to the line, signal the flagger that we're ready, he lowers the green flag, and-" The engine again revved to several decibels above what most would call deafness-inducing, and then Toby popped the clutch. Newton's 'equal and opposite reaction' ground them into the leather bench seat as the truck nosed into the air and took off like a rifle bullet. The shifter made short work of the first three gears while the orange speedometer needle climbed past eighty-five.

"Toby!"

"Woo-hoo! Wake me up when we get there!" They passed the one hundred mile per hour mark. Out the window, tall roadside weeds had dissolved into nothing but a greenish yellow blur.

"Toby, slow down!"

"Novello disappears in a blue ball of fire! His head has exploded!"

Jenna was clutching her stomach. "Toby, *please!*"

Toby glanced over at her and his beaming smile faded when he noticed that her eyes were beginning to well up. He immediately let off the gas. The speed needle fell rapidly.

"Hey…" He reached for her hand, but she pulled it away. "Take it easy… I'm just playing around." After backfiring, the truck's engine slowly returned to its normal cackling purr.

Jenna turned toward him. A tiny tear had forged a trail down her cheek. "Toby, all you ever think about is yourself." A small sniffle escaped. "Please stop," she whispered.

"Alright… just, just take it easy."

"Please…" She was still holding her stomach.

"Are you gonna be alright? You're not gonna be sick in here or anything are you?"

Her shoulders slumped and she wiped the tear stream off of her cheek. Then, hesitantly placing her hand in his, she said slowly, "Toby, I… I'm sorry, yes… no, I'll be fine."

The remainder of the trip consisted of an obeyed speed limit and unreserved silence. Toby hated it when he made Jenna mad or angry or hurt. It seemed like he was always apologizing for something that could easily have been

avoided had he thought through what he was doing before
he actually did it. Other times, like now, he thought Jenna
was just being too sensitive. He sighed out loud. The dusty
country road made its dead end on a bustling four lane
highway that they rode all the way into Mapleton, one of
Blossom County's largest cities. After successfully
navigating through its convoluted maze of buildings, one
way streets, and what seemed to be an inordinate amount
of Greyhound buses, they passed out of the city, their
proximity to the airport confirmed when a DC-8 passenger
plane rumbled over their heads at an altitude of about
seventy five feet. About a mile later, they finally reached a
large blue sign that read 'Mapleton Regional Airport'.
Toby made a right turn into the complex.

"I think we're here." he said, finally breaking the
unusually weighty silence. The parking lot they pulled
onto was a vast expanse of steamy asphalt and dozens of
sun-catching vehicles. They were separated from the two
runways by a large white terminal and a chain link fence
that was beginning to rust near the ground. Behind the
fence sat several planes, each one a different size, shape,
and color than the rest.

Jenna cleared her throat. "What airline was she flying?"

"Uh, I don't know." Toby found an empty parking spot
near the entrance of the terminal and with a jingle of the
keys the truck's engine coughed to its death. "Let's go find
out together." Both doors creaked as they opened and shut.

After throwing their empty Coke bottles in the bed of
the truck, Toby and Jenna crossed the parking lot to the
all-glass terminal entry arm in arm, stopping briefly so
that Toby could rescue an orphaned penny from the
ground. "Dang it… tails." He slipped it into his jeans
pocket, and then pulled the door open for Jenna. "After
you, Madame."

"Mademoiselle," she corrected.

Toby followed behind her. "Okay, so Spanish wasn't my goodest class…" The airy, sunlit desk area opened up before them after they had passed through the entryway. Inside, the crowd count was considerably below capacity and Toby was able to catch an idle airport attendant immediately.

"Uh, excuse me Ma'am, could you tell me what gate the morning flight from Burbank will disembark at?"

"Let me see… B Gate, but the plane unloaded fifteen minutes ago."

"Oh…" Toby glanced at a wall clock behind her; it read ten-fifty-five. "Thanks." He and Jenna turned and entered a corridor that was marked with an arrowed 'B'.

"Will she be upset?" Jenna asked.

"Nah, she'll be so glad to see my gorgeous mug, she won't have time to be mad," Toby hoped.

They followed the hall until it emptied into a spacious gate room filled with vacant chairs. Mostly vacant. In a corner by the window, half hidden by a potted palm tree, an elegant-looking, well-dressed woman in her early thirties sat perched on one of the blue vinyl seats, surrounded by three large, alligator skin suitcases. A sheer white scarf was tied around her slender neck and an expensive-looking pair of black sunglasses rested on her forehead. Gazing wistfully out the window, her graceful features set aglow by a soft, indirect sunbeam, she was the single most beautiful woman Toby had ever seen. It was easy to see how she was so often compared to his imaginary sweetheart, Grace Kelly. She was flawless. He slipped up beside her in silence.

"Pardon me, madam, but you're stopping traffic."

The woman turned in surprise, and then a gleaming smile spread across her face. "Toby!" She stood and embraced him, speaking with the soft, slightly English accent that she had acquired in theatrical school.

"Hello, Mrs. *Rosegarner*." He whispered her last name, the one Paramount had assigned her when she landed her first major role, and then melodramatically looked around to make sure that no one heard him.

"Shh…" She put a finger to her still-smiling lips.

Toby stepped aside. "Aunt Shelly, you remember Jennalyn."

"Yes, yes how are you?" Shelly's white-gloved hands reached for Jenna's.

"Fine, thank you. It's nice to see you again."

"It's so nice to see the both of you." She stood back and looked them over. "I was beginning to wonder if you had forgotten about me. And what's this?" She stroked Toby's somewhat shaggy sideburns.

"Well… I'm going for the rugged mountaineer look."

"And this?" She asked, pointing to his bandaged arm.

"Don't miss a thing, do you? Come on, I'll carry as many of your bags as I can." He moved to pick up the closest suitcase.

"Oh, no, I can get that one. Could you take those two?"

"Sure…" He pulled on the handles and grunted, "Jeeze! When did you start selling anvils?" With a slight struggle, they lifted off of the floor. "This it?"

"No, no… um, Jennalyn, could you take these?" She produced two previously unseen handbags. "I'm sorry."

"You building a house?" Toby jibed.

"Sure, it's no problem." Jenna took the bags.

Shelly picked up the last suitcase. "There," she breathed a sigh, "I think we're ready."

After successfully navigating back through the airport corridors, with a brief stop at the restrooms, they reached the exit and Toby backed up against one of the glass doors, pushing it open for the two ladies.

"Thank you, kind sir," Shelly said, but as soon as she walked into the sun, her squinting green eyes locked onto Toby's truck. "I, um…" She cleared her throat and slid her sunglasses into place. "I was happy to hear that you were the one coming to pick me up."

Toby was sure that behind those large, dark glasses he was receiving his second raised eyebrow of the day. "Well, I guess they heard I was pretty good at picking up chicks."

"At least he was awake when he came to get you, Mrs. Rosegarner," Jenna said.

"Oh, please call me Shelly. Why?"

"Jenna, come on, I was just… leak-testing my eyelids."

"I think he needs his eight 'o clock bedtime reinstated."

Jenna was the first to reach the truck. "Maybe then he'd actually sleep at night. Can these go in the back?" She held up the handbags.

Toby glared at her. "*You* can go in the back." He lifted the travel cases into the truck bed.

"Yes they'll all be fine back here… although I don't think that we really have much of a choice. You don't have a blanket or something to put down…?" Shelly sat the last suitcase next to the other two.

"For what, a picnic? The gators are dead, Aunt Shelly." Toby walked to the passenger's side door and opened it. "Pile in!"

"How?" Jenna asked, getting in first.

"Ha, ha."

"Was something wrong with your mother's car?" Shelly asked as she slid in next to Jenna.

"Yeah, it's my mother's car." Toby slammed the door shut behind her and walked around to the driver's side. "And it was made for her. The thing's a frickin' automatic. Automatics are for deaf people." He squeezed in behind the wheel. "Cozy, huh?"

"Yeah," Jenna said, "this would be really great if it was

December. Ow! You're jabbing me with your elbow…"

"Sorry."

"Toby, did you, um… ouch, I *was* happy that you were the one picking me up," Shelly said, twisting to coax the most comfort possible out of her tiny allotment of leather seat.

Toby started the engine. "Hey, Jenna, you've gotta get your feet away from the gas pedal. And either put your legs on that side of the stick or you'll have to shift for me."

"I'll shift. There's no room for my legs over here."

"Well, if they weren't so damn long…"

"Toby!" Shelly exclaimed.

"What?"

"Oh, don't be fooled, Mrs… Shelly. He loves long legs… I think he'd rather date a burn victim than a short girl."

"Yes, I'm *deeply* shallow. First gear, sweetie pie."

Jenna shoved the shifter forward, and with a slight grinding of the transmission, they pulled away from the parking spot.

"I think there's something wrong with your engine, Toby," Shelly said.

"What makes you say that?"

"Because I can barely hear myself think over the sound of it."

"Oh, don't worry… You get used to it. After a while your ears go numb and then you can't hear anything."

"Wonderful…"

Toby let out a huge yawn. "Ahh… I'm ready for bed," he groaned, resting his head against the door as they left the airport parking lot and began retracing their course. The breeze that flowed in through the open windows was becoming more turbulent with their acceleration, and to Toby, its sweet coolness was refreshing.

Shelly didn't have quite the same feeling. Her once neatly styled, honey blonde hair was being whipped about like a tornado-engulfed windsock. She struggled to roll the window up. "So, um… excited about graduating, Toby?" The draft subsided slightly as the window squeaked shut.

"I don't know… I might miss all those really neat tests and quizzes and french-fried bean burritos and stuff."

"I remember the night that I graduated…" Shelly said in a quiet, somewhat wistful tone. She drew out a pack of Chesterfields and put one of the long, thin cigarettes to rest between her cherry lips. "Don't ever start smoking," she said, rummaging through her purse.

"Need a light?" Toby pulled a book of matches out of his pocket.

"Toby…" She tore out a match and struck it to the cigarette in cupped hands "Please tell me that these are only for setting off fireworks."

"Okay…" He took the book back. "They're only for setting off fireworks."

"Do you have any idea what this does to you?" She inhaled, and then held the cigarette on display, a blue ribbon of smoke slithering off of its tip.

"What are you talking about?"

"Just last week my doctor was telling me about some new studies that are coming out. They're linking prolonged smoking with lung cancer."

"Hmm. So, uh, how's Uncle Jim and everybody?" Toby asked, changing the subject.

Shelly put the cigarette back in her mouth. "Zasu and Sookie are doing well."

"Wow, I haven't seen them since they were puppies. They didn't hardly even have spots then. And Mom said you bought a new house in Malibu."

"Yes," Shelly said, nodding slowly. "I go there to be- to get away from everything. It's beautiful, Toby. I'll have to send you some pictures. How is everyone here?"

"Oh you know The Creek, nothing ever changes. Had one hell of a storm a few weeks ago; tornado touched down in Mainer's field; our basement flooded."

"Yes, your mother told me about that."

"You should'a seen it. What a mess."

"How's your brother?"

"Alright, I guess. He and Gwen bought the house across the street from Grandpa Dale. Tizzy Ralston's old place on Clelland, remember? He's still driving ambulance; mostly nights."

"And Tracy?"

"I think Satan's still looking for her replacement."

"Oh, come now, Toby. She can't be all that bad."

"Yeah, well, you never had a little sinister. I mean 'sister'."

Shelly turned away, smiling. Outside, the various structures that formed the city of Mapleton were flowing by, including a large cinema at which Toby pointed.

"There's Uncle Mick's. I heard he's been doing a Gary Cooper tribute thing all week. Like three movies in a row or something." He whistled out the theme from High Noon. "Did you know him at all?"

"Gary? Well, yes, but not very well. We'd occasionally bump into each other…"

"Did you go to the funeral?"

"Yes."

"What's it like," Jenna cleared her throat, "to be around people like that all the time? I mean, you're like America's royalty."

"Well, once you get to know them," Shelly said, "you realize that only two things separate most celebrities from street people: money and fame, both of which are very volatile entities." She unconsciously removed her gloves. "Some people are just in the right place at the right time, that's all. They're no different from the rest of the world." Then, turning to look out the window, she added softly, "We all have the same demons…"

They talked small for the remainder of their route through and out of Mapleton, with Shelly often pointing out bits of architecture or landscape that had been changed since her last visit.

"How long has it been since you were here last?" Jenna asked.

"Oh, let me see… Christmas of '58… I think. It was the year we had that terrible blizzard, remember Toby?"

"Yeah, when me and Uncle Jim got stuck on the way back from the butcher's, and had to walk all the way back home through three feet of snow- carrying a fresh, thirty-five pound turkey." He smiled at the memory. "We probably dropped that thing ten times."

"It was the most tender turkey I've ever eaten," Shelly laughed. "And then Toby and family were supposed to come and visit last summer, but something came up, hmm Toby?" She paused for a moment. "How is your leg?"

"It's fine," he said with a slap to his thigh, "I hardly notice it anymore. Just don't expect me to win any foot races."

"I'm glad. You're lucky you can still walk, I hear."

"Hey, my tummy's growling," Toby said, rubbing his stomach. "Where should we stop for some eats?"

Shelly pursed her lips. "Well, I had hoped that-"

"Interruption!" Toby interrupted, "I'm going to read your thoughts! Hmm, let me zee…" He furrowed his brow and pretended to close his eyes. "Ah-ha! You vant to stop at ze Strawberry!"

"How did you ever guess?"

"Well, let's just say a little birdie told me… no, no wait, it was a nasty old-"

"Now it's my turn to interrupt," Shelly interjected. "Your *wonderful* and most *gracious* mother said that you would be much obliged to stop there for a malt. What do you say?"

"I say 'whatever Lola wants, Lola gets!'"

"Take me home, daddy." She smiled, the phrase sounding funny after passing through her soft accent.

Toby mimicked her, "It woon't be loong, sweethaaart."

Chapter 5

The gleaming, zenith-perched sun was beaming down through a dusty haze as Toby and company passed back by the drag strip, where Willie stood next to the fence, struggling against the breeze trying to hang up an uncooperative, race-announcing banner. Toby stuck his hand out the window and pounded on the truck roof. Willie heard the racket and turned to offer his huge palm in an enthusiastic wave that followed them as they zoomed by.

"Dang horn doesn't work," Toby said, pulling his bandaged arm back inside.

"Willie seems to be doing well," Shelly mused.

"Well, he spends most of his time there now. After Marion died, he just kind of... I don't know... I guess he gets lost in his work."

"I can't imagine anything in life being worse than losing your husband or wife," Jenna offered. "Especially after being married as long as they were."

"Thirty-four years," Toby stated. "Over half of his life... Then all of the sudden 'poof'- gone."

"Thirty-four years..." Shelly said softly.

"But it has been nice having him around the track so much. He really is a great mechanic... I need a downshift, Miss Gibson."

With the drag strip slowly disappearing behind the long, curving slope, the truck shuddered up the steep grade and past the ornately decorated 'You Are Now Entering Willowgrove' sign. They soon slipped beneath a canopy of lush, street-bordering foliage. The sunlight, when not filtered through the leafy, apple green umbrella, lay in bright patches on the brick street, the slate sidewalk, and across the many well-manicured lawns that were flowing past. The truck hummed along like an enormous bumblebee.

"Oh, no…" Shelly exclaimed to herself, picking up one of the white cotton gloves she'd taken off in Mapleton.

"What?"

"Look." She held it on display. A black ring about the size of a half dollar marred the otherwise snowy white glove near the inside of the palm. "It would appear that your lovely vehicle has left its mark on me."

"My lovely vehicle- how? Besides, that'll wash out, won't it?"

"Hmm-mm, darling. I don't think so."

"Did you bring another pair?" Jenna asked.

"I brought three, but one pair are black, and the other are elbows."

"My dad sells some very nice-"

"Uh, can't you…" Toby cut Jenna off, "…I mean, but the other ones still keep your hands warm, don't they?"

"Maybe we could stop and see what he has," Shelly said.

Toby cut in again, sounding slightly nervous, "But I'm sure Mom or Aunt Sue could lend you a pair, I mean, there's no reason for you to go spending your hard earned money on things you could get for free somewhere else…"

"Toby," Jenna said angrily, "can't you see I'm trying to make a sale here? Besides, I'm sure you're dying to see my father."

"I love it when you use those two words together…"

"Well, Mr. LaRue," Shelly asked, "May we take pause for a bit of shopping? Can your stomach wait for ten minutes?"

Toby blew out an irritated sigh. "California must be beautiful this time of year…"

The aroma of fried chicken, wafting from the open windows of Lexie's Grill, seemed to permeate the entire downtown square of Willowgrove. The streets were even more congested than they had been that morning, due to an influx of hungry weekenders eager to commence their lunch break, either in one of the five, longstanding restaurants or out of a picnic basket in the shade of an oak on the courthouse lawn. Toby found a recently vacated parking space across from Gibson's.

"Well, Happy New Year, here we are," he grumbled.

"Wonderful," Shelly said. "Thank you, sweetheart." The door seemed to pop open when she pulled up on the chrome handle. She stepped out. "Oh, it feels good to stretch. After a six hour flight and your, um… the ride home, I just want to walk around a little."

"Yeah, well, do you mind if I just wait here? My legs aren't done cramping."

"No, Toby," Jenna said, sliding out after Shelly, "You have to tell her what pair you like best. We need your masculine advice." She slammed the door shut.

"Yes dear, you know what men like," Shelly said, walking around to the still-closed, driver's side door.

"I also know what they don't like."

"Come on, sweetie," Jenna coaxed. "For me?" She floated him a surefire, doe-eyed look. He stared at her, jaw clenched. Then, muttering some indistinguishable profanity under his breath, he jerked open the door.

They had to dodge a few fast moving cars as they walked across a shady Vellshank Boulevard, their contorted reflections being caught in the polished black marble and tinted glass that formed the bulk of Gibson's Fine Fashions. The address '302' was spelled out in flowing gold script above the deep-set double doors.

"Ladies first," Toby said, pulling on one of the brass

handles. "I insist."

The air that swept over them as they entered was cool and clean, smelling like a blend of sweet perfume and new cotton. A thick, navy blue, floral print carpet stretched out before them, disappearing from view beneath the slender, elegantly clad mannequins and garment-laden clothing racks that filled the quarter block-sized store. Florescent ceiling lights cast their milky glow upon the wall-bordering rows of hats and purses and cellophane-wrapped stockings. The sultry sound of Jackie Gleason's Orchestra quietly saturated the room. Behind a very large sales desk occupying the center of the store, a pretty young woman, one of only four people in view, stood thumbing through the latest edition of Vanity Fair. She looked up.

"Jenna!"

"Hello, Claire," Jenna said musically. "Where's Dad?"

"He's at lunch, but he should be getting back soon. Hi, Toby."

"Hi."

"Well, if he doesn't, tell him we just dropped by to look at the gloves."

"Shalimar just delivered a new rack full…" Claire's eyes flitted from Jenna to Shelly, who was still sporting her dark sunglasses.

"Oh… Claire, this is Toby's Aunt Shelly. Shelly this is-"

Claire's mouth spread into an irrepressible smile. "Claire Anne Halladay! I'm very pleased to meet you Mrs. Rosegarner!" She shook Shelly's hand vigorously. A few of the other customers raised their heads.

"Thank you, Claire. It's nice to meet you, too," Shelly said in a hushed tone.

"I just saw you in Shadowbox; you were fantastic!"

"Oh, you're too kind."

"No really, I mean it! That part when you came through the waterfall with the moon behind you- it was amazing!"

"Thank you."

"Yeah, thanks," Toby cut in, "Which way are the gloves?"

"They're over here," Jenna said, walking around the counter towards the back of the store. Toby and Shelly followed, stopping in front of a tall display rack loaded down with various sizes, hues, and lengths of dress gloves.

"Hmm…" Shelly stepped forward, slid her sunglasses up onto her head, and began to skim the choices one at a time.

"Great…" Toby mumbled. Just then, he heard the stockroom door swing open and a man enter the store, speaking to someone. A corner blocked his view, but he didn't need to see; he knew. "Double great…"

"Dad!" Jenna called.

"Shh!" Toby hushed.

Seconds later, a tall man in a dark blue flannel suit strolled around the corner. His hair, a graying crew cut, had recently been covered by the brown fedora he now twirled on his finger. His features were handsomely well-chiseled. "Hello," he said cheerily.

"Hi, Dad. Shelly, this is my father… Dad, this is…"

"Pleased to meet you," Shelly said, extending her hand.

"Ed Gibson, Mrs. Rosegarner; the pleasure's entirely mine." He returned the shake, and then turned to Toby. "Hello, Toby." He offered his hand.

"Good afternoon, Mr. Gibson." Toby and Ed engaged in a very firm, almost duel-like handshake. "It's… good to see you. Sir." Toby forced a cough so he had an excuse to let go, covering his mouth.

"So what can I do for you ladies?"

"We're just looking at the gloves," Jenna said

"I can see that. Looking for any particular style?"

"Just plain, white, wrist length."

"Cotton, lace… satin, silk?"

"Hmm… I think maybe I'd like silk," Shelly said.

"Silk? Wait here." He walked back around the corner. A short question to Claire was followed by the swaying stockroom door.

"How easily does he get lost?" Toby grumbled.

"What is your problem with him, Toby? He seems like a fine gentleman." Shelly whispered with a creased brow.

"*I* don't have a problem." Toby whispered back.

"Well, it certainly seems like someone does."

"'Someone' does."

"Toby, stop," Jenna said, joining the hushed conversation. "He hasn't even talked about you lately."

"Yeah, well he-"

Ed returned. He was carrying a thin, black box in his hands. "Here you go, Mrs. Rosegarner. I do believe you'll find these quite satisfactory."

Shelly took the box and removed the lid. "Oh, Mr. Gibson…" Inside, a pair of exquisitely crafted silk gloves, each sporting a small constellation of pearl embroidery on top, lay wrapped in a leaf of red tissue paper. "They're perfect." She drew one out and slipped it on. "They're absolutely perfect. I'll take them." She removed the glove and placed the lid on the bottom of the box.

"Wonderful."

"How much are they?"

"Hmm… I seem to have misplaced the price tag…"

"Oh, I couldn't possibly-"

"I insist, Mrs. Rosegarner. I'll be the one getting the deal once people see you wearing them."

"Mr. Gibson…" Shelly searched for a fitting expression of thankfulness. "I'll inform everyone I know exactly where they may obtain their own pair. Thank you."

"No, thank you. I'll have my mail order boxes standing by." He laughed slightly. He was about to say something to Jenna, but was interrupted by a ringing telephone. "Oh-

I'll get it Miss Halladay!" He began walking away. "Please excuse me; I'm expecting a very important call."

Jenna followed him, as did Toby and Shelly. "Well, we're just going down to The Strawberry for some lunch, okay? Do you need me to come back here when we're done?"

"No, no, Jenna. I'll see you at dinner." Ed reached the desk and picked up the phone. "Hello...? George!" He waved goodbye to them.

"'Bye," Claire said to Shelly.

"Goodbye, Claire. It was wonderful meeting you." Shelly clutched the new gloves against her chest. "Maybe I'll see you again sometime." She pulled her sunglasses down into place

"That would be wonderful!"

Ed gestured Claire to silence with his flapping hand and angry brow.

"That would be wonderful," she whispered.

Toby was the first one to push back through the doors. *"Zippity do dah..."* he sang softly, eagerly leading the way out across the sidewalk and into the street. *"What a wonderful day...* I was nice, wasn't I, Jenna?"

"You were the epitome of geniality."

"I shook his hand, didn't I?"

"Toby, I don't understand why you don't like him," Shelly said.

"Aunt Shelly... he can be such a-" he paused and thought for a moment, "Jenna, cover your ears." They reached the truck and piled back in.

"Oh, Toby," Shelly said, slipping on her new gloves after she'd gotten situated, "Just you wait until you have a daughter, then we'll see how protective you are."

"Me? Have kids? Are you crazy?" Toby laughed. "If I wanted to subject myself to a lifetime of slow torture, I'd refurbish septic tanks." He started the truck and, after glancing over his shoulder, pulled away from the curb. "Really, could you see me changing diapers and getting puked on and stuff?"

"I think you could be a wonderful father," Shelly said, "I think it would be good for you, too."

"Yeah, this coming from someone who has how many kids?"

"Toby," A quiet fervency crept into Shelly's voice. "Just because some people don't have children doesn't mean that they don't want them."

"Yeah, well…" Toby thought for a moment, "that statement would be just as true without the 'don'ts'."

Shelly leaned her head against the window and sighed. "Sweetheart, I've attained everything I could ever want in life…" She looked down at her new gloves, and then ran her fingers over a bulge formed by the large diamond on her left ring finger. "Unfortunately, things that I need are much more elusive."

"And just what do you need?"

She turned back toward him. "The same things that you need, Toby. Joy, peace, happiness… love… We all need them. We all need to give and receive, receive and give." She resumed her window gazing, and a sad smile crept across her face, reflecting back at her in the window. "Don't ever take love for granted, Toby. Life without love isn't life at all."

Even with the truck's engine raucously chugging down the street, a sober silence descended in the cramped cab. Toby uncomfortably scratched the back of his neck. Jenna continued to command the shifter with robotic precision. Shelly fumbled with another cigarette, having found her lighter. After several minutes, unable to stand the stillness any longer, Toby switched on the radio. A Pepsi commercial, followed by another weather report. The tension began to lift gradually as Kenwood Avenue abruptly turned from brick to asphalt and, with houses giving way to thick foliage on both sides, began a steep, downward slope as they drew near to the eastern edge of town. After a sharp, shady curve, the road evened out and the trees on the left opened up into a large, gravel lot surrounded by woods on three sides. At the center of this rocky field, resting atop a patch of cracked blacktop, sat a gleaming, red and white drive-in diner. The smell of grilling burgers seemed to lay like a cloud in the afternoon heat.

"My…" Shelly exclaimed, "I'd forgotten…"

The building's outline was circular, complimented by two, twin-peaked awnings that stretched far out into the lot like the hands of a quarter-till-twelve clock. They turned off of the blacktop onto the dusty gravel. It seemed like more people were leaving than arriving, and Toby was able to procure a parking spot not far from the jingling door.

"Hey…" Jenna said, "There's Smoosh!" She pointed to a rather tall, hefty young man emerging from the diner. He was sipping on a monster-sized milkshake.

"Who?" Shelly asked.

"Eddie Vinsen," Toby said, "He's one of my many friends. And a third of our racing team: Krindle, LaRue, and Vinsen, remember? We all call him 'Smoosh' so we don't get him mixed up with Jenna's dad." He removed the keys from the ignition and rolled his window up. "Ready?"

"More than." Shelly said, adjusting her sunglasses and head scarf.

"Then let us now partake of heaven on earth."

Chapter 6

"Hey, Smooshy!" Toby called to the chunky young man who was squeezing behind the wheel of a khaki-colored Volkswagen Beetle. The boy stuck his head back over the car door, searching the crowd of drive-in diners for the source of the call. "Over here," Toby said, waving his hand.

"Suzy-Q!" Smoosh called back after spotting Toby.

Toby glanced hesitantly at Shelly's puzzled expression, and then cleared his throat, fighting the smile that was tugging at the corner of his mouth. "You're not already done eating are you? It's only one 'o clock."

"Huh? Me? Done eating?" Smoosh got back out of the car, waving a wallet around. "I just came up for air, mm'kay? And my dough. I only took a few bucks in with me." He slammed the door and began walking over towards them, still nursing his milkshake.

"You had me worried for a second, thought you were already done," Toby said, leading Jenna and Shelly towards the door.

"Don't worry. I'm never done. I'm a pro, mm'kay?"

"Mm'kay."

"Mm'kay."

Toby pulled the door open and a girl on roller skates carrying a full tray of food rolled out. "Thanks, Toby baby," she said, winking.

"You bet." Toby shot Jenna a sheepish smile and a shrug. She didn't look amused. They stepped through the door. The first thing that hit them, besides the heavenly fragrance of burgers, fries, and hot dogs, was the music. A neon-faced jukebox was pumping *'Heart and Soul'* into the somewhat hazy diner. Carhops and customers flitted to and fro across the narrow isle way that snaked between the table rows.

"We'll sit back here," Toby said, leading them to a secluded corner bench that was right next to the swinging kitchen doors. "I have reserved seating here." He stepped aside so that Jenna could slide across the vinyl bench seat. "Oh, Smoosh, you remember my… my, uh, Aunt… Shirley."

"Nice to meet you, Aunt 'Shirley'. I'm 'Uncle' Eddie," Smoosh said with a boyish grin, letting Shelly slip into the booth first. Sitting his shake on the chrome-rimmed table, he squeezed in beside her. "Everyone calls me 'Smoosh', though. I haven't figured out why…"

"Maybe it has to do with that football game last year," Toby said, sitting down next to Jenna, "You know, the one where three players from the other team went to the hospital? Remember that kid, uh… what was his name? The one who didn't wake up 'til the next day."

"That was a light tackle!"

"Smoosh, the guy was six-two, two hundred and twenty pounds, and it took four guys to carry him off the field."

"Anyway…" Smoosh looked at his watch. "I'm starved. I haven't eaten in ten minutes." Just then, a waitress on skates rolled up to their table. "Hey, guys," she said.

"Hey, Angela," Toby said.

"The usual?"

"Yep."

"Okay…" Angela began scribbling on a small pad of paper. "Jenna?"

"The same. The usual, I mean."

"Alright… I already know what you want, Eddie. Ma'am?"

"Well, I was just going to get a malt, but… do you still have the Moonburger?"

"Yes we do."

"I'll have the meal."

"And to drink?"

"Just water, thank you."

"Alright, I'll be back in a few minutes." She left, jotting down the rest of the order as she skated through the kitchen doors.

Toby waited until she was gone, then turned to Shelly, nodding in approval. "The Moonburger? Dang… you're my kind of skirt."

"I've got to make my trip cross-country worthwhile, Toby."

"Well, if something were ahead of me on your list of important stuff, a Moonburger would be the only one I'd approve of."

"What are you having?"

"My own special recipe: The Tobyburger."

"The what?"

"Ah-ha. You start out with a plain quarter-pounder, then add lettuce, tomato, mayonnaise, uh… barbeque sauce, a couple slices of cheese, and top it off with a big pile of chili fries. Then you lovingly nestle the whole thing in a toasted and buttered egg bun."

"Hmm… sounds interesting."

"It's taken years of research and close collaboration with Chef Petey to get it just right. He even measures out the ingredients. Makes it himself."

"Peter Larson? Is he still chef here?"

"What do you mean? Pete Larson is The Strawberry. If anything ever happened to him, I think the earth would plunge headlong into the sun."

"I'd love to see him."

Toby thought for a moment, and then leaned forward. "Really? Well, come on." He stood up.

"Now?"

"Would you rather wait until they tear the building

down?"

"Alright…" she said.

Smoosh wiggled out to let her by. "I'll keep your seat warm, mm'kay?"

"Thank you."

Bouncy rock and roll was replaced with sizzling burgers and the rattling of pots and pans as Toby pushed through the free-swinging double doors. The haze, understandably thicker in the kitchen, was being swirled about by a faint breeze floating in from the open back door. People were everywhere. One of them, a young man in the process of lowering a basket of raw french fries into a vat of hissing oil, threw a casual glance their way. He blinked in disbelief when he saw Shelly.

"Howdy, Chuck," Toby said.

"It's… it's true…" the boy stuttered, eyes glued on Shelly.

"Yeah, it's true. And what was it that I'm full of again?"

"Uh, I, I don't remember…" Chuck slowly lowered the fries into the oil.

"Uh-huh…" Toby's eyes skimmed the busy kitchen until he caught sight of a short, somewhat rotund man who was hunched over one of the steel counters. "Hey, Pete!" he called.

The man turned. If Lou Costello had a balding identical twin brother, Pete Larson would be him. He put a stocky finger to his lips. "Shh… Don't distoib the magic…" He moved aside to reveal Toby's Tobyburger under construction.

"Hey, it's looking good," Toby said, pulling Shelly over by the arm. "Uh, I brought someone to see you."

Pete squinted, then reached into his shirt pocket and pulled out a pair of heavy, thick-rimmed glasses. He put them on. "Well, whadaya know! What do ya know! If it idn't lit'le… lit'le…"

"Hello, Mr. Larson," Shelly said, stepping forward with a smile. "It's been a very long time."

"It soitainly has, toots, it soitainly has! Why, da last time I saw you, you was knee-high to a beef stick! Where've ya been keepin' y'self?"

Shelly cast a glance at Toby. "Oh, I've been… away."

Pete furrowed his brow, and began snapping his fingers. "Hmm, hmm," he mumbled to himself, "Naw, no… Suzy… Shirley, naw, no… Shelly! Shelly Rainesburg! I knew it'd come to me one of dese days!"

"Uh, well… actually, I got married. It's… it's not 'Rainesburg' anymore. I changed it for my… work."

"Oh! Wondaful, wondaful! Who's the lucky shish kabob?" Pete removed his grease-spattered glasses and turned his attention back to Toby's lunch.

"Um… uh, well, his name is… is James."

"Ah-ha, dat's a good strong name. You two got'ny tater tots?"

"I'm sorry?"

Toby crossed his arms. "Kids, Aunt Shelly, kids."

"Oh, no. No, not yet."

"Uh-huh, how long ya been married?" Pete set aside the mayonnaise and began measuring out the barbeque sauce.

"Nine years."

"Ump, ya betta get busy, toots, dey don't pop out forever, ya know." He laughed loudly.

"Yes, yes, I know. How's- how is Warren doing?"

"My Warren? Oh, he lives up in Cleveland now, he's got a family of his own. I'm a grandad three times over!"

"Oh. That's… nice."

"Well, ya boiger's about ready, Tobe. How's it lookin'?"

Toby pulled his eyes off of Shelly. "Uh, looks good enough to eat, Pete. I'll be waitin'- waiting for it." Toby began to walk back toward the dining room, and then stopped to wait for Shelly.

"It was wonderful to see you again, Mr. Larson. Next time you see him… tell Warren I said 'hello'. I really miss this place. And the people here… "

Peter wiped his palms on his apron and then took Shelly's hand in both of his own. "Da pleasure's all mine, toots. You're welcome anytime. Bring Mr. James wit you next time, I need ta make sure dat he's good'nuff for ya."

"Maybe I will… goodbye, Peter." Shelly turned and joined Toby, seeming slightly out of sorts.

"See ya 'round, toots."

"I was hoping maybe you'd get lost, Toby," Smoosh said, standing to let Shelly slide in. "You're lucky you came back when you did. I was about to start entertaining your shake.

Toby sat down behind a tall, perspiring strawberry milkshake. "It's the thought that counts," he said as he took a sip through the candy cane-striped straw. He turned to Shelly. "You sure you don't want a Coke or something?"

Just then, Angela skated up with a tray of food and began to lay it out. "Here you go, Jenna…"

"No, Toby. I'm on this special diet." Shelly said, pulling off her new gloves as a plate-sized burger and a giant side of ketchup-laced fries was placed before her.

With eyebrows slowly furrowing, Toby stared at her plate for a moment, looked at his own food as it was being set in front of him, then glanced back to hers. "Diet?" He cocked his head. "So, uh… should I talk to my doctor before I start?"

"You don't think I'm going to eat all this at once do you?" Shelly said, unwrapping her napkin-enveloped silverware.

Toby picked up his own burger. "I don't know. Have

you ever eaten your weight in food in one sitting before?"
He sunk his teeth into the sandwich, a bit of burger juice
dribbling down his chin"

"I can't say that I have."

"Unfortunately, neither can I," Toby said, wiping his
mouth. He looked across the table at Smoosh, who was
hard at work on a plate full of chili dogs. "Hey, have you
talked to Dean at all today?"

"No, why?" Smoosh asked with his mouth full.

"Give him a ring at the garage when you get a chance.
He'll have something very interesting to tell you about the
dragster."

"Like what?"

"Just give him a ring."

"Can't you just tell me now?"

"No, call him later," Toby said, arching his eyebrow.

Smoosh threw down a half-eaten hot dog and stood up.
"Mm'kay, fine. You know I have no patience." Flustered,
he stomped away towards the pay phone at the front of the
diner.

"What did Dean say?" Jenna inquired.

"Uh..." Toby took a sip of milkshake. "He found a way
to lighten the frame."

"How is your racing going?" Shelly asked, spearing a
french fry with her fork. "I keep forgetting to ask your
mother."

"Oh, it's going. We made it to the semi-finals last
Saturday night. Last night we got knocked out second
round."

"How long has it been since you've won a race?"

"Over a month. We won the opening event at B.C.D.
this year; that was pretty neat because there were a lot of
cars there, like thirty-something fuel dragsters."

"Why so many?"

"Well, partly because it was the season opener, and

partly because Blossom County Dragway is one of the few strips around here that'll let you run nitro."

"What does that mean?"

"Nitromethane is an exotic fuel that makes something like three times the horsepower that pump gas makes, and a lot of strips, like Stardust, won't let us use it because they're sanctioned by the NHRA, who has a ban on it. Not that we haven't ever tipped the scales in our favor before…"

"Why do they have a ban on it?"

"I don't know, something stupid like safety or something. Boy, I wish I could take you guys for a ride in the dragster."

"Why?" Shelly asked. "What's it like?"

"I can't even really explain what it feels like. Like if you took the tallest, fastest roller coaster ever, and then multiplied it by ten. It literally takes your breath away. Really. I mean you seriously can't breathe, 'cause you're getting smashed against the seat by the acceleration… Sometimes it feels like your face is gonna slide right off your head. It's bitchin."

"It… seems like it could be fun," Shelly replied, without much conviction.

"It is. But, only one seat, so unless you guys are gonna sit on my lap…" The end of Toby's shake was announced with a loud slurp. After one last bite of burger, he looked down at his plate. It was now empty save for a few fries and a puddle of ketchup. "Where did it go…? It never seems to be big enough. Maybe a banana split…"

"Shouldn't you leave a little room for the special dinner your mom's making you tonight?" Jenna asked, wiping the condensation off of her lemonade.

"Yeah, she doesn't think I know but I saw a list of… Oh, sh- dang it!"

"What's wrong?" Shelly asked.

"What time is it?"

Jenna tinkered with the watch on her slender wrist. "One-fifty. Exactly."

"Dang it... we need to go!" Standing, Toby wiped his mouth and threw the napkin onto his messy plate. "Mom wanted me home no later than two!"

"Oh," Shelly said, looking down at the four-fifths of her burger that remained untouched.

"I'll get you a box." Toby said. He turned and nearly knocked a roller-skating Angela and her tray full of food to the floor.

"Toby! Jeeze!"

"Sorry, Angie- uh, I need a box."

"Well, just wait a minute and I'll get you one."

"Alright, but make it snappy, okay?"

Just then, Smoosh returned, face flushed with anger. Throwing a brief 'I'm in the loop' glance to Toby, he sat down in fuming silence.

"What's wrong with you?" Jenna asked.

Smoosh's hooded gaze shot her way. "I just found out that..."

Toby cleared his throat.

"...That we could have been winning a lot more races if the frame wasn't so dad blasted heavy!"

"But Dean already fixed it," Toby said, leaning over to pull Jenna out of the booth by her elbow. "Smoosh, we gotta split..." He fished out his wallet and produced a few dollars. "Here, can you pay for us too?"

"Sure..." Smoosh took the money.

"Now, remember; that's for *our* food, not another round of chili dogs"

"Yeah, yeah, book it, Suzy-Q, mm'kay?"

Angela returned with a white cardboard box in her hands. "Here." She gave it to Toby and began skating away.

"Gracias, mademoiselle. That oughta bump your tip up to a nickel."

"Thanks," she called over her shoulder.

Toby handed the box to Shelly. "Where do you want me to take you? I know Mom said that you were staying at Grandpa and Grandma Rainesburg's but I didn't know whether or not you wanted me to drive you all the way to Catalpa."

"Um…" Shelly slid her burger into the box. "If you need to get home, I can have your mother take me to Mom and Dad's."

"Alright, then we'll take the short cut."

"The short cut?" Jenna asked.

"Yeah, right out of here and down Mendenhall."

"Mendenhall? That way's three miles longer!"

"Yeah, but with never a cop, it goes a lot quicker. Ready?"

Once again, Smoosh had to get up to let Shelly out.

"I'm sorry." Shelly said, sliding out.

"Don't worry about it. At least I'm getting my exercise in today." He turned to Toby. "Catch you later, Suzy-Q. Have fun graduating."

"Yeah, take it easy, putty butt. Have fun working."

Toby took Jenna by the hand and began weaving his way back through the tables toward the door, Shelly following close behind. But just as he was about to exit the diner, his attention was caught by someone calling his name.

"Hey, LaRue!"

His head swiveled around in search of the source.

"Over here!"

He noticed a hand waving out of the corner of his eye and turned to see two men in their early twenties lounging at a table near the jukebox. They looked tough, but sociable.

"What's your hurry?" One asked. His arm lay on top of his head; a smoldering cigarette was being flipped through his fingers. "How's it going, Jenna?"

"Well, well, Bell and Hawkins," Toby exclaimed, walking over to them. "My favorite least favorites. What brings you guys off the mountain?"

"I like to pick on kids." The man took a drag and blew smoke out of his nose. "But I won't bore you with things you already know, Toby."

"Thanks, Gary, I appreciate that. You and Frankie here," Toby mock-punched the other young man, "have a lovely afternoon, okay? I've gotta book."

"Who's…" Gary began, pointing his cigarette at Shelly. His sleepy-looking gaze widened a bit as his eyes roved up and down her partially disguised form. "Who's the new chick?"

Shelly put a hand on her hip and sighed, not in the least bit intimidated.

"A backup. Toodle-loo." Toby began leaving.

"Hey, you gonna be at the strip tonight?"

"I don't know yet. Why?" He twisted back around.

"Well… we've been testing out some new stuff, and I thought maybe you'd like to be our first victim. Mary Jane's been itchin' to whoop your ass."

"Well, I don't know yet. I'm graduating this afternoon, remember?"

"Oh, yeah… I forgot you still wore a diaper. Hey, that reminds me, Krindle invited us to his bash and whatnot tonight. Probably won't be there. Pass it on, okay?"

"Sure."

"And if you feel like being a loser this evening, you know where to find us."

"Thanks, Gary. I'll keep that in mind. Take it easy." He turned away and pushed through the jingling door with Jenna and Shelly close behind.

Chapter 7

"*Dang it, dang it, dang it…*" Toby said, pulling the truck keys from his pocket. "The last time I was late for supper, they fed my food to Tracy's stupid dog." The air outside of the diner was noticeably warmer now than it had been an hour ago, and stuffy, unventilated heat rolled out of the truck cab when he opened the passenger's side door for Jenna and Shelly. "Whew, it's like a steam bath in here…"

"I'm used to hot air…" Jenna said, trying to create some elbow room between Toby and her after he got in.

"Try not to dent the roof once I stick you up there, okay?" Toby said. After rolling down his window, he started the truck and backed out from beneath the awning, the engine's rough, low idle drawing more than one envious stare from The Strawberry's male clientele. After pulling off of the gravel lot, instead of going back up the hill into Willowgrove, he made a left and followed the shaded, undulating curves of Kenwood Avenue until it dead-ended on Mendenhall, where he hung another right. The tachometer rose and fell very quickly as the truck picked up speed at an obviously illegal rate. Dust and gravel spewed out in their wake.

"Who were those young men back there?" Shelly asked. "Friends of yours?"

"Well… kind of, I guess. They're just a couple of guys I race with all the time. That cherry deuce sitting outside was Gary's; he calls it 'The Cottonmouth'. It's the baddest ass car in The Valley." Toby licked his teeth. "Hey, can you get in the, uh 'glove box' there?"

Not having to reach very far, Shelly flipped up on the toolbox's latch and the battered metal flap fell open.

"There should be a buck in there somewhere…"

"Oh, jeeze…" Jenna sighed.

Shelly produced a crisp, half-folded dollar bill. "This?"

"Yeah, that's it." He took the bill, and, with Shelly looking on in curious disbelief, began flossing his teeth with the stiff, clean edge. Jenna stared straight out the front window, wearily shaking her head.

"My, how you've changed, Toby," Shelly said. "You…"

"Is woks gate," Toby spoke with the bill in his mouth, "Ou shou ty et omtime." He spit something out the window and then handed the dollar back to Shelly, who, careful to pick it up by one of the dry corners, returned it to the glove box.

"Um, who is Mary Jane?" she asked, trying several times to get the flap to latch.

"Who? Oh, that's the name of their dragster. 'Mary Jane Three' actually; the first two are in race car heaven."

"Oh. I thought you were actually being beat by a woman."

"*Pfft.* I don't think so."

"Not in drag racing anyway," Jenna pitched in.

"Okay, lets not tear open old wounds," Toby said, rolling his eyes.

"Old wounds? I just beat you yesterday!"

"At what?" Shelly asked.

"Never mind." Toby gave Jenna an angry looking warning stare that went unheeded.

"Tic-tac-toe," she said, turning to offer Toby a loving smile. "We keep a tablet at the garage, and right now I think the score stands at… 304 to 12."

"Oh-ho…" Toby growled, "One of these days, Jennalyn; one of these days! Pow!"

"Right in the kisser?" Jenna asked, puckering her lips.

"Ha. You wish."

As the woodlands began to dwindle and give way to the ever present tree-bordered fields, Toby slowed for a shiny new stop sign at the Mendenhall-Indiola intersection, meaning that they still blew through an uneven crossroads at a bone-jarring fifty miles-per-hour. The truck fishtailed around an all gravel corner.

"Take it easy, Toby," Jenna said, grabbing on to the hand that Toby wasn't using to drive. "I'd like to live until *my* graduation."

"Cool your jets, sweetheart. I know what I'm do-" Toby's bragging was violently cut short by a loud, 'popping' explosion followed by a brutally abrupt plunge of the truck's rear driver's side. Toby ripped his hand away from Jenna's in order to wrestle the swerving truck away from the deep, cattail-filled ditch on their left. He slammed on the brakes. "Whoa, whoa, whoa…" he said to himself, trying to control their rapid deceleration while gravel spewed from the locked-up, wavering front wheels. He glanced out into his cracked side mirror. Large chunks of rubber were being thrown from the rear wheel well. "Hang on!" Toby jerked the steering wheel and the truck finally came to a wobbling halt sideways in the center of the road. Uneasy silence, save for heavy breathing, filled the cab as the dust slowly descended outside.

"Uh…" Toby coughed. He looked at Jenna, who turned to him, her big, turquoise eyes standing out against her suddenly pallid face.

"W- what happened?"

"I, uh…" He gulped. "I, uh… think we blew a tire."

Shelly had one hand clutched against her heaving chest. Her boxed Moonburger was laying on the floor.

"Aunt Shelly? You okay?"

"Yes… yes, I'm… I'm fine." she said, opening her eyes. "What happened?"

"I think we blew a tire." Toby opened the door and got

out, gravel crunching beneath his feet. A brief glance into the wheel well told the whole story. All that was left of the rear tire was a few rubber strips that clung to the rim like the last shreds of meat on a bone. "Ahh sh-... damn it. Son of a..."

Jenna leaned out the door. "Is it flat?"

"A little."

"Do you have a spare?" She got out to look at the damage. "Wow..."

"Of course I have a spare- back at the garage. I just took it out Thursday." Toby looked around at their surroundings, shielding his eyes from the beating sun. Locusts buzzed throughout the fields that encircled them. "Damn..." He walked back to the cab and stood on the running board. "Well, we're about as far from any help as possible..."

"How far?" Shelly asked.

"About four miles on the road, but if we cut across old man Mainer's land, it'd be a little shorter." He sat down on the running board and began tightening his shoe laces.

"What do you mean? Walk home?"

"Yeah, unless you have a spare tire in your purse. But first we've got to get the truck off the road."

"I, I don't know if... Maybe someone will come by. Maybe you could..." Shelly retrieved her burger from the floor. "Someone might come by..."

"And someone might not come by. This is mostly a tractor road. Pretty much just farmers use it, and I don't see anybody out today."

"But..."

"We'll be fine. Come on, what are you afraid of, swamp monsters?" He stood and motioned to the west. "I know where some horse trails are over that way. We'll be home in no time."

Shelly looked down at her white high heels, then in a

slow silence opened her door and stepped out, Moonburger in gloved hand. "Are you sure you know the way?"

"I think I'm pretty sure I'm positive. Uh, just sit on that fender over there, the front one." He turned the steering wheel to the left, and pulled the transmission out of gear.

"Why?"

Toby moved back toward the rear of the truck. "I need you to take some weight off this rim. Come on, Jenna."

"I just *love* this truck," Jenna said, taking her place beside Toby.

"Ready? One, two three, push!" Together, they leaned into the tailgate. For a moment it seemed as if they were walking on a gravel treadmill, but after the loose stones were pushed from beneath their feet, the truck began to inch forward. "That's it, that's it…" Toby said, "Tell me when it's getting close to that ditch, Aunt Shelly." A few more feet were traversed.

"Alright, it's getting close! Easy, easy!"

"Alright, that's good." Toby and Jenna stopped pushing and began to catch their breath. Ignored, the truck still crept forward, slowly pulled toward the ditch by the soft, grassy edge.

"Stop!" Shelly cried.

"Whoa, whoa! Get it!" Toby yelled to Jenna. They both grabbed a hold of the tailgate, but against the weight of the truck, it fell open, throwing their grip off.

"Oh, no!" Jenna exclaimed. Unable to prevent it, she and Toby watched as the front passenger wheel, above which Shelly was sitting, dropped over the edge of the three foot deep, weed-clogged ditch. The rest of the nose quickly followed.

"Shhhh…oot!" Toby hissed, moving along side the truck toward the front. "Aunt Shelly?" Behind a curtain of cattails, Shelly rose, her green eyes aglow, and her lips forming a very definite frown. Toby jumped over the trench. "Are you okay?"

Shelly pulled a long, green weed from her tousled hair and looked up at him. "Why, yes, Toby, of course I am," she answered in a wavering voice. "In fact, I feel so good, I think I'll walk the rest of the way barefoot." She held up the broken heel of her shoe.

"Ahh, jeeze, Aunt Shelly, I'm sorry. Here, I'll help you out." He took her hands and pulled her out of the ditch. "There. Don't forget your food. It's over there." He pointed to a patch of tall grass where the white cardboard box was laying.

"My poor little friend," Shelly said, scooping it up. After hopping over the gap with Toby's aid, she slipped off her shoes and tossed them and the burger through the open truck window.

"Damn it, I'm going to have to get Dad to tow this thing out now." He looked at Shelly, who was removing her gloves. "I didn't know you did your own stunts."

"Neither did I. *Ouch!*" Her bare foot recoiled from the jagged road rocks. "I don't!"

"You'll have to walk along the edge." Jenna said, retrieving her and Shelly's purses from the cab.

"Yeah, sorry I don't have an extra pair of high heels," Toby said, as he rolled up the window and locked the doors. "Come on, let's- oh, dang it! I forgot we've got all your junk, uh, luggage in the back." He reached into the bed and pulled out two suitcases. "Hey... shouldn't you have another pair of shoes in one of these?"

"Not any that match this outfit! And not any that are suitable for gallivanting about the countryside!"

"Oh, come on! It's just for... Don't be such a, such a... a..."

"It wouldn't do to ruin another pair, would it Toby? Just give me that handbag."

"Fine. Do we have to lug all of this stuff with us?"

"Well, I don't want to leave out here in the middle of nowhere!"

"Alright, alright! Don't pass a cactus… Judas Priest… Here, Jenna." Toby handed her a case.

"I can carry two," Jenna said.

"I won't fight you for 'em. Here, Dear Auntie."

"I guess you can leave that one big one, Toby," Shelly said, pointing to one of the ones that Jenna was holding. "But you'll have to lock it inside the truck."

"Alright." He unlocked the truck and took the suitcase from Jenna, sitting it on the seat. "Okay, let's beat feet. Now I'm really gonna be late." With a slam of the door, they were off.

"There's a tractor path up here a little ways," Toby said, getting a better grip on one of the suitcases that he was carrying. "It'll be a little easier on your feet." He kicked a baseball-sized rock into the ditch.

"And then what?" Shelly asked.

"Then we take one of the horse trails that cut through here. I know there's one that comes out right at the end of our road, it's just a matter of finding the right one. Oh, and, uh, watch out for snakes."

"Snakes?" Shelly looked down at her bare feet.

"Yeah, especially when we get to the river. Me and Dean saw a water moccasin down by the bridge last summer, but don't worry about that."

"What's that supposed to mean? What happened?"

"It's dead."

"How do you know?"

"It, uh… it got lead poisoning."

"You never told me about that." Jenna said.

"Well, I didn't want you to fear for my mortal flesh. I mean, just try and imagine your life without me."

"Don't tempt me."

"Hardeeharharhar," he said, lending Shelly an arm as she teetered across the rock-toothed road and stepped upon the dusty, tire-gouged soil of the tractor path.

The fields that began on either side of them were green with freshly sprouted corn. On one side of the path, a row of tall, leafy trees grew, shielding them from the afternoon sun. Shelly removed her glasses as a circling hawk caught her eye.

"You know, even though it may not seem so, I do miss the country; all of the birds and trees and streams and…" She looked down at her already dusty feet. "…and dirt."

"Dirt?" Toby exclaimed. "How do you miss dirt?"

"Well, just the smell of it… The smell of freshly plowed fields and gardens… I guess it's not the dirt I miss… it's the soil."

"Oh."

"I miss the rain…"

"Yeah, well, then you should have been here a few weeks ago." Toby stopped and sat down one of the suitcases. He uprooted a bushy, green foxtail growing in the center of the path and, after pinching off the soiled end, stuck it in his mouth. "Lines down all over the place. No power. And then John Ingram comes by in a panic, saying that he can't find his daughter Shelia." He picked the suitcase back up and continued onward.

Shelly ran her hand through the tall, roadside grass beside her while gazing into the birdsong-filled woods that were beginning to take shape on their left. "Did he?"

"No, I found her. Seems she tried to take a short cut on the way home from school, but was cut off by mean old Mr. Funnel Cloud."

"And you found her? How romantic, Toby!"

"Ha. Yeah, right. The whole thing was about as romantic as the field full of dead cows that I had to walk through to get to her. Besides, she's only like ten or something."

"And if she wasn't?" Jenna asked.

"Then it would have been nice and cozy on the way home, huh? Instead, I gave her my coat and half froze to death myself."

"Was she alright afterward?"

"Oh, yeah; *she* was fine. *I* was sick for a week. I guess that's what I get for trying to help someone out, huh?"

"The sacrifice of aid is the womb of compassion." Shelly said, poking Toby in the shoulder. "And altruism is the virtue of virtues."

Toby thought for a moment, and then his nose and lips curved into a sneer. "Yeah, thanks, Aunt Confucius. Where'd you read that? Plato Weekly? What the hell's 'altruism' anyway?"

"I didn't read it. I wrote it."

"You wrote it? In what?"

"My book of proverbs."

"What?" Toby threw her a skeptical glance.

"My book of proverbs. Someday I'll get it published." She swatted away a bee that was buzzing around her head.

Toby laughed. "I can see it now…" He stretched his suitcase-laden arms out like a headline writer. "'Aunt Shelly's Book of Fortune Cookie Wisdom: Everything You Need to Know About Everything You Don't Know'."

"Go ahead and laugh. You'll see."

"Yeah, well, good luck." He spit out the foxtail. "Here's the horse trail…" The trees at their left were broken open by a narrow, hoof-marked bridleway nearly choked to death by overgrown foliage. "Don't worry, it gets wider."

"If you say so…" Shelly said, following single file behind Toby through the foot wide gap. The songbirds met her with their convoluted symphony.

"Keep an eye out for poison ivy, Toby," Jenna said. She

held the suitcase in front of her and stepped onto the trail.

"I am. Believe me, I am. I don't feel like being a giant red marshmallow for graduation."

After several hundred feet, the trees did begin to thin out somewhat, causing the path to open up to a more comfortable, suitcase-friendly width, with beaming shafts of hazy sunlight piercing through the leafy ceiling all around them. The leaf-littered land began to gently, but pronouncedly, rise and fall.

"So, Aunt Shelly, ever hear from the princess anymore?"

"Grace? No, not for several months now. I was in Monaco last September and spent a few days with the family. That was about all I could stand."

"What do you mean?" Toby asked.

"I feel so bad for her, Toby. When we were in school together in New York, she was so free-spirited, so, so... fun to be with... full of life."

"And now she's not?"

"I don't think she knew what she was getting herself into. She seems... it seems like she had everything she wanted for a moment, and then reality came along and slowly began eating away at the whipped cream."

"Now you're using words I can understand."

"But, my, does she love her children."

Toby pushed aside a low-hanging branch. "Children? Now I feel bad for her, too. Hey, Jenna, what time is it?"

"Don't you own a watch?" Jenna asked.

"Of course. I keep it with my spare tires. What time is it?"

Letting out a sigh, Jenna glanced at her wrist. "Going on three."

"Well, I'm supposed to be at school now, putting on my dress. Of all the days to be late... that I *have* been late..."

"You know what Mr. Derwitz says," Jenna said, "'Tardy makes re-tardy'."

"Yeah, he would know. If he spent as much time being principal as he did thinking up stupid sayings like that, our school would rival West Point." Just ahead of them, the earth gave way to a gaping, stone-walled ravine. The horse trail disappeared over the mossy edge. Toby put down a suitcase, wiped some sweat off of his forehead, and blew out a lungful of air. "Here's where the party starts…"

Chapter 8

"How are we going to get across *this?*" Jenna asked, coming up to the winding gorge's edge. At her feet, the horse trail began its snaking course down the steep incline, finally leveling out on the ravine floor some thirty feet below, only to immediately zigzag up the even steeper opposite side. A wide creek ran down the center of the gully.

"Jump and pray that you die on impact, I guess," Toby said. "I don't know, it might be easier to walk down backwards." He tested the grip of his Converse on the treacherous-looking trail. "I'll go first. Just remember that if one of you starts to fall, don't hit me on the way down."

"Toby, where's your sense of chivalry?" Shelly asked, looking down at him from behind Jenna.

"The same place my sense of water pressure is," Toby said, grunting. "At the bottom of the ocean. Just keep your feet sideways and you should be alright. Don't try to go too fast."

"Be careful with my suitcases, Toby. They cost me a fortune."

"Ha. You and the alligator both."

"How can they even ride horses down this?" Jenna asked, following behind Toby. She wrapped her free hand around a gangly oak sapling for stability. "I wonder if Heidi ever rides this way. Do you think?"

"Don't know."

"Who's Heidi?" Shelly asked, her bare feet beginning to warily find their way down the incline.

"Dean's girl," Toby said.

"Dean? Isn't he your best friend? I think I- *ouch!*- met him once."

"Once? He's only been my best friend since I... stopped, uh... since a long time ago. You've met him a lot of times."

"Well, I can't keep track of every new person I meet, Toby."

"You'll remember him once you see him. He's pretty much known as the James Dean of Blossom County. Although, it seems like lately Gary's been fighting him for the title..." Toby finally reached the shady, pebbled floor of the ravine. He sat the suitcases down on a long stone slab. "At least it's a lot cooler down here."

"What do you mean by that?" Shelly asked, still halfway up the side.

Toby tossed her a confused look. "It means it's not so hot." He shook his head.

"No, no, no. I mean about him being the- *ouch!*- 'James Dean' around here. Ouch!"

"Oh. Well, he's just kind of got that 'don't give a...' look, you know? And everybody wants to be his friend, but, uh, he's not much of a 'people person'."

"To say the least," Jenna said.

"What? He's always nice to you." Toby took the suitcase that Jenna was carrying and lent her a steady hand for the last few feet of her decent. "If you do fall into favor with him, he'll be one of the best friends you could ever ask for. I owe him a lot... But you didn't hear that from me." Jenna stepped onto level ground. "There, you're still alive."

"Mmm, it *does* feel good down here."

Shelly let out a few more yelps before she joined them at the bottom of the gully. Her hands were now grimy and her once-pristine white skirt was sporting dirty little knick-knacks that she had picked up on her way down. The satin hemline had turned a cocoa-like hue.

"Now to cross the Delaware," Toby said. "Come on,

don't stop to rest."

"For goodness sake, Toby, have a little mercy," Shelly panted. "I need to catch my breath."

"Ah, you've been walking on red carpets too long." Toby sat down next to the suitcase. "I guess I might as well take it easy too; I'm already up to *here* in it."

Shelly leaned against a tree. "Well, you know if you had driven your mother's car, none of this would have happened, I'm sorry to say."

"Oh, so this is all my fault, huh?"

"Well, who else would you blame it on?"

Toby thought for a moment. "Some guy in Akron." He picked up a pebble and tossed it into the stream.

"What?"

"Too bad it wasn't your day to have the car, Jenna."

"Why? My car has less room than your truck."

Shelly rolled her head toward Jenna. "What kind of car do you have, Jenna?"

Jenna was pacing back and forth in front of Toby and Shelly, tying her hair into a ponytail with a long white ribbon. "Actually, I don't have a car. It's my sister's and mine, but the first one of us to get married loses it. And when we're both married, my dad gets it. I guess that's his way of keeping us serious."

"And being guaranteed a hot set of wheels," Toby pitched in. "It's a Corvette- a '59. Come on, let's go. You've had your nap." He stood.

Shelly pushed off of the tree and, behind Toby and Jenna, slowly picked her way across the pebbled ravine floor toward the stream. With a suitcase in each hand, Toby began to hop across on a few of the dry stepping stones that jutted out of the crystal clear water. Jenna followed behind.

"How deep is this?" Shelly asked, standing at the edge.

Toby looked back at her, then down at the water.

"Hmm, 'bout four inches. Can you swim? Maybe we should build you a raft." He continued onward. "Just step on these stones here."

"No, I thought that if it wasn't too deep, I'd just walk across. It would feel good on my feet."

"Well, I don't think you're in any danger, just watch out for sharks."

"Very funny." Shelly dipped her toes into the flow. "Oh, it's cold!" She eased the rest of her foot into the water and began traversing the stream. The icy flow lapped at her ankles. "You know when I was a little girl, I used to walk through the streams around our house all the time. I can remember one summer when me and my friend Irene-" She inhaled sharply. Toby and Jenna hopped a few more feet before they turned to see why she had fallen silent.

"What?" Toby asked.

Shelly was standing completely still, her face as white as her clothes had been before she'd come down the ravine wall. Her lower lip was quivering.

"What? What's wrong?" Toby asked again.

"I…" She clutched tightly at the handbag she was carrying. "I, I…"

"Shelly?" Jenna said, starting to retrace her steps back across the stones.

Shelly pressed her hand against her stomach. "I, I… think I'm going to be sick."

"Sick?" Toby exclaimed. "The water's not that rough!"

"I think I stepped on something sharp…" She lifted her left foot out of the water; a stream of blood was gushing out from between her toes.

"Oh, my God…" Jenna said, covering her mouth. "Don't move! Toby come here- she has a piece of glass in her foot!"

"Glass? Oh- Hang on, I'm coming!" He started to move towards them.

"Uh, umm…" Shelly stuttered, and then, between heavy breaths, fired off, "Toby, take the suitcases to dry land!"

Toby swung around, hopped to the other side as fast as he could, sat down the luggage, and hopped back. "Come here…" He stepped into the stream, shoes still on.

"Ahh, ah, ouch…" Shelly gave the handbag to Jenna and then slung her arm around Toby's neck.

"Ready?" Toby asked.

"Mmm-hmm," she whimpered as Toby put his arms under her and lifted her up out of the water. "Ooo…"

"Be careful, Toby," Jenna said.

"I am, I am."

Shelly clung to Toby, a steady stream of blood still dribbling off of her foot. "Don't go too fast, Toby…"

"I'm not, I'm not." He reached the water's edge a few moments later and sat Shelly down on a large rock, her pale feet dangling over the flow. "Put it in the water for a second," he told her.

With a slight gasp, Shelly dipped her bloody foot into the stream. A crimson cloud plumed into the water around her toes and then stretched out, whisped away by the steady current. "*Ow, ow, ow…*"

"Alright, alright, that's good enough." Toby lifted her foot back out of the water. Gingerly, he examined the wound. What appeared to be a piece of green bottleneck had sliced its way into, and remained embedded in, the sole of her foot directly behind her big toe. "Hmm… et loogs like ve vill haz to ampyootate zis…" He pushed her foot back under water. "Ready?"

"No…"

Jenna took her hand. "Here, squeeze my hand, Shelly."

"Okay?" Toby asked again.

"Umm… alright…" Shelly closed her eyes, tears brimming onto her lashes, blurring her mascara. "Okay, do it quick…"

Toby reached into the stream and, firmly pressing his thumb into the direct center of her foot, grasped a hold of the glass shard and quickly drew it out.

"*Mmmrrr…*" Shelly gritted her teeth.

"There," Toby said, holding up the jagged, quarter-sized bottle chip. "Better?"

"No, not yet…"

Toby washed the blood off of his hands and sat the piece of glass on the rock beside Shelly. He pulled her foot out of the stream. It was bleeding freely now. "Now I gotta give up my cigarette holder…" He grabbed onto his shirt sleeve, ripped it off, and began tying it around Shelly's foot.

"*Uh, mmm, mmm…*"

"There. Now we match." He stood. "You can look now."

Shelly cracked her eyes open one at a time. The white t-shirt sleeve sufficed as an effective, if somewhat bulky, bandage. She moved her toes around and looked at him through slowing tears. "Do… do you think it will need… stitches?"

"Nah. It wasn't even that deep. But, see," he pointed to his bandaged forearm, "now we both have big Band-Aids."

"You don't think it will need stitches?"

"Hey, relax, it'll be fine."

"Jenna, do you think it will need stitches?"

Jenna was still holding her hand, and now gave her a reassuring squeeze. "No, I think it'll heal up okay. But I don't think you'll be able to walk the rest of the way home."

"No, *I'll* have to carry you," Toby said. "Come on. Can you grab one of your suitcases?"

"Yes…" Shelly reached for one of the handles.

"I'll carry the other one," Jenna said.

Toby put one arm around Shelly, one arm beneath her legs, and gently lifted her off of the river-side rock. The suitcase that Shelly held in her joined hands dangled against his back. She tucked her face beneath his chin.

"It... *ouch*."

"Well, it's not exactly very comfortable for me, either. You're not exactly... I mean, uh, that suitcase is pretty heavy." He walked a few feet to where the trail started to climb up the ravine wall, his shoes making a '*squish-squish-squish*' sound. "I don't know *how* the hell I'm gonna do this. Hang on." He put his left hand out to stable himself and began, slow and carefully, to ascend the winding path. Shelly hung on to his neck with both of her hands. Somehow, though not without difficulty, he was able to keep his feet planted firmly on the trail all of the way to the top. Here, he sat Shelly on the edge and went back down to help Jenna.

"If you'd just grab one of these I can get up by myself," Jenna said, holding a suitcase out for Toby to take.

"Give me your hand." He took the case and then grasped a hold of Jenna's hand, pulling her up the trail behind him.

"I said if you just- ahh!" Jenna's foot gave way beneath her, but Toby's firm grip kept her from tumbling back down into the ravine.

"What was that, *dear?*" he said as he again reached the lip of the gully, hauling Jenna up the rest of the way.

"Nothing." She grabbed the suitcase from his hand, appearing slightly shaken. "Let's go, *darling*."

"Right. Now for the hard part."

"What?" Shelly exclaimed. "Wasn't that hard enough for you?"

"Haven't found anything that ever was," Toby said, picking her up again. "Let's go, Jenny-pooh."

After they had walked about a mile, the trees began to thin out, and a grassy, untended field started to peek through at them from the woods' sloping edge. The dirty, leaf-strewn floor was slowly overtaken by soft, green, gently waving meadow turf.

"Ahh-ha. Almost there, my pretties!" Toby said after stepping out of the woods and into the thigh high grass. The field that spread out before them was hundreds of yards wide, with a river-cradling valley running across the middle. On the other side of this river, the field rose again to crest at the oak-lined end of Webber Road.

"Oh, great," Jenna moaned. "Just what we need—another river."

"What do you mean 'another river'? You think that last little trickle was a river? This is *the* river: the Carson Valley River."

"How deep is it?" Shelly asked.

"Well… let's just say that we might have to ride the dolphins across."

"Oh, no…"

"Relax, it's only a few feet deep. You won't feel a drip of it. But, uh, keep your eyes peeled for crocodiles, okay?"

"This is Ohio, Toby," Jenna said. "We're not stupid."

"Keep walkin', punk."

As they traversed the sun-drenched field, beads of sweat began to form on Toby's brow. He looked up at the cloud-dappled, sapphire blue sky. "Whew, it sure doesn't feel like seventy-five degrees out here. More like eighty-five."

"I heard that it's supposed to rain tomorrow," Jenna said. "We could definitely use that."

"Yeah, it's weird that after that big storm, everything dried out so fast."

"It's probably all in the river we're about to cross…" Shelly said, still sounding worried.

"Ah, come on, relax. I won't let you drown- you've still gotta win me that Oscar for a hood ornament, remember?"

Shelly leaned her head back and sighed. "I'm afraid that you'll have to find someone else to get you one, Toby."

"What? Why? Getting selfish on me all of the sudden?"

"No…" She focused her eyes on the grass passing beneath her. "I think I'm finished."

"Aw, come on. Don't say that. You're one of the best actresses I've ever seen- and not just because you're related to me. W-whoa…" He nearly tripped, but caught himself. "What… what makes you think you're finished?"

"Because I *want* to be finished, Toby. I want to… to…" She looked him in the eye. "I guess I don't really know what I want except for that. But I'm tired…" A desperate edge began to creep into her voice, but she calmed quickly, almost in defeat. "I need to get away for a while- for a long time. Do you know what it's like not to be able to go anywhere? To have no privacy at all?" Her eyes widened as her temper flared slightly. "To have kiss-and-tell article upon kiss-and-tell article written about your private affairs? Would people care if *your* husband had a so-called 'fling' with someone like…" She trailed off.

"Uh… well…"

"Would they write about it in deep detail? Revealing and inventing with utter abandon?"

"I hope not…"

"They wouldn't. Because you aren't stupid enough to do what I've done, Toby."

"Well, uh… what- what do you mean by that?"

"You aren't stupid enough to jump into the lion's den that fame and fortune can be."

"Says who?"

"Says me. You want to be happy and satisfied with life, don't you?"

"Yeah…"

"Then find out what makes you happy and satisfied- not what everyone else says will make you happy and satisfied- not what everyone else says you should strive for. Find something you love and love it with your whole heart, Toby." She poked him in the chest.

"Right, right, I dig it."

"Toby, I'm being serious! Very serious!"

"I know! Jeeze…"

"Good. I wouldn't want…" Shelly's voice drifted off as they neared the somewhat murky looking river. The weeds grew thick and tall on each side.

"Let's hope that the swimming lesson I took in third grade was worth something…" Toby said. "Okay. Aunt Shelly, I'll take you over, and then," He turned to Jenna. "Then I'll take you over."

"And my suitcases?"

"And then I'll make an extra special trip just for Luggage the Alligator, alright?"

"Alright…" Shelly gave Jenna the suitcase she'd been holding, and tightened her grip around Toby's neck.

"Eww…" Toby said, stepping through the weeds and into the water. His shoes sank into the thick mud of the river bottom. "It's squishy. I hope I don't slip."

"Toby, If you do, I'll never ever, *ever* forgive you," Shelly said.

"Well, jeeze, I might pass out if you don't give me some air! Hang loose!" The dirty water crept up past his knees.

"At least it's not too cold. Wanna feel?" He dropped Shelly a few inches.

"Ahh! No! Toby, I swear if you do I'll, I'll-!"

"Come on, you're all dirty; you need rinsed off." He lowered her a few more inches, just above the water.

"Toby! You-! So help me-!"

Toby reached mid-stream and stopped. The water now came up to his thighs. "How long has it been since you've washed your hair, Aunt Shelly?"

Shelly squealed again as he tipped her head back towards the murky flow. "Don't you dare!"

"Toby, stop!" Jenna yelled from the river's edge.

Toby thought it was funny until Shelly grabbed a fistful of his hair and pulled herself back up. "Ahh, ahh, ahh!" he yelped.

"If you'd be so kind as to take me to shore, Mr. LaRue."

Without a word, Toby hurriedly sloshed to the other side of the river, trudged up through the tall, rustling weeds, and carefully let Shelly down. Instead of sitting in the field, she opted to stand on one foot.

"Thank you," she said, letting go of him.

"You sure you've never had kids before?" Toby turned around, gently stroking his hair, scowling. "'Cause you're acting just like my Mother." He waded back across the river to where Jenna stood and held out his arm.

"Toby, if you even think about it…"

"Fine, come on. This water's getting wet."

"You promise?"

"I promise."

"You swear? Remember, I know where you sleep!"

"I *swear*, okay? Come on!" He picked Jenna up as he had Shelly. Immediately, she grabbed a light hold unto his hair.

"Insurance," she said.

"What, you don't trust me?" Toby began traversing the river again, this time without antics.

"Umm, let me think about that. No."

"Well, I've never seen such ungratefulness! After all that I've done to help you two through the big bad wilderness…" He stood Jenna on dry land. " I feel like Sasquachagia or whatever the hell her name was. There. Happy?"

"Quite."

Shelly put a hand on Jenna's shoulder for stability.
"Don't forget-"

"I know, I know. I'm going. Okay?" Once again, he
crossed the stream. Somehow, he managed to get all three
suitcases and the handbag in one trip. "If I had time for
revenge, I'd send your pet alligators down the river." He
walked out of the water, legs soaked and dripping wet.
"You're lucky I don't just-"

"Shh!" Jenna said, tilting her head. She turned around.
"Someone's coming up the road!" Quickly grabbing two
of the suitcases and the handbag, she began running
towards the road as fast as she could.

"Hey, wait for us!" Toby picked up Shelly and the last
suitcase. He didn't quite take off running, more like a very
brisk, grass-swishing walk. "Hey, slow down!"

"It's Ace!" Jenna yelled from far ahead of them. "Come
on!"

Toby and Shelly finally caught up with Jenna beneath
the oak trees, just as a gleaming white, long-finned
Cadillac eased to a stop in front of them.

The cigar smoking, tweed-clad man inside stuck his
head out the window. "Toby! Where in the goddamn hell
have you been? We've been looking everywhere for you
for an hour!"

"I blew a tire!"

"I know you blew a tire- your pop found your truck!
But why in the hell didn't you stick to the roads? And why
in the hell are you all wet?"

"I, I…" Toby glanced at Shelly and then Jenna

"Never mind, just get in! They've already started
calling kids up for their diplomas, and your mother will be
pretty damned mad if you're not there in time for yours!
Let's go, come on, come on!"

"Okay, okay! We're coming!" Toby ran around to the
other side and Jenna opened the door for him. He sat

Shelly in the back seat and crawled in beside her. Jenna got in the front, both of the suitcases on her lap.

"Ready?" Ace said.

"Yeah! Let's go!"

Ace punched the gas pedal and did a tire-smoking u-turn in the center of Webber. He glanced at Toby in his rearview mirror as they picked up speed. "All I have to say is that'd better not be piss…"

Chapter 9

Ace was rivaling Toby in the crazy driving category as they zoomed over a rickety wooden bridge that left the Cadillac rocking like a wind-tossed boat.

"Are Mom and Dad already there?" Toby asked, pulling off his still-dripping shoe. He peeled the soaked sock off as well.

"Your momma is. Your pop's still out looking for you." Ace chomped down hard on his cigar and tried to coax a little more speed out of the car. "Talk about a wet hen…"

"Dang it…" With both socks off, Toby glanced out of the window. The fields were nothing but a green blur. "What about Mom? Was she mad?"

"Does Jimmy Durante have a nose?"

"Dang it…"

Two minutes later, they swerved into Carson Valley High's packed-out parking lot. Ace screeched to a halt in front of the main entrance. Jenna swung the car door open and got out.

"Thanks, Ace," Toby said, stepping out too. He turned to Shelly. "Are you coming in now?"

Ace answered for Shelly. "We're not gonna have any reason to come in if you don't get the hell in there!"

"Alright!" Toby grabbed his shoes and started walking toward the doors.

"Run, goddamn it!" Ace called after him.

Toby picked up the pace, his bare feet slapping against the pavement, leaving a trail of damp footprints behind him. Through the glass doors ahead, he could see his mother and someone else rushing toward him. The school's auditorium loudspeaker echoed out into the air as she burst through the double doors.

"Toby! Where have you been? You were supposed to be here over an hour ago!" A black gown hung over her arm. "And why are you all wet?"

"I was-"

"We don't have time now, come on!" She grabbed his hand and pulled him through the doors and into a dimly lit hallway, where his home room teacher was waiting with a mortarboard in her hands.

"Tobias!" she exclaimed, looking at his soaked pants. "What...?"

Applause escaped the auditorium.

"It's a long story, Mrs. Durham."

"A long story that will be told later," Elaine said, dropping the silky black gown over him. She took the cap from Mrs. Durham and sat it on his head. "There."

Toby's arms fished around for the balloon-like sleeves. "It's a little long, isn't it?" He kicked at the dragging hem.

"We don't have time for a tailor, Toby." Elaine began pulling him toward the auditorium.

"But what about my shoes?" He said, holding up his dripping Converse.

"Bring them with you!" Elaine's fingernails dug into his wrist as they ascended a flight of stairs and approached a set of wooden, single-windowed doors. She stopped and looked through one of the windows, a patch of artificial light illuminating her face.

"...*Mr. David Beachler*..." a muffled voice filtered through, followed by a hearty round of applause.

"Okay?" she whispered

"Okay."

Elaine pushed against the door as the clapping began to die down. Toby followed her into the well-stocked, gymnasium-turned-graduation hall. They stood at the top of a flight of aisle steps that led down to the honey-colored basketball court, upon which the black-clad graduates were grouped, sitting on rows of uncomfortable wooden folding chairs. The school band sat to their left, and several well dressed adults stood on the green-curtained stage that broke open the wall in front of them.

"Where am I supposed to-?"

"Right down there," Mrs. Durham whispered, "right between Mr. Krindle and Miss Lucas."

Toby peered down across the rows of tiered seats. "Between Dean and Heidi?"

"Yes, between Dean and Heidi," Elaine cut in, "Your father and I are over by Mary, see? See where Grandpa and Grandma are?"

The speaker continued to check off graduates. "…*Miss Jane DeLoy…*" More applause.

"Where's Grandpa Dale?"

"He's right over… well, he was here a minute ago… Never mind, he's here somewhere, don't worry, alright?"

Toby adjusted his cap. "Alright…"

"You look wonderful," Elaine kissed him on the cheek.

"Mom, not in front of the… jeeze…"

"Good luck," she said, leaving for her seat as another burst of clapping filled the high-ceilinged gym.

"Hey, I own good luck," Toby called after her with a smile.

"Go now, Toby," Mrs. Durham waved him down the steps, "while they're clapping."

"Alright." Toby began descending the steps.

Toby's vacant seat was waiting for him in the fourth row. He was able to make it most of the way down without much notice, but apparently 'Buckeye' Harkins wasn't quite as popular as some of the other kids, because the applause for him fizzled out quickly, before Toby could get to his row. He reached the court and had to traverse the last ten feet in a painfully naked silence. Luckily, the adulation over Miss Naomi Hoagland erupted, covering up the struggle he was having as he passed over his fellow fourth-row graduates.

"Where the heck have you been, Toby?"

"Hey, watch my gown!"

"Take it easy, LaRue!" came the whispered complaints as he shuffled past. Finally, he reached his unoccupied seat between Dean and Heidi and plopped down.

"Well, well, well. Look who decided to grace us." Heidi said.

"My, isn't this cozy?" Toby said, letting out a long-contained sigh. He looked at Dean and then at Heidi. Fortunately for Dean Krindle, Toby already had a girlfriend. Heidi was gorgeous; the kind of girl that people see in suntan oil advertisements, the kind of girl that other girls hate, and the kind of girl that Toby would have if Jenna didn't exist and Dean wasn't his best friend.

"Where the hell have you been?" Dean whispered.

Toby turned to see Dean's stern-looking face. "Deanie Boy!"

"Don't give me any of that 'Deanie Boy' bilge. Where the hell have you been? What's with the shoes?"

"It's a long story."

"Shh!" someone hushed.

"I'll tell you later."

"Yeah, well," Dean leaned forward and looked at Heidi, then back at Toby, "Keep your hands to yourself."

"What? You mean nothing like this?" Toby put his arm around Heidi and pulled her closer to him.

"Yeah, or something like *this* might happen…" Dean grabbed Toby's thigh and squeezed hard.

"Alright, alright!" Toby said, letting go of Heidi. "Jesus… we'll just hold hands."

"I'm warning you, LaRue. And don't you encourage him," Dean said to Heidi.

Mr. Derwitz, the principal, began calling up graduates whose last names began with the letter 'K'.

"Hey," Dean said, turning slightly, "Is my tie straight?"

"It's fine," Heidi answered.

"Yeah, it's fine. How's mine?" Toby asked.

Dean's eyes fell to the triangle of white t-shirt that was peeking out from beneath Toby's gown. He turned away, shaking his head. "Judas Priest."

"I didn't have time to change," Toby told Heidi. He lifted the edge of his robe, revealing his still-wet jeans and bare feet. "See?"

"What-?"

"It's a long story."

"*...Mr. Dean Krindle...*" Mr. Derwitz's voice bellowed out. Dean rose and Toby and Heidi joined in with the vigorous clapping. Toby put his fingers in his mouth and let out an ear-splitting whistle. They watched a rare smile tug at Dean's lips as he edged out of their row and ascended the temporary stage steps to shake hands with the gray-haired principal and several other faculty members. He graciously received his diploma, and was then directed off stage, not back down the steps, but off to the right side, behind the curtain.

The butterflies in Toby's stomach took flight as Mr. Derwitz glanced down at a piece of paper and then at Toby.

"Mr. Tobias LaRue."

The crowd erupted as a beaming Toby stood and shuffled up to the stage. Several flashbulbs lit up the auditorium. He paused for a split second at the base of the steps, realizing that the last twelve years of his life had led to this moment. Slowly and deliberately, hoping that no one would see his bare feet, he made his way up onto the stage, where a stiff-looking Mr. Derwitz was holding a rolled-up piece of manila paper. The audience continued to applaud as Toby took his diploma and shook the principal's hand.

"Gook luck, Toby," Mr. Derwitz said. "My office won't be the same without you."

"Thanks."

Toby moved on to the other men and women on the platform.

"Good job, Tobias," said Mr. Green over the crowd.

"Thanks."

"Congratulations, Toby," said Mrs. Lloyd

"Thanks."

Mrs. Flanagan just shook Toby's hand and smiled.

"Thanks.

"Well done, Mr. LaRue," Mr. Bowman said. "Right that way." The social studies teacher pointed toward another set of stairs at stage side, dimly lit and hidden from the audience's view.

"Thank you." As Toby began walking away, he saw a familiar silhouette standing at the bottom of the steps. His smile widened. "Gramps!" he said, reaching the shadow.

"Hiya, kiddo!" The old man said, giving Toby a hug.

"What are you doing here?"

"Well, I wanted to be the first one to say 'Hiya, kiddo' to Toby Dale LaRue, high school graduate. How does it feel?"

"Like twelve years for twelve seconds."

Grandpa Dale laughed, slapping Toby on the back.

"Oh, hey, can you hold these for me?" Toby pulled off his cap and held out his diploma.

With a puzzled expression, Dale hesitantly took the two articles. "What for?"

"I've got a debt to collect."

"What?"

"You'll find out. Just wait for me here, okay?"

"Alright…"

"I'll be back in a minute," Toby said, finishing out the tiny corridor. Instead of turning right and going back into the auditorium, he went through another doorway and found himself in a dim hallway. The slap of bare feet and the shuffling of his gown echoed off of the walls as he made his way down to the janitor's closet, where the slatted door stood slightly ajar, allowing a sickly yellow light to spill out into the hall.

"Sam?" Toby whispered.

"That's Mr. Jones to you, wise guy," said a flat, gravely-sounding voice from behind the door.

"I'm here to collect my debt."

"I know why you're here, jackass." A thin-haired, bespectacled man in his late forties stuck his head out of the closet. He was a few inches taller than Toby. "You're here to get me fired, ya little ingrate."

"Ah, ah, ah. You promised. You lost fair and square, now come on, let's have it." Toby held out his hands.

The man chewed on a growl, snorted through his big, purplish nose, and then, disappearing out of view for a moment, produced a plastic-shrouded record turntable with two long, hastily spliced wires trailing out of it. "Here, ya dirty…"

"Great!" Toby examined the tip of the wire. "And…?" He held out his hand.

Mr. Jones produced a black skeleton key from his pocket and slapped it down into Toby's open palm. "Ya little bastard."

"Great! Now, you dig the drill?"

"What?"

"Do you know what to *do?*"

"Yeah, sure! Now scram before somebody sees ya!"

"Alright! Thanks, buddy!"

"I'm not your buddy, ya bum! Now beat it!"

Toby started to leave, and then turned back around.

"Now, remember- leave the fuse unplugged until he's talked for two minutes, okay? Two minutes exactly."

"Will you get outta here, Stella?"

"I sure hope this works." Toby pulled the turntable close.

"Well, if it don't, ya never knew me, ya hear?"

"I'll see you around," Toby said, continuing down the cream-colored hallway.

Mr. Jones turned out his closet light. "I hope not!"

The sounds of graduation continued to reverberate throughout the building as Toby rounded a corner and headed for a door with a small sign reading 'School Office' hanging over it. The mahogany door, slightly ajar, opened with barely a creak of its metal hinges. Once inside the small, aqua-hued room, Toby set to work executing his mischievous plan. Sitting the record player on a desk, he pulled the public address system away from the wall and located the cobwebbed microphone wire, which he tugged out and pushed aside. Working quickly, tongue sticking out in concentration, he plugged the record player first into the wall, and then into the recently vacated microphone jack. He wiggled it in place to be sure that a good connection would still be made. Sliding the P.A. system back against the wall, he chuckled slyly to himself, glancing through the tinted plastic shroud that covered the turntable. A shiny, black forty-five peeked back at him; it read *'Johnny B. Goode- Chuck Berry'*. The needle was resting on the album's outer edge and the turntable's power switch was in the 'on' position. "Perfect..." he snickered.

After quietly pulling the office door shut, Toby locked it and then kicked the skeleton key under the door, back into the office. Trying to stifle his laughter, he retraced his steps through the long hallway, returning to the small, dark corridor beside the stage where his Grandpa Dale was still waiting for him.

"What in the world are you up to?" Dale asked, returning the mortarboard and diploma to Toby.

"I…" Toby contemplated telling him. Grandpa Dale was, after all, his favorite living relative. "You'll see in a few minutes, but you can't tell anyone, okay?" He put the cap back on.

"Can't tell anyone what?"

"You'll see, uh, hear it in a few minutes…"

"Toby…"

"I've got to get back to my seat. Walk out with me so they think I've been talking to you this whole time."

"Toby…" Dale followed Toby out into the auditorium. Principal Derwitz was on the letter 'W'.

"Alright, I'll see you after this is all over, okay?" Toby whispered, reaching his row. Not waiting for Dale to reply, he slipped down the row and into his seat.

"Were the hell have you been?" Dean asked.

"You know, I'm really getting sick of that question."

"Well?"

"Just watch."

Heidi jabbed Toby with her elbow. "You weren't here to see me get mine." She held up her diploma.

"I was just lucky to be here to see *me* get *mine*."

"You also missed Stuart Novello almost fall off of the stage."

"What? Now *that* I regret not seeing." Toby turned his eyes back toward the stage.

Before long, Mr. Derwitz was shaking Natalie Zimmerman's hand. Dean leaned over to Toby. "Great, here comes Mr. Dimwitz's three hour speech."

"Heh, heh. Not if Chuckie B. has anything to say about it." Toby said with a wink, followed by a slightly evil grin.

"Huh?"

"Just watch."

The graduates began to squirm as soon as Mr. Derwitz stepped up to the microphone and cleared his throat. The other faculty members made their way off stage. Toby glanced up at the white-faced, grate-covered clock hanging high on the gymnasium wall. It was 4:35.

"I would like to begin here at Carson Valley High School this afternoon," Mr. Derwitz cleared his throat again, "by updating the friends and family here at Carson Valley High School of what we have been doing here at Carson Valley High School all year long here, and about how we here at Carson Valley High School plan to improve here at Carson Valley High School in the years to come..."

"Jesus Christ..." Dean groaned, tilting his head back.

With every move of the clock's second hand, Toby's wicked smile grew; 4:36.

"... and I'd like here, as principal of Carson Valley High School, to thank one by one all of the teachers here at Carson Valley High School that have held their students to the level of discipline that has come to be expected here at Carson Valley High School..."

4:36 and a half.

"... and, as principal of Carson Valley High School, I am obligated- no honored, to one by one thank each and every child who helped with the fund raising here at Carson Valley High School in February here at Carson Valley High School..."

"Ten... nine... eight..." Toby counted down under his breath, "six... five..."

"...because we here at Carson Valley High School believe that when we put responsibility into the hands of

one of our students here at Carson Valley High School we
are putting the future into-"

The auditorium lights dimmed slightly.

"-their hands. And if I may say so-"

The ear-splitting blare of Chuck Berry's electric guitar
cut into Mr. Derwitz's speech like a supercharged
chainsaw. He, along with the entire audience, jumped
about six inches into the air as the P.A. speakers began
thrusting out the intro of the song at full blast. Toby let out
an irrepressible laugh when the drums and bass kicked in
and the basketball court started to vibrate beneath their
feet. He laughed even harder when, unheard to all, Mr.
Derwitz, who, as was well known, hated rock n' roll,
began yelling with his hands over his ears, in exact
synchronization with Mr. Berry's vocals.

"What the hell-?" Dean yelled to Toby. A look of
realization crossed his face. "You didn't!"

All that Toby could do was wipe the tears from his eyes
and laugh harder.

"SHUT THAT GARBAGE OFF!" Mr. Derwitz roared
over the music, finally using the microphone.

Several school staff members rushed out of the gym.
Meanwhile, without fear of punishment, the graduates
were beginning to get up and dance around.

"…*Go, Johnny, go! Go! Johnny B. Goode*…"

Kids began tossing their caps into the air.

"NO! NO! NOT YET! STOP!" bellowed Mr. Derwitz.

Toby grabbed his cap and fired it off like a Frisbee;
Dean and Heidi followed suit.

"Who did this?" Heidi shouted, a wide smile gracing
her face.

"Not I said the goose!" Toby replied and then looked at
Dean. He put his fingers to his nose and made a stretching
motion.

The school staff members ran back in, and one of them

screamed at the top of his lungs, "IT'S A RECORD PLAYER, BUT THE DOOR'S LOCKED!"

"WELL, THEN FIND A KEY!" came the principal's irate reply.

They ran back out.

By now, many of the brothers, sisters, and cousins of the graduates, at the protest of their parents, had come out of the bleachers to join in with this wild, spur-of-the-moment rock n' roll party. The hats and feet were flying like there was no tomorrow. Toby looked for his sister Tracy. She, along with all of the other musicians, was being held at bay by the bandleader, Mr. Marshall. Toby stood up and waved at her. As he did, a mortarboard fell at his feet; he stooped to pick it up. He turned around and located Stuart Novello.

"Hey, Dean," he said, elbowing his friend. "Watch this." He curled the cap into his arm and then flung it at Stuart's face with all of his might.

Stuart didn't even know what hit him. He just fell back into his seat, which in turn collapsed beneath him. Several dancing grads blocked him out of view.

Dean gave Toby a double high-five. "That was too perfect!" he yelled over the blaring music.

"Naturally!"

One of the staff members ran into the gym. "THE KEY! WE… CAN'T FIND IT!"

"YOU -- IDIOTS! GET THIS TRASH OUT OF THESE SPEAKERS NOW! BREAK DOWN THE DOOR IF YOU HAVE TO; I DON'T CARE!" Mr. Derwitz's face was as red as a tomato.

Frustrated, the staff member ran back out, but by now the song was nearing its end and no force on earth was going to get the kids back into their seats, let alone the parents and family members who were milling about the bleachers, shouting to one another.

When the closing chord of the song was struck, the crowd of kids erupted in deafening applause. The volume continued to increase as Mr. Derwitz threw up his hands and stormed off of the stage.

Heidi and Dean were standing beside Toby, hands clapping over their head.

"I don't know who did this," Heidi said, "but God bless them!"

"Amen!" Toby yelled with a wink to Dean. "God bless him indeed!"

Chapter 10

The applause died down to a loud murmur as a hundred different conversations began simultaneously, most of them centering around who the mischief maker might be and how thankful they were for him. Mr. Derwitz came back and tried several times unsuccessfully to get everyone seated in order to finish his speech, but he finally gave up, stomping off backstage.

"Well," Dean said, "that was short."

"I can't believe anyone had the guts to do that!" Heidi exclaimed.

Toby sat down and began putting on his shoes. "I guess some gots it an' some ain't."

Dean crossed his arms. "Yeah, well, the one that *gots* it is gonna *get* it if they ever find out who *he* is."

"Better that one should die for the people."

"Toby!" The sound of Jenna's voice pulled Toby to his feet. She was trying to make her way to him, pushing against the flow of people exiting the row. Her face looked serious.

"What's up?" he asked, moving toward her.

"I have to go; my mother's here to get me."

"Why?"

"She had to take my Grandma to the hospital; they don't know what's wrong with her…"

"Oh… Well, do you want me to come along?"

"No, no, I just won't be able to make it to your party."

"Oh… What about Dean's?"

Jenna began to leave. "I'm not sure. I'll call you, okay?"

"Alright… I guess I'll see you later"

"I'm sorry," she called over her shoulder. "Bye!"

"See ya…"

Dean tapped Toby on the shoulder. "Hey, I've gotta go too. I've gotta have dinner with my folks before they go to work. They're both working tonight."

"Well everyone's leaving me…" A fake grin spread across Toby's face. "Except for Heidi here!"

"Sorry, Tobe, I'm going with Dean to dinner." Heidi picked up her purse and took Dean's hand. "I'll see you later."

"Fine. What time tonight?" Toby asked Dean.

"I figure somewhere between seven and eight. Don't forget the chips and dip."

"Right-o, daddy-o."

"Let Smoosh know, okay?"

"Right. See ya."

"Yep." Dean disappeared into a swarm of graduates, Heidi in tow.

Suddenly devoid of people to make fun of or impress, Toby became aware that his leg was throbbing. He eased back into his chair. It took about ten minutes for the remaining grads to shuffle off of the basketball court and out into the halls. After the junior high band finished putting away their unused instruments, he was left alone with his thoughts. He glanced down at his diploma and then up into the emptying bleachers behind him. His family was no longer there; they were probably out in the hallway waiting for him. After massaging his leg for a few minutes, he stood and began moving out of his aisle. As he did, the huge auditorium drop lights above him began to fade out one by one, and by the time he reached the doorway, only one, in the center of the court, remained lit. He turned and watched as it too slowly traded its milky white glare for a soft, warm glow, and then gently joined the other lights in darkness. The wooden folding chairs disappeared into the blackness.

The emotions that welled up in him now were definitely unexpected, as memory after memory seemed to join the darkness before him. A sick feeling of insecurity filled his stomach. As he turned and stepped across the threshold, suppressing a tear, he realized that he was finally crossing over into the uncertain and unforgiving freedom he had been waiting for his entire life. He cleared his throat and walked into the hallway of goodbye-ing graduates.

"Heyo, Toby! Twelve-O-C.!"

Toby looked up to see the freckle-faced, gangly-framed person of Frankie Grossi flopping toward him. "Hey Frankie, what's up?"

"Dig to bug out over t' my pad after black?"

"Huh?"

"Sano job-ee to my jap flap puncher?"

"Uh, I don't think so…"

"Neg-o?" Frankie's shoulders slumped and he turned away. "Check… Jiffy-jop on the flippy-flop, 'kay?"

"Yeah, Frankie… Right." Toby shook his head and began to make his way through the crowd.

"Toby! Toby!" a girl's voice penetrated the mob of people at Toby's right.

"Hey, Trixie," he said, following the voice to a honey-haired, smokey-eyed girl leaning against a row of lockers. She was happily surrounded by four drooling guys. "What's up?"

"Oh, I just wondered if you'd like to come over to my graduation party later… my parents aren't invited…"

"Uh…" Toby coughed, "I- I don't think so. I'm all booked up tonight."

Trixie's face clouded over and she turned away in disgust.

"Sorry." Toby continued through the hall. He heard someone else calling his name, and was going to ignore it until he saw a waving hand and realized that it was his mother. She, along with the rest of his family, was standing at the end of a long line of crowd-reflecting trophy cases. He began knifing his way in their direction. He was greeted with a big hug and kiss from his teary-eyed Grandma Rainesburg, followed by a firm yet loving slap on the back from his white-haired Grandpa Rainesburg.

"Congratulations, Toby," they both said.

Toby moved on to his Grandpa Dale's finger-crushing handshake. At first, Dale's face was stern, but it soon melted into a strange kind of 'You're an idiot' slash 'That's my boy' expression. Toby winked at him.

"Hey," his sister Tracy said, picking up on the exchange, "*you* didn't have anything to do with that music in there did you?"

Toby smiled a fake-looking 'shut up if you know what's best for you' smile and began greeting the rest of his relatives, some of whom he hadn't even been aware were there. He moved through his Uncle Mick and Aunt Susan, his cousins Charlie and David, his Great-Aunt Violet, Ace and his wife Mary, their kids Al and Linda, and finally his older brother and sister-in-law, Jack Jr. and Gwen. Gwen was cradling Toby's ten-month-old nephew, Joey.

"Well, Tobe," Jack Jr. said, shaking Toby's hand, "you finally made it."

"Yeah, well, I would have made it four years ago if Mom and Dad would've had the good sense to have me first."

"Yeah, too bad."

"Congratulations, Toby," Gwen said, leaning over to kiss Toby on the cheek.

"Whoa, hey, don't do that! Jack'll label me wife stealer!"

Gwen kissed him anyway. "Why were you so late? We

were afraid you weren't coming."

"Long story." Wiping off his cheek, he held up the diploma. "But this is all that matters, right?"

Elaine pitched in, "What about the dinner that's sitting at home on the dinning room table?"

"I had a few problems, okay? I'm sorry." He started to pull off his gown, and then realized that he didn't want to be standing in the middle of all his classmates in a pair of wet jeans. He turned around and nabbed Mrs. Durham as she was passing by. "Mrs. Durham?"

"Yes, Toby?

"Do you mind if I, uh, bring this back later?"

"Just make sure that you have it back by Monday afternoon. Oh, and here." She handed Toby a red and gray tassel with a silver '61' charm hanging in it.

Toby took it with a smile. "You sure this one's mine?"

Mrs. Durham rolled her eyes. "Please, Toby, please."

"Well, I'll see you around, Mrs. Durham. Thanks."

"Goodbye, Toby. And good luck."

"Thanks."

Elaine took Toby by the elbow. "Are you ready to go?"

Toby took one last look down the crowded hall. He waved goodbye to fellow drag racer Cal Rillings and then turned to his mother. "Yeah… let's go."

"So where's Aunt Shelly?" Toby asked as then began filing out of the building. The air seemed slightly cooler now; partly because of Toby's damp clothes. The reddening sun hung halfway down in the sky.

"She watched from the projection room," Elaine said. "She's probably waiting in your Grandpa and Grandma's car."

"I haven't even seen her yet," Tracy said with disgust.

Toby's family and friends began splitting off to go to their own cars. "We'll see you in a few minutes, Toby,"

Mr. Rainesburg said, tugging at the brim of his hat.

"Alright, Grandpa."

Jack Jr. and Gwen stayed alongside; they had parked their brand new Ford Galaxie right next to Elaine's black Nomad.

"See you at the house," Jack Jr. said, opening the passenger's side door of his car for Grandpa Dale. Gwen got into the back seat with Joey in her arms.

"Okay," Elaine said, opening her door as well. It was a two-door station wagon, so she had to wait for Toby to pull off his gown before she could get in.

"Whew... at least I'll never have to wear this thing again." Toby tossed the gown on the back seat and climbed in.

Tracy got in behind him.

"Wow, that was exciting, wasn't it?" she asked. "Why are you all wet?"

"I went swimming, okay?"

"In your clothes?"

"It's against the law to skinny dip in the Carson Valley River."

"You swam in the river?"

Jack started the car.

"Why don't you shut up?"

"Why don't *you* shut up?"

"I wasn't talking!"

"Hey!" Elaine cut in, turning around to face them. "Simmer down."

"Dad," Tracy whined, "Toby pinched me!"

"I did not!"

"Did to!"

"Quiet!" Jack yelled, speaking for the first time since the graduation ceremony. Silence descended as he lit a cigarette and steered out of the school's parking lot, pointing the car toward home.

Toby glanced out the back window. Five cars formed a sparkling, multicolored train behind them, each one carrying graduation presents; *his* graduation presents. A warm feeling began to grow in his stomach. They made the transition from Webber onto Briggle, where the road began to twist and turn and rise and fall, snaking over little hills and valleys through a tunnel of long-branched trees.

"Did you get to talk to Aunt Shelly at all?" Toby asked Elaine. He twirled his red and gray tassel around his finger.

"Just enough to give her a hug. She was changing her clothes."

"What? She didn't even get wet!"

"Her skirt was torn and covered with dirt, Toby." Elaine rolled down her window as the smoke from Jack's cigarette started to drift in her direction.

"What happened?" Tracy asked again, "Why is everyone all wet and dirty?"

Toby sighed long and loud. "My truck blew a tire and we had to walk home, okay?"

"In the river?"

"No, dim bulb, across the river."

"Dad! Did you hear what Toby called me?"

"Daddy! I'm a little tattle-tale whiny baby!" Toby mocked, squeezing Tracy's knee.

"Ow! Mom!"

"That will be quite enough you two!" Elaine said. "Unless you don't want any cake and ice cream…"

"But…"

"Enough!"

A line of pine trees next to a colorless barn marked the beginning of the LaRue property. The glistening old farm house sat at the top of a hill, on the right side of the one lane road, with a leafy maple shading the tiny front yard. A rusty mailbox adorned with '7975' in blocky white letters was planted on the opposite side of the road. The gravel driveway that they pulled into actually had two entrances, one by the barn and one beside the house. Jack took the barn entrance, climbing a short, steep hill, looping around beneath a massive oak, snaking by the vacant chicken house, and finally joining the other entrance in front of the garage. The convoy of cars followed behind, minus Ace's Cadillac; he had turned into his own driveway at the bottom of the hill. Pulling up beside his blue A&L Automotive work truck, Jack shut the car off and they all piled out.

"Ah," Toby said, "My leg's bugging me again…"

Elaine slammed her car door. "You can take a hot bath after everyone's left."

"Huh-uh, I'm going to Dean's, remember?

"In what?" Tracy sneered. "You wrecked your truck."

"I did not. It just needs a new tire, which I happen to have. Hey, Mom?"

"Yes?" Elaine was following Jack up the stone path that connected the driveway to the house.

"Did you get the chip dip mix and cream cheese?"

"Yes, it's in the refrigerator. I already mixed it up." She reached the concrete slab in front of the door and turned around, addressing all of the guests that were getting out of their cars. "Just come in everyone!"

Tracy reached the door first and held it open for Toby. "Age before beauty, big brother.""Then I guess your dog goes after you?"

"Ha, ha."

Before stepping into the house, Toby glanced over his shoulder at all of the gift bags and boxes being carried toward him. He looked at Tracy and raised an eyebrow. "At least school was good for something…"

The kitchen still smelled like sugar cookies when he came through the door, except that now it was mingled with the heady aromas of corn dogs and cake and cheesy potatoes. The small porcelain tabletop was covered with all kinds of appetizers and condiments, and, looking through the doorway into the dining room, Toby could see that his mother had went all-out decorating and laying out the food.

"I hope you're hungry," Elaine said, pulling a pitcher of lemonade out of the refrigerator, "Because you're the only one I know that likes his green beans mixed with mayonnaise." She disappeared into the dining room.

"I'm starved." Toby held open the wooden screen door for his Grandma Rainesburg. Her pale, almost ice colored blue eyes sparkled as she took his hand and stepped up into the house.

"Oh. Thank you, Toby. You're such a gentleman."

Toby helped his Grandpa in as well. "I've got everybody fooled."

Elaine came back into the kitchen. "Oh, here, Dad, let me take your hat."

"Thank you, dear," Mr. Rainesburg said. He was a tall, stately man, with his silvery gray hair and finely crafted goatee. His knobby fingers were adorned with several exotic-looking rings.

It only took Toby a minute to run up to his room and put on a dry pair of jeans and some clean shoes. When he came back downstairs, all of the guests, including an unsullied Aunt Shelly, had gathered in the house, some finding a friendly chair in the living room, others content to carry on a conversation leaning on a door frame. Elaine, Tracy, and Gwen were serving the cake and ice cream on blue china plates, while Toby found a comfortable spot at the table behind a bottle of Coke and a plate piled high with homemade corn dogs. His gifts had congregated on top of the cedar chest that sat in front of the dining room window, and several more congratulations and pats on the back from friends and family were thrown his way. His two cousins, Charlie and David, joined him at the table.

"So, how's it feel, Toby," sixteen-year-old Charlie asked. "Now what are you going to do that you don't have to go to school?"

"Oh, I don't know, Charlie Bob. I figure I'll just go to work for Dad for a while, you know."

"You're not going to college?"

"Are you kidding? That'd be like walking back into prison and asking if I could use the electric chair!"

Charlie laughed.

Ten-year-old David spoke up from behind a mouthful of cake. "But what do you want to do when you grow up?"

"I don't think I'll ever have to worry about growing up, Davey."

"Toby," a random voice called from the living room. "Toby, come here. Aunt Violet wants to take your picture…"

"Great," Toby sighed. "I'll be back. Hey, make sure you guys try the green beans." He stood and, carrying his Coke and half a corn dog with him, weaved his way through the guests and into the living room. His Great Aunt Violet was cradling a little Kodak Brownie in her lap.

"Now stand over there, Toby. Beside the Victrola."

Toby moved to the spot that she was indicating. "Like this?" He struck a debonair pose.

"Oh, no, no, no! You can't be holding that food in the picture!"

"Oh, right." Toby slid the rest of his corn dog off of the stick and popped it in his mouth. He sat the Coke on one of the pillared wooden ledges that separated the living room from the den. "How's that?"

"Much better! Now, smile!"

Toby swallowed his corn dog and then cracked his lips into a lop-sided grin.

"Okay… one, two, three!"

The camera flashed brilliantly, sending Toby into a short blinking spree. "How was that?"

"Wonderful, Toby, just lovely. Now one more."

Toby repeated the procedure and, shaking his head slightly from the flash, picked up his Coke.

"Thank you, sweetheart." Aunt Violet said.

"You're welcome." Thinking that the room needed a little more atmosphere, Toby cranked up the antique Victrola. The Glenn Miller record that his mother had been listening to that morning began playing again, coming up to speed right in the middle of 'String of Pearls'. He sat down on the piano bench beside Grandpa Dale as Elaine walked into the room.

"Has everyone had cake and ice cream?"

She was answered with a unanimously hearty 'yes'.

"Anyone for seconds?"

A few people accepted the offer, including Grandpa Dale who, holding out his plate said, "Let the kid open his gifts! We can eat and watch at the same time."

A smile spread across Toby's face. "Yeah, mom, they can…"

"Alright… Tracy, will you help me bring the gifts in here?"

Tracy grumbled to herself, putting her half-eaten cake on the coffee table. "Fine." She and Elaine began to bring the presents into the living room, sitting them in front of Toby. The guests in the kitchen, dining room, and den all came in to watch.

"Come on, Toby! We all thought this day'd *never* come!" a lighthearted Uncle Mick said.

"You're telling me!" Toby answered. "This is the day I

was born for!"

"Well, come on," Grandpa Dale urged, lighting his pipe. "Get the show on the road!"

"Which one should I open first?" Toby asked.

"Here." Dale leaned forward and produced a small package from his back pocket. "Here, open this'n first."

Toby took the present; it was surprisingly heavy for its size. The room became silent as he tore at the brown paper wrapping. The paper fell away to reveal a tarnished, six inch pocket knife with the initials 'D.W.L.' carved into the wooden side. "Wow…" Toby said, pulling open the blade.

"Your great-grandfather gave that to me on the night I left for Europe," Grandpa Dale said almost reverently. "It saved my life twice… That little blade killed two Huns during the war."

"Wow…" Toby exclaimed again, eyes widening. He folded it back up and slipped it into his pocket. "I'll take good care of it, Grandpa Dale."

"And it'll do the same for you."

The gifts that followed were slightly less sensational, but a few of them made Toby wonder. The new watch from Grandpa and Grandma Rainesburg, and the dress shirt from Aunt Violet came as no surprise; it was the drapes from Uncle Mick and Aunt Susan, the bedding from Ace and Mary, and the pail of cleaning supplies and wall clock from Jack Jr. and Gwen that puzzled him. The pile of presents soon dwindled down to a patch of balled-up wrapping paper strewn out on the avocado carpet.

"May I go next?" Shelly asked. She reached into her purse and drew out two envelopes and, standing from her chair, walked across the room and sat down on the piano bench beside Toby. "Now, this one is from me." she placed one of the envelopes in his hand. "Go ahead, open it."

"Okay…" Toby stuck his index finger beneath the flap and pulled it open. Inside he found a sentimental card, but more importantly two crisp, one hundred dollar bills. "Wow!"

"That's from James and me for a good head start in life. This one," she gave him the other envelope. "is from a secret admirer…"

"Secret admirer?" Toby said, flipping it over in his hands. "Who?"

"Go on, open it!"

"Okay…" Toby did the same as he had with the previous envelope, but the contents of this one were slightly different. After tearing the flap, he pulled out a white card with some sort of crest embossed on the front. He opened it. Within that unadorned white cardstock was nestled a small, three inch lock of silky blonde hair and a handwritten message in simple cursive that read:

To Toby, best wishes and all my love -Grace Kelly

"Get outa town!" Toby rocketed to his feet. He turned around to face Shelly. "Is this really real?"

Shelly beamed. "One hundred percent."

"But… how?"

"I told you I was in Monaco last fall. I've had it since then."

"Thank you!" He threw his arms around Shelly.

"You're welcome, Toby." She laughed, returning the hug.

"Wow…" Toby said again, gingerly cradling the lock of hair in his palm. He walked it around the room so that everyone could get a good look. "I can't believe it! This is even better than the picture you gave me of her! Look, Mom!"

"It's wonderful, Toby!" Elaine said.

"Let me see," Tracy whined. "I want to see!"

"Fine… just don't breathe on it."

Elaine whispered something to Jack and he got up and hobbled out of the room. Toby, carefully refolding the card, returned to his seat between Grandpa Dale and Aunt Shelly, still awestruck.

"Well, Toby," Elaine said, "I think that you've made out pretty well."

"Yeah, me too!" Toby answered.

"But…"

Jack limped back in with what appeared to be a heavy canvas body bag with a wire hanger sticking out of the top. Elaine stood up beside him and motioned Toby over.

"This," Elaine said, "is from your father and me. Go ahead, unzip it."

Getting back up, Toby walked over and grabbed a hold of the large, silver zipper and slowly pulled it down. He knew what it was before he even finished. "I… but… you…" The black canvas parted and fell away to reveal a glowing, coffee-colored, leather fighter pilot's jacket and a pair of silver-rimmed aviator's goggles. The sweet smell of old leather rolled off of them.

"Do you like them?" Elaine asked.

Toby was temporarily struck silent. "But this… these were Uncle Joe's…"

"And now they're yours." Elaine pulled the jacket off of the hanger and helped Toby put it on. "This will protect you while you're racing; better than that old denim one you wear."

"I don't know about… I wouldn't want to ruin it…" Toby said, slipping into the jacket. It fit him perfectly, hanging on his frame like a glove. He touched the cracked black ace of spades that had been applied to the right shoulder. "It's perfect, but I don't know what to say…"

"You're lucky Uncle Joe was a shrimp like you," Jack Jr. said, laughing. "Otherwise, I'd be wearing that right now."

"Try the goggles," Elaine prompted.

Toby pulled the goggles over his head, the leather jacket creaking as he moved. He slid them into place and everyone cheered and started clapping.

"Wonderful!" Grandma Rainesburg exclaimed. "You look wonderful, Toby!"

"Do you think so?" Toby tapped on the goggles. "These are a lot tougher than the ones that I've been wearing. And this…" He ran his hands up and down the front of the jacket, finally sticking them in the pockets. His hand touched something inside. "What's this?" He drew from the pocket an envelope very much like the ones Shelly had given him, except that this one kept bending on itself, weighted down in one corner. "What's this?" He held it out.

"That is your last gift, Toby; from everyone."

"From everyone?" Toby pushed up the goggles. "What is it?"

"Well, open it!"

Toby tore open the envelope and a small, round-headed key fell out onto the floor. "What…" He stooped to pick it up. "What's this for?"

"Look at it, it should look familiar."

Toby flipped the key over in his hand and examined it a little closer. The numbers '392' were stamped on the copper head. The realization of what he was holding flooded into his head. "This is the key to the apartment over the garage! Over A&L!"

"It's the key to *your* apartment over the garage." Elaine corrected. "Everyone helped clean it up. And it's yours for as long as you can pay the utility bill."

"Holy-! Wow! You're kidding, right?! You mean I'm really gonna have a place of my own?"

"Like I said, everyone helped in some way."

Toby turned around. "Thank you, everybody!" He looked at the key in his hand. "This is bitchin'- I mean, uh, this is real neat!"

"Congratulations, Toby," Elaine said, giving Toby a hug.

"Thanks, Mom." He turned to the rest of the guests. "These are the best presents I've ever gotten in my whole life! These are the best presents that anyone could *ever* get!"

"Well," Grandpa Rainesburg said, standing, "you deserve it, Toby. You've become a fine young man."

Grandpa Rainesburg's comments were eventually repeated by all of the guests as they slowly began to stand and find their way out of the living room. A few of them hung around, picking at the leftovers and conversing, while others said goodbye and left. Toby sat back down with his Grandpa Dale on the piano bench and Elaine began picking up the wrapping paper.

"Toby, your father said if you want to get your truck out of that ditch get ready to go. He wants to get it before it gets too dark."

"Okay. You want to come, Gramps?"

"Well," Dale grunted, "maybe it would be a good idea to move around a bit after eating all that cake. Where's your truck stuck at?"

"Over on Mendenhall. Between Mainer's and Grissom's."

"Alright…" Dale put his hands on his knees and rocked forward, standing up. "Let's get going before I fall asleep."

Chapter 11

The old grandfather clock began chiming seven as Toby and Dale got up off of the piano bench and walked into the dining room. Toby couldn't resist the urge to grab the last corn dog off of the table.

"Alright," he said before taking a bite. "I'll see you later, Mom."

Elaine was tying her apron on. "Okay, sweetie. Be careful."

"You probably won't see me until-"

Just then, Tracy burst into the house through the kitchen door. "Toby! Come look what Dad found hanging on the back door!"

"What?" Toby asked.

"Come on! Come see!"

"What?" He followed her through the kitchen. The back door was nestled, along with the basement steps, in a tiny hallway between the kitchen and the bathroom. Pushing aside the curtain that covered the door's window, Toby could see his father picking up a pile of heavy chain off of the back porch. Jack pointed to the knob on the outside of the door. Toby pulled the curtain back a little farther, craning his neck to see what his father was pointing at. The crown of a black felt cowboy hat peered back.

"You know who that's from?" Tracy asked.

Toby didn't answer. He carefully turned the squeaky metal knob and pushed open the door. "I don't believe it…" he said, stepping out onto the porch. The child-sized cowboy hat, with the name 'Hopalong Cassidy' emblazoned on its dome, was hanging on the doorknob by its once-white chinstrap cord. Toby gently lifted it up. "I do not believe it… I was ten years old the last time I saw this!" He flipped it over and a piece of paper fell out. "Hey, grab that!" he exclaimed, as the breeze began to carry it away.

"I've got it," Tracy said, snatching the paper out of the air.

"Give it here! Give it here!"

"You're welcome." She handed it to him. Toby scanned over it, a wide smile slowly forming on his face. "Well? What's it say?"

"It's from Mr. Kimball."

"I knew it!"

"He says congratulations on graduating…"

"How did he know you were graduating?" Tracy asked.

"He knows… somehow, he knows everything that goes on. Anyway, he says congrats… he says that he's had my hat since the night he found me in the woods… uh, thanks again for the Christmas present… and he says I'm welcome to visit him any time I want. That's it." He held the hat up again. "I don't believe it…"

His mother and Grandpa Dale filled the door behind him. "What's this?" Elaine asked, and then caught sight of the hat. "Oh, my goodness…"

"Look, Gramps." Toby handed it to Dale.

"Jiminy Krauts," Dale exclaimed, "My, my, my… Old Ben Kimball, isn't it?"

"Yep," Toby said, gazing out across the back yard. A barbed wire fence separated their well-trimmed lawn from a rising, hillside horse field, which in turn separated the lawn from the dense, almost foreboding woods that enveloped the rear of their property. There, where the field-encircling fence disappeared beneath a clump of wild blackberry bushes, a narrow, almost invisible trail cut into the trees. "What'd he do? Walk all the way from the lake?" Toby wondered aloud. "It's almost ten miles from here to his place."

"Well," Dale said, "he knows his way around." He gave Toby the hat back.

"Here," Toby handed it to Elaine. "Can you put this in there? Somewhere safe." He stuffed the note in his jacket pocket. "I'll have to give him a visit sometime next week."

Still shaking her head in wonder, Elaine took the hat with care and turned back into the house, a smile playing at her lips. "I remember the day we bought this for you…"

The sound of Jack clearing his throat came from behind Toby's back.

"Alright, kiddo," Dale said, "Let's go."

"Okay."

Jack, walking across the yard with the assistance of his cane, threw the chains in the bed of his blue pickup and got in the driver's side. Toby scampered over the empty trailer that had already been hitched up to the truck and was promptly forced into the middle seat by Dale's jerkily directing thumb. Giving his grandpa a disgusted look, he scooted into place.

"Why's ever'body always pickin' on me?" he asked in a deep voice.

"You're not gonna wear that coat in this weather are you?" Dale asked, winded from getting in and slamming his door.

"Of course I am!"

Jack started the engine. He threw the shifter into reverse and began backing out of the driveway, but slowed when Elaine popped her head out of the kitchen door and waved for them to stop. She held up a brown grocery bag.

"Oh, crap," Toby said, "I forgot the chip dip."

Elaine gave the bag to Tracy, who then ran it to the truck. "You forgot the chip dip!" she said, pushing the bag through Jack's window. "And Mom said Jenna just called and said that she'd meet you at Dean's."

"Alright." Toby took the bag.

"You're welcome."

"Yeah, thanks."

Tracy stepped away and Jack continued backing out of the drive, using his mirrors to swing the trailer into the road.

"What do you need chip dip for?" Dale asked.

"Dean's throwing a graduation party tonight. I'm supposed to bring the chips and dip."

"Where're the chips?"

"I'm picking those up at Peppy's."

"Oh."

Jack put the truck in first and they began rolling down the hill, the cool evening air whipping through the open windows. The sky overhead was gradually darkening and the blazing orange sun that hovered just above the trees lit the cab from their left. They passed the Axemberg house on the way down the hill, where Ace and Mary, who both waved, were enjoying a drink on the front porch.

"You seen any lightning bugs yet, Gramps?" Toby asked Dale.

"Nope," Dale said, striking a match to his pipe. "You probably won't for a few more weeks."

"Hmm." Toby brought out the new apartment key and began affixing it to his key ring. "Do you ever miss living in the country?"

Dale took the pipe out of his mouth and unconsciously tapped his chin with the mouth piece. "Sometimes… but that was a long time ago, Toby. I haven't lived out here since before the war."

"Yeah, I guess you're right."

They bounced over a narrow bridge and then Jack downshifted as they began climbing the steep hill near the end of Briggle. The empty trailer danced along behind them.

"How come you moved to the city anyhow?"

"Well, Toby… it's a long story."

"Oh."

A brand new stop sign marked Briggle's end and brought them to a halt. After checking for traffic in both directions, Jack eased the truck into a left turn. The short stretch of Webber that they traversed passed smoothly beneath them, but then they came to the pine tree-shrouded entrance of Mendenhall Lane, where Jack hung a right onto the rutted, one lane gravel road. The truck and trailer started bouncing around as they picked up speed.

"Take it easy, boy," Dale warned Jack. "We don't need two trucks in the ditch."

After driving several bone-jarring miles over the field-checkered countryside, the dark, lopsided form of Toby's little truck came into view. Jack slowed to a stop beside it.

"Get out," he said to Toby, "and hook the chains up."

"Alright."

Dale opened his door and slid out. Toby followed. He walked around to the trailer and, after removing his new jacket and handing it to Dale, wrestled the mass of chain onto the ground. They stepped back and Jack pulled away.

"Okay…" Toby said, locating the hooked chain ends. "Alright…" He grabbed one of the hooks and yanked it towards his truck.

"You sure you know what you're doing?" Dale asked.

"I'm pretty sure I'm positive." He stomped out the tall weeds that were in his way and then lay down on his back. "But how hard could it be, right?" He rolled beneath the truck. The dying sunlight didn't aid him much in finding a sturdy tow point, but after feeling around he finally found a satisfactory place to hook onto. "Alright," he said, struggling out from under the truck, "I think I got it."

By now, Jack had unhitched the trailer and backed up into towing position. Brushing himself off, Toby picked up the loose end of the chain and looped it around the greasy trailer ball on the back of his father's truck. Jack called him up to the cab. A fresh cigarette bobbed up and down as he spoke.

"You push; let your grandfather back it out."

"Alright." Toby walked back to his truck and fished the keys out of his pocket. "Here." He handed them to Dale. "I'll push."

"Okay," Dale said.

"Oh, uh, you'll have to unlock it. Aunt Shelly's suitcase is in there."

"Right." Dale stuck the key in and opened the door. "Jiminy Cripes, you could've left a window down for me, kiddo." He squeezed in behind the steering wheel and started the engine.

"Just a second," Toby said loudly, high-stepping through the weeds to the front of the truck. He planted his feet solidly on the ditch bank, and then gave his grandpa thumbs up. Dale revved the '34's engine and slowly let the clutch out. Jack did the same in his truck.

"Come on…" Toby said to himself, palms pressing against the bumper. The right rear wheel started to spin and kick up chunks of sod. The truck lurched slightly. "Come on…"

Dale stuck his head out the window. "Just had to put those baldies on it didn't you?" he yelled, wrestling with the steering wheel.

"I never planned on- ouch! I never planned on off-roading with it!" He grunted and groaned, pushing for all he was worth, and then, finally, with Jack's truck tires spewing gravel all over the place, and both engines roaring on the red line, he felt the pickup start to rise out of the ditch. "That's it! That's it!" With one last jolt, it pulled free, amid a flurry of grass, rocks, and his grandfather's profanity. "Woo-hoo! That did it!"

Jack got out and unhooked the chain from his truck. "Think you can get it on the trailer?" he asked Toby, who was kicking the mud off of his shoes.

"Yeah, if we've got the long ramps."

Jack cleared his throat, spit out a wad of phlegm, and took another drag on his Camel. "We do. And we have the winch." He got back in his pickup and drove over to where he'd dropped the trailer.

"Well," Toby said to Dale, "that wasn't too hard."

"You're lucky," Dale said, getting out and handing Toby his jacket. He left the engine running. "I remember one time when we was out in the field, way out there plowing, and we got the tractor stuck in a big ol' mud pit. Sunk the tires in that much." He held his hand about three feet off of the ground.

"What'd you do?" Toby slipped back into his coat.

"Took four horses and five men to pull it out."

"Wow." Toby slid in behind the wheel and slammed the door. He pushed Shelly's suitcase across the seat. "I'll bet that was fun."

"Huh. About as fun as a three-legged..." Dale trailed off and slapped the truck's roof.

Toby watched through the front window as Jack re-hitched the trailer and began backing up towards him. "Well," he said, his hand on the shifter, "here goes nothing."

Jack stopped about ten feet away, and then got out and slid the two metal ramps into place, lining them up with Toby's front tires. When he was finished, he began pulling cable out of the trailer-anchored winch and motioned for Toby to pull forward, which he did. Jack held up his hand when the wheels touched the ramps. He hooked the cable onto the front of the truck and signaled Toby to continue. With Dale manning the winch's hand crank, Toby gave the truck some gas and it began climbing the ramps.

"Come on, baby," he said. It did fine until the shredded left rear tire touched the steel incline; there it began to spin the wheels.

"Whoa! Hey!" Jack yelled hoarsely, arms flailing. "You're gonna come off the ramps!" He turned and said something to Dale, who sped up his cranking pace. Toby felt the winch's tug.

"Alright," Jack gestured. "Now. Slowly."

"Judas H. Priest…" Toby mumbled to himself. "Like I don't know how to put something on a trailer…" He slowly let out the clutch and, with the winch's aid, finished ascending the ramps, coming to rest squarely on the trailer without further struggle. He shut the engine off. "How's that?" he asked.

"Fine," Jack answered, already fastening the pickup down with the tow chain.

Toby opened the door and stepped out onto one of the trailer's four tires. He pounded the side of the truck with his fist.

"Come on," Jack said. "Let's go."

The ride back was no less bumpy, but at least the weight of Toby's truck kept the trailer from bouncing wildly as it had before. Jack was largely unsuccessful in his attempts to avoid Mendenhall's potholes. Finally, the smooth, welcome asphalt of Webber met them, bathed in the rapidly fading afterglow of the China-bound sun. Faint yellow house lights, nestled against the growing navy blue darkness, began to speckle the shadowy countryside.

They rode Webber all of the way into Carson Creek, where, upon reaching A&L Automotive, Jack swung the rig onto the dark lot and backed up to one of the bays. The garage looked very different by night; a neon Valvoline sign hanging in the otherwise dimly lit salesroom colored the glass red and blue, with the chrome window trim brilliantly reflecting every light source on the street. Toby, having this time procured a window seat, got out and rolled open the heavy garage door by the yellowish light of the corner streetlamp, the brown paper bag of chip dip in hand.

"Okay…" he said, feeling his way through the dark, gasoline-scented garage for the light switch. Dean had left the radio on, as usual, and it was trying its best to eke out *'Come Go with Me'*. He located the little round switch box and flipped the toggle. The florescent beams flickered to life, illuminating the entire shop area and casting a glowing patch of artificial light out of the garage and onto the rear of his truck. He walked back outside. Ever the productive one, Jack was already throwing the tie-down chains to the ground.

"Go get in," he said.

"Alright." Toby climbed up on the trailer and slid back into his pickup. Sitting the chip dip on the seat beside him, he pushed in the brake pedal and wobbled the shifter out of gear. "Okay, all set."

"Hold your horses," Dale said. Bathed in the glow of Toby's brake lights, he and Jack finished lining up the ramps. "Alright, now."

Toby let off the brakes and started the engine.

"Go easy!" Jack yelled through the window. "You don't have any brakes on this one!" He jabbed his finger at the shredded tire.

"Alright." Toby eased his way off of the trailer and down the ramps. The truck leveled out just inside the garage door, the engine echoing off of the walls, and, after a few revs, he turned the key. "Whew. There." He opened the door and stepped out. "Now I think I can…" A red Corvette pulled onto the lot, its brilliant headlights washing over Jack's truck and the now-empty trailer. "Is that Jenna?" he asked.

"Just make sure you lock up." Jack said, throwing one of the ramps into the bed of his truck.

"Right. I'll see you later," Toby said. "Oh, wait! Take this with you." He yanked Shelly's last suitcase off of his seat and walked outside. The passenger side door of the still-running Corvette opened and Jenna got out.

"Hello," she said.

Nodding, Jack took a hold of the leather handle and sat the suitcase in the bed with the ramps. He got in the truck.

"See you later kiddo," Dale said, following Jack's lead. His twinkling eyes glanced at Jenna and then back to Toby. "Don't stay up too late."

"Bye, Gramps."

With a bounce of the trailer, Jack and Dale pulled out onto the street and disappeared into the darkness. Toby turned to Jenna, who stood silhouetted against the Corvette's headlights.

"Hi."

"Hi," she said, returning his hug and kiss. "Nice jacket."

"Nice lips. What are you doing here? Tracy said you'd meet me at Dean's."

She let go of him and started moving towards the passenger side of the idling Corvette. "I was going to, but we saw you were here anyway, so we stopped." She leaned through the open window. "Besides," she spoke from inside the car, "Callie won't go to Dean's house."

Walking closer, Toby bent down and looked at Callie, who sat in the driver's seat. "What's the matter, Cal? Still sore at little ol' Dean?"

"Oh, no," Callie said in a sarcastic tone, "but could you give him a message for me?"

"What do you want me to say?"

She held up her middle finger.

Toby cleared his throat. "Uh… short and sweet, huh? Alright, but it won't mean as much coming from me."

Jenna backed out of the window with a small bag in her hand. "Okay, Callie, I guess I'll see you at eleven-thirty."

"Okay."

"Why?" Toby asked. "What's at eleven-thirty?"

"We're staying with my Grandmother tonight."

"Where's she?"

"Toby!" Jenna exclaimed, "I told you that they took her to the hospital!"

"Oh, right, right! I forgot. Sorry. Uh, what's wrong with her?"

"They think that she has the flu again."

"Oh." He stuck his hands in his pockets.

"Anyway, I'll need a ride home at eleven-thirty. 'Bye, Callie."

"'Bye," Callie said, and then backed out of the parking lot.

"Eleven-thirty? At the height of the party?"

"Sorry, Toby. What can I do?"

Toby walked into the garage. "Send her a nice card that says 'Get well before midnight'. Jeeze…" He wheeled a jack under his truck and started pumping the handle. The rear wheels began inching off of the garage floor. "Damn it… Eleven-thirty. Just my luck. *I'm* not the one with the flu…"

"Well that's a fine thing to say!" Jenna said, crossing her arms. "And what happens if I got sick? I hope that wouldn't bother you too much!"

"Alright, alright, I'm sorry… Jeeze." He walked over and pulled a tire iron off of the wall.

"You know what, Toby? Sometimes I get sick of hearing you say 'I'm sorry' all of the time."

"Fine. Next time I won't." He dropped the wrench and

walked to the back of the garage, where a stack of mounted tires sat. "Next time I won't say anything, or maybe I'll just sign language something, like Callie does." He selected a wheel and pulled it to the ground. Jenna stepped aside as he rolled it past her to the side of the truck.

"I just wish that you'd think of someone besides yourself every once in awhile."

"Jenna, I don't want to argue."

"Then don't start an argument!"

"I didn't!"

"Yes you did! When you said that about my Grandma!"

Toby affixed the tire iron to one of the lug nuts. "Look, will you just get in the truck and put on the brakes? Thank you."

Letting out an angry sigh, Jenna complied. With her depressing the brake pedal, Toby was able to loosen the wheel without it spinning. When finished, he pulled the naked rim off of the wheel studs and set it aside. He then rolled the new wheel into place and began putting the lug nuts back on. With two bolts to go, he heard Jenna begin to sniffle.

"Ahh, jeeze… Come on, Jenna… I said I was sorry." He spun the last bolt tight, and then, throwing the wrench on the floor, stood up and moved to the driver's side window. "For cryin' out loud… Aren't you overreacting a little?"

Jenna held a small handkerchief to her nose. She looked at him with angry, tear-filled eyes. "I wish I hated you."

Toby's brow furrowed. "Well…" he stammered, running his finger along the dusty window sill, "Why don't you?"

"I can't. I'll always love you, Toby."

"Wh- Why?"

"Because I'm afraid."

"Afraid of what?" He opened the truck door.

"Of being lonely."

"Lonely? Give me a break, Jenna. You could drop me tonight and have any one of the ten thousand guys in line behind me…" He put his hand on her arm. "And you'd probably be better off. You'll never be alone, Jenna."

She sniffed. "I know. But that's not what I said I was afraid of."

Toby exhaled and ran his fingers through his hair. "Ahh, I'm a moax. I've got two words of advice for you, Jenna. Two words."

"What?"

"Dump me. You'll be the happiest person in the world." His eyes fell to her wristwatch. "Damn, I'm late again. Listen, I'll make sure that you get home at eleven-thirty. Alright?"

Jenna nodded silently.

"Okay. Now can you pull the truck out? I'm going to lock up."

"Okay."

As Jenna started truck and slowly pulled it out of the garage, Toby hung the tire iron back on the wall. Then, with one last casual glance around the building, he flipped the lights off, leaving the radio to echo in the dark.

The garage door came down easily behind him, hitting the pavement with a loud 'clang'. He turned the silver handle in the center of the door to lock it.

"Building secure." he said, walking over to the idling truck. Jenna had scooted to the passenger's side. "Ready?" Toby asked, getting in.

"Yes."

"Alright." He revved the truck into a crawl. "Then, as all of my reefer addict friends say, lets get rollin'!"

Chapter 12

The truck bounced slightly as Toby drove over the curb and off of A&L's parking lot. Once at the traffic light, he made a left onto Main Street. It was a typical Saturday evening in Carson Creek; the small town was brightly lit and still quite active, but tonight the atmosphere was even more celebratory as kids everywhere rejoiced in their graduation. Even underclassmen had something to celebrate, having only one week of school left before summer vacation. Toby and Jenna rolled past the Indian Head Arcade, where, through the huge glass windows, kids could be seen pounding away at rows of flashing pinball machines, and next door, in Jinx's Record Shop, young people were dancing the evening away to the bouncy sound of Rock 'n Roll. Car radios blared in unison, as did car horns.

"Hey," Toby said, "Here comes Cal…" He pointed out the front window at a station wagon coming toward them in the opposite lane. Tagging along behind it on a tow bar was an old Ford coupe-turned-drag car. "Hey, Cal!" Toby yelled out the window at the slowly passing car. "You're goin', the wrong way! The strip's that way!"

"Eat pus, Toby!" the dejected looking young man yelled back.

"Heh, heh." Toby pulled his head back in the window. "Must not've been his lucky day."

"Hmm. What's this?" Jenna asked opening the brown paper sack that was sitting between them.

"Oh, thanks. I almost forgot; I've got to get the chips for that."

"Where?"

"Right…" Peppy's Pizzeria, a small restaurant making

up the first floor of a three story building, came up on their right. "…here." Toby turned into the narrow, dimly lit alleyway that separated Peppy's from Main St. Pool House. "I'll be right back," he said, getting out and leaving Jenna alone in the running truck.

He followed the sidewalk up to the glass door, above which the restaurant's name had been lettered in dark green paint. His entrance was announced by a leather strap full of jingle bells attached to the door. Inside, the wood paneling and lamp-lit, wall-recessed booths gave the tiny restaurant a very warm and inviting feel. Toby walked past several happy looking diners as he made his way toward the back of the building, where a middle-aged man with slicked back hair and a half-ash cigarette poking out from his bushy handlebar mustache was tossing a floppy pizza crust in the air.

"Hiya, Burt," Toby said, resting his elbows on the counter. A small television set, broadcasting a blue-toned Indians vs. Athletics game, hung on the wall above the cash register.

"Well'a, well'a, well'a," the man said, his voice drowning in an Italian accent, "if it is not'a my old delivery boy."

"I just quit on Tuesday, Burt."

"And already I have four complaints for about late'a pizza." Burt slapped the crust on a wooden tray and then turned back to Toby, holding up four fingers. "Four. How am I to replace you? You were fastest deliverer I ever have. You were almost too fast.

"It's a curse I've been blessed with."

"I will never forgive'a you."

"Okay," Toby said, casually flipping through a dinner menu. "But I need some chips."

"Chips? Chips?"

"Yeah. Ruffled ones."

"Why you need'a chips for?"

"I'a need'a them'a for'a Dean'a's party'a."

Burt squinted an eye and pointed his dwindling cigarette at Toby. "You are delinquent kid."

"That's what the 'D' stands for. But anyhow, could I have some?"

"Hmmm," Burt growled. "I guess for sake of old time I give'a you a couple. You know where they are."

"Thanks, Burt. You're a peach."

"Heh. That is what 'B' stand'a for."

"Right…" Toby said, walking around the bar and into the open kitchen. Without problem, he singled out the pantry door containing the no-bake appetizers. He sorted through bags of pretzels, jars of un-popped popcorn, and sacks of old Halloween candy until he found two unopened bags of Peppy's famous rippled chips, imported by Burt from an unknown Californian source. Toby tucked them under his arm and shut the pantry door. "Thanks, boss," he said to Burt.

"Those Cola-Cokes that'a you left in my cooler are going in the trash if you don't'a take'a them with you."

"Oh, right. I forgot about those." Toby opened the cooler and pulled out a half-empty six pack. "Thanks."

"Now go and leave'a me to die in peace."

"Right. I'll see you around. Maybe I'll stop in for lunch on Monday."

"I can't'a wait."

Instead of going out the way he came, Toby exited the building through the side door, which opened right into the alley. He picked up one of Burt's trash cans that had fallen over and got into the still-running truck.

"What took you?" Jenna asked.

"We were reminiscing. Here." Toby handed her the

chips and sat the six-pack on the floor. Then, looking over his shoulder, he backed out of the alley and into the street.

"Was Burt busy tonight?"

"Ahh, so-so." Toby didn't make it very far before a red light brought them to a halt. Taking advantage of the break, he drew out one of the frosty Coca-Colas. "You can have one too if you want."

"Thanks, but I'm not thirsty."

"Suit yourself." He popped the cap and took a swig. "Ahh…mm-mm-mm. Slushy."

"You always say that," Jenna said. "It isn't always slushy."

"Sure it is; it's all in your head."

"What? Slush?"

"If you say so."

The town whipped by and soon they were cruising along the river, steadily climbing into the hills above Carson Creek. The quarter moon now shone hazily through the clouds that were beginning to blanket the star-studded sky, and, drifting from the river on their left, the operatic whine of frogs and crickets filled the night air. After about a mile, the trees began to thicken into dense woods.

"It's starting to cool off," Toby said, coming to a four-way stop, Ormsby Corners, where he turned left onto West Riverside Drive and crossed over the water on a rusty, steel-girded bridge. He had to downshift in order to ascend the steep incline that followed. "Are you planning on swimming?"

"I'm not sure," Jenna said. She picked her bag up off of the floor. "I brought my swimsuit, but I don't know. I'm not really in the mood."

"*In the mooood- ba-dah-ba-da-do-da-da,*" Toby sang. "Dean told me to bring my trunks, but I haven't been swimming since my leg... It's not very... cosmetically appealing."

"I know."

"But I forgot to bring them anyway, so it doesn't matter. Maybe I'll just sit around and watch all you girls have fun. Maybe I'll volunteer for lifeguard duty."

"I knew I should have brought a blindfold along." Jenna said.

"Why would you need a blindfold?"

"Not for me... for you."

They continued on for about a half mile. "Oh... Hey, hey, ho," Toby said as they rounded a sharp corner, "Here's our spot..." The trees to their left gave way to a small, grassy plateau that overlooked Carson Creek, which now spread out below them like a checker board lit up for Christmas. He slowed down.

"A minute ago, you just said 'Damn, I'm late'." Jenna said as Toby pulled off of the road and onto the grass.

"No. I said that twenty minutes ago." He shut the engine off and opened his door.

"I don't want to stop here."

"Come on, lets just look around."

Jenna sighed and got out, not bothering to shut her door. "That's what you said last time..." She walked around to the driver's side and leaned against the front fender. Toby put his arm around her.

"It's beautiful, huh?"

Jenna didn't look up, she just played with one of the rings on her finger. "Yes. It's very nice. Can we go now?"

"Ahh," Toby growled, pulling away. "What's the problem with you today? Ever since I picked you up this morning you've been about as affectionate as a gallon of prune juice! No kisses, no hugs, not even an 'I love you more than life itself'! Where's the cork, sister? Come on, spit it out!"

Jenna stood up straight. "What's wrong with *me?*" she shot back. "What's *my* problem?"

"Yeah!"

"I'll tell you- *you* are my problem!" She stuck her finger in Toby's chest.

"Me?!"

"You! The way you're always acting! Everything that you're always bragging to your friends about, like about how *far* you got or what you'd like to do that night! Everything you're always saying about me to everyone at school! Like 'She's all mine and can't help it'." Jenna stepped out into the grass and gestured to the clearing. Her voice quivered slightly. "Everything that this place means to me now! You don't care what we do just as long as it's what *you* want to do! Don't you see that? Can't you see I'm-"

"Whoa, whoa, wait a minute!" Toby interrupted.

"No, *you* wait! Toby, I'm just a toy to you! According to you, you can say whatever, go wherever, and do whatever with whomever you please, but I have to remain completely loyal to you and what you want. Don't you think I have dreams and goals and hopes and fears of my own? That's what love is, Toby! It's two people coming together and holding each other up, even when it's not what we feel like doing! Even when it hurts!" Tears of anger, glistening in the pale moonlight, began crawling down her face, but she kept talking, pointing again to their surroundings. "Do you think what happens here stays here? It doesn't, Toby. Everything that we do in life, big or small, good or bad, affects us somewhere down the road. *Realize* that."

"Jenna, you knew what you were doing! I mean, you knew who I was from the beginning! How come all of the sudden you're going off like this all the time? Every time I want-"

"I didn't -" Jenna started.

"No, you wait. Now Toby's got something to say!"

"Toby *always* has something to say!"

"That's right. And always is right now, so shut up for a minute. Listen-" Toby pointed at himself. "I am me. If you don't like me, then why did you ever agree to go out in the first place?"

"I have never said that I don't like you, Toby. I've never said that. I said that I don't like the way you act."

"How do I act that's so wrong?"

A look of incredulity spread across Jenna's tear-streaked face. "Haven't you even been listening to me?"

"Right. I only care about myself. How?"

"Toby, you… When was the last time you did something for me that didn't benefit you in any way?"

"I… uh," Toby thought hard for a moment. "Just last week!"

"What was it?"

"I gave you my little blue record player! And all those 45's!"

"Only because you bought yourself a new one the day before! And Jack gave you all of those 45's! And the ones you gave me were the ones that you hated! You said so yourself, remember? And that's just one of *many* examples."

"But, I… that was…" Toby put his hand on his forehead. "You know what, Jenna, let's just forget this whole conversation ever even took place, alright? Just get back in the truck. Get in the truck; we were never even here, okay?" He opened his door and got in.

"No, Toby, you can't… you can't just run away from everything all the time!"

"Get in the truck, Jenna. Let's go."

She pushed a lock of hair aside. "Fine. But I don't know

how much longer I can stand this, Toby. I'm not trying to control your life, I'm not trying to change you, but the way you act... it... I wanted-" she choked, "I wanted to spend the rest of my life with you. But now I'm not sure anymore."

"Sweetheart, please get in. I'm sorry, okay? I'm sorry I *ever* stopped here." Toby started the truck.

Jenna just stared at him for a moment and then cleared her throat. "I'm sorry too." She then walked around to the passenger's side and slid into her seat, slamming the door as hard as she could.

"We'll just forget about all this, okay? Alright? I said I was sorry, and I meant it."

"Fine. I forgive you." she said. "For the millionth time."

As West Riverside continued to climb, they began to pass extravagant-looking houses, mostly log cabins, that were nestled in the shadows among the various pines, oaks, and other trees that choked up the hills around Whitefeather Lake. This dark, leafy foliage swayed in a growing breeze. Natural stone walls, some of them covered in thick moss, occasionally jutted out of the earth to form great barriers that sometimes flanked the road on both sides, and as they rounded a corner Toby slowed at a break in one of these walls, where a steep driveway had been carved through the rock.

"What the hell is this?" he asked as he pulled up the drive to a clearing in front of the Krindle cabin. The front yard was jam-packed with seemingly dozens of vehicles. Lights were flashing, music was blaring, and partying kids were everywhere.

"What in the world...?" Jenna exclaimed, coming out of her seething silence. "Where did all these people come from?"

Toby slowed to a stop. "That's what I want to know..."

"Did Dean invite all of them?"

"Are you kidding? Mr. Iceheart? He's probably hiding in the basement." Toby grabbed the chips and dip. "Come on, let's go see."

As they were walking up the driveway, a young man's voice called out from the smoky backseat of a new Chevy.

"It's about time you showed up, Toby."

Toby craned his neck to see in the car. "Hey, Johnny. Nice lipstick. Hi, Betty. Did Dean invite you guys?"

"Is that who's place this is? I just followed the cars."

"Uh-huh. Speaking of cars, who's is this beauty?" Toby rapped his knuckles on the silver Chevy.

"Beats me. It's sure got comfy seats, though."

"Right… I'll see you around, John. Betty… take care of yourself."

Toby and Jenna continued to weave through wildly parked cars as they made their way towards the house.

"This is crazy," Jenna said.

"You're tellin' me. Look up there." Toby pointed to a second story balcony where someone was standing on the railing, getting ready to dive into the pool below. "Judas Priest…" he exclaimed. They pushed through a gate that separated the front yard from the back, and followed a winding, bush-lined walkway that led to the rear of the house. A cement patio, doubling as a outdoor dance floor, encompassed the large, in-ground pool that was churning like a washing machine full of people. A heat-powered lamp shade made of translucent, multicolored plastic sat on a table, spinning vivid colors across the patio.

Toby took Jenna's hand. "This way." He led her through the crowd and up to the house's sliding glass back doors. He yanked on the handle. It didn't budge. Putting his face to the glass, he could see the dimly-lit recreation room inside, where a small group of people were gathered around a pool table. He located Dean, sitting in a chair in the corner, his arms crossed tightly against his chest. He was watching Perry Mason on a blue-hued set.

"Told you." Toby said to Jenna, knocking on the glass. Inside, Dean jumped up from his seat and came over to the door. "Is this where I get the booze?" Toby asked through the glass.

"Did you do this?" Dean yelled back.

"What?"

"That!" Dean pointed his Dum-Dum pop at the throng behind Toby. "Did you invite all them?"

"Me? Why would I…? What the hell's goin' on here?"

Dean threw the lock and slid the door open. "Get in here. Quick." He pulled Toby and Jenna inside.

"Alright, alright. Jeeze." Toby said. "Here's your chips."

"I'm dead." Dean said, re-locking the door. "What the-what am I going to tell my parents when they get home?"

Toby looked back out at the pool scene, just as someone cannon-balled off of the balcony with a bottle of beer in his hand. "I don't think you'll have to do much talking. They can read the morning paper for themselves."

"Son of a bitch… I told that bastard…" Dean turned away from the window, a look of disgust on his well-tanned face. "Anyhow…"

"Anyhow, here's your chips and dip." Toby held up the bags.

"Just set 'em over on the bar. You want a Pepsi or something?"

"Pepsi?" Toby said, putting the food down. Jenna went and sat in the corner with Heidi and some other girls who were watching the television. "You know I'm a Coke boy. Pepsi's too hard."

"Too hard? What? We're not talking about Jack Daniel's here."

"Okay, its too fizzy."

"Soda is supposed to be fizzy."

"Drop it. I brought my own drinks, I just left them in the truck."

"Have it your way. Hey, Arvel! Get the ash tray off the felt!"

Arvel, a black man in his mid twenties, turned toward Dean and Toby. "I ain't had a smoke all night. Tha's Ju-Ju's 'cig."

"Jude," Dean said to the other man playing pool, "You have any idea how much that table cost?"

Jude sent the cue ball careening into a group of balls, sinking two. "'Course I do, I'm the one that helped you pick it up, 'member?" He picked the ash tray up off of the table and sat it on a coffee table. "Suit you?"

"Yes, thank you."

"Hey, how come you two guys aren't at the strip?" Toby asked.

"I was," Jude said, trying to rub a spot of blue chalk dust off of his white t-shirt. "But I left when Cal did. He went out second round. Blue in the side pocket." He lined up another shot, but missed. "Damn. That's when I stopped by here."

"Huh." Toby sat on the corner of the table. "What about you Arvel? I saw your pop this morning."

A smile spread across Arvel's face as he prepared to launch the cue ball. "Yeah, I heard that. 'Bout what you did to Novello. That was cherry. He called me up at work an' tol' me 'bout it."

"Can you guys keep it down over there?" One of the girls said.

Just then the phone rang upstairs.

"Dang it," Dean said, jumping up from his chair. "I wish they'd run a line down here." He disappeared up the steps.

"Hey," Toby said. "Where's Smoosh?"

"Don't know." Jude answered. "Haven't seen him all day."

Toby walked over to the door and looked out at the bouncy crowd. "Good Lord. Remind me never to swim in that pool again. Animals." The 'thump-thump-thump' of Dean running back down the carpeted steps turned his head back around.

"We've gotta go!" Dean yelled, grabbing a jacket off of the wall. "Come on, Toby!"

"What? What's goin' on?"

"Bell and Hawkins' rail just ran 185!"

"What?"

"One hundred and eighty-five miles per hour?" Jude exclaimed.

"One hundred and eighty-five miles per hour!"

"You're kidding me!" Toby said. "That'd be a national record!"

"Yeah, and they've got one round left, so come on! It may happen again!" Dean zipped up his jacket and threw open the sliding door. "Alright!" he yelled to the kids outside. "Hey! Listen! I just called the cops! Anybody not out of here in ten minutes spends the night in jail!" He pulled the door shut and locked it again. "Come on, we'll go out the front. Heidi, let's go!"

Toby was right behind Dean. "Jenna, let's go!"

"But we just-" Jenna started.

"I'm comin' too," Arvel cut in, throwing his pool cue on the table.

"Hey!" Jude said, "You- we're not finished with this game! Aww… wait up! I'm coming!"

"Don't turn any lights on, you guys," Dean said, exiting the stairwell into the dark living room. All eight of their small party followed him to the front door: Toby, Jenna, Heidi, Arvel, along with Bess, Arvel's love interest, and

Wendy, Jude's on-again-off-again, love-hate girlfriend.

"What are you driving?" Toby asked, reaching the door first.

Dean stopped for a moment. "Those mothergoosers better not have me parked in."

"That's what I'm saying. I don't think you'll be able to get out." Toby slowly opened the door. "All clear. Come on. Hurry up." He pulled Jenna behind him.

"Leave the arm," she said. They crossed the large, enclosed front porch and then descended a long set of wooden stairs to the driveway.

"We had to park way out there." Toby pointed toward the road. "Hey! There's Smoosh's VW! It's about time he showed up!"

Dean jumped over a row of small, sidewalk-lining bushes. "Well, didn't you tell him eight or eight-thirty? Damn it! They *did* park me in!"

"Uh, no. I must've forgot that…"

"Stay cool, Dino," Jude spoke up from behind. "You can ride with me."

"How the- how do you expect us all to fit in that T-bucket?" Dean asked, pounding his fist on the hood of his blocked-in car.

"I didn't drive my T. It's in the shop. I'm borrowing my Aunt Flossie's new car."

"Well," Toby rushed, "Where is it? Come on! We're gonna miss the final round!"

"Cool your jets, LaRue," Jude said, continuing down the driveway. "It's right… over… Hey! Who the hell's in the backseat of my car?"

"Uh-oh," Toby said. He looked at Jenna. "John and Betty. Come on, let's go. We'll never get out of here if Jude starts a fight. Dean, we're leaving! I'll see you there!"

"Hey," Dean said. "Find Smoosh and tell him what's

up!"

"Keep going," Toby whispered to Jenna, picking up his pace. "Act like you didn't hear him."

"Toby! You can't just-"

"Never mind, Smoosh is still in his car anyway. Hey Smooshy!" Toby ran over to the Volkswagen.

Smoosh stuck his head out the window. "What in the heck is goin' on here, Suzy?"

"Never mind. We're all going to the track; Bell just ran 185 miles per hour!"

"Holy- Are you serious?"

Toby continued down the driveway, yelling over his shoulder. "Yeah, and he's going to the final round. Maybe he'll do it again! We're all going over right now!"

"Wait for me!" Smoosh started his car.

Toby and Jenna finally reached the truck and hopped in. "One hundred and eighty-five miles per hour... I'll have to see it to believe it," Toby said. He brought the engine to life and quickly backed out of the driveway, switching on his headlights.

Chapter 13

The old '34 Ford wasn't exactly made for the kind of high speed cornering that Toby squeezed out of it on their way back down into Carson Valley. They twisted and turned along the dark, deserted road, and Jenna, as usual, hung on for dear life around the guardrail-less curves of Suicide Hill, where she couldn't stop herself from sliding across the seat and into Toby.

"Well, hello," he said, putting his arm around her. "I am getting a little cold over here all by myself."

"Then why don't you try rolling up your window?"

"Because you're more fun."

Jenna pulled away. "Just watch where you're going, okay?"

Finally, they reached the rusty, steel girder bridge. Toby made a left turn. Ello Lane stretched out before them, its narrow gravel path disappearing over a steep hill.

"I hate this road," Jenna said.

"What for?" Toby asked, shifting into second. "This is one of the best racing roads around, after you get past the orchard."

"It's always so creepy; even during the day."

"Aww, that's just 'cause we used to tell a lot of ghost stories about it. I don't think anything bad ever really happened here. Well, except for Red Mackenzie's wreck…"

"And Greg Bodart's and Phyllis Lowell's and the list goes on."

"Yeah, but at least they found their bodies; Red's still sitting at the bottom of the swamp." Outside, the jagged branches of unkempt apple trees whipped by overhead, caught in the cold yellow glow of Toby's headlights. The speeding truck bounced over a small hill.

"I hate this road," Jenna said again.

"Don't worry, I'll try and make it short." Toby slowed to a crawl around a double hairpin curve. "I wouldn't even go this way if it didn't cut out so much hassle. All the streetlights and traffic and stuff." After the curves, the road straightened and became more level; the trees thinned out slightly, and a large cemetery passed by on their left.. "See," Toby said, "this is the perfect stretch for a drag race."

"Why can't you just race at the track?"

Toby thought for a moment. "Well, sometimes you just… it's like… uh… Oh, a girl wouldn't understand anyway."

"Uh-huh."

"Like what if it's winter, or raining or something like that?"

"It's against the law, Toby."

"Law, shmall. It's not like anyone lives out here. Whoa…" Toby tapped a gauge on the dashboard. "Uh-oh."

"What?"

"It looks like we're running on fumes." He eased back on the gas pedal.

"You mean we're almost out of gas?" Jenna exclaimed.

"Uh… 'almost' is such a nice word." He downshifted. "We're only a couple miles away. I think we can make it."

"You *think* we can make it?"

"We'll be fine." Toby patted Jenna's hand.

"I hate it when you say that!"

They went for another mile before the truck began to stutter.

"Must be this dusty road…" Toby said, casting Jenna a

crooked grin. He shook his head. "It always acts up on dusty roads."

Jenna looked much more serious. "We're never going to make it up the big hill."

Toby coughed. "Let's climb that mountain when we get to it." He brought their speed down to about twenty miles per hour.

"I can't believe this!" Jenna said. "Don't you watch the gas gauge?"

"Sure." Toby overcame a small incline and, once on the other side, put the truck in neutral and coasted for awhile. "When it's moving." He turned the radio down. The sounds of the swamp filled their ears as they freewheeled along through the darkness. "So, Jenna… did I ever tell you about the three teenagers who broke down out here…?"

"Toby, don't even start."

"It was a lot like this out, and they-"

"Toby! Knock it off! Now is not the time!"

"…started walking down this road…"

Jenna began humming loudly. "I'm not listening…"

"But they didn't know that every, uh… twenty-seventh of May… that all the people who'd died in this swamp come out like zombies and look for fresh people to possess…"

"*Bum-bum-bum, I'm a walkin' in the rain…*" Jenna sang to herself.

"Yeah, that's right! It *was* raining! That kept the kids from smelling the rotting flesh until it was too late, until-"

"That's enough! I don't think you're funny!"

"Until the zombies were right behind them… Then they grabbed them and dragged them one by one under the water and started- Wait!" Toby stopped. "Did you hear that?"

"What? Hear what?"

"There it was again!"

"I didn't hear-"

Toby began moaning like a swamp monster.

"Knock it off!"

"And you know what the scary part is? They came back out of the water without any skin! They were all green and gooey and had organs hanging out and…"

"I'm going to tell your mother on you!"

"They say that they're still roaming this swamp, looking for revenge. That's how come so many people've died down here. They come up to your car when it's dark and push their oozing faces against the windows and then… then they drag you out and down into the swamp! Ahhh! I see one! It's walking outside your window!"

Jenna covered her ears. "Stop, stop, stop! Stop it! You're going to make me sick!"

They rounded a bend, where the base of a large hill was waiting for them.

"Okay," Toby said, "Stop fooling around, now. Back to business."

Jenna sat up and punched Toby in the arm as hard as she could.

"Ow," he said, putting the truck in gear. "If you're that tough, you can get out and push." They began to inch up the steep slope. "Come on, baby…" They made it nearly halfway before the engine stalled. "No, no… come on," Toby coaxed, starting the truck again. Several hundred feet more were traversed. "You better start rocking," he said to Jenna, looking in his rearview mirror. "It's a long way back down into the swamp if we don't make it." The thirsty engine groaned.

"Toby Dale LaRue," Jenna said, "I swear, if this stupid truck doesn't make it up this hill, I'll push it *and* you into the swamp myself!"

"We'll make it, we'll make-" The motor died again. "…

it. Oh, come on, honey, come on… Just a little more…"
Toby turned the key. The truck coughed to life once again.
The top of the hill was now in sight, marked by a break in
the trees where the cloud-shrouded crescent moon shone
through. "Almost there…" Inches turned to feet as Toby
manned the gas and clutch pedals with skillful precision,
working them just enough to yield forward motion. Three
car lengths, two car lengths, and then, finally, with one last
gun of the engine, they crested the hill, where the truck
rolled to a stop. "Wee-haw!" Toby whooped in triumph.
"We are now officially out of gas!"

Jenna let out a sigh of relief. Luckily, this side of the
hill was just as long and steep, and the lights of Blossom
County Dragway were waiting for them at the bottom,
shining through the trees. Toby opened his door and
stepped out.

"What are you doing now?" Jenna asked.

"Just giving us a little push start…" He leaned against
the truck's door frame "And… awaaay… we go!" Toby
jumped back in and they began to roll down the gravel
slope. "What did I tell you," he said, easing back into his
seat. "No sweat."

As the truck picked up speed, it began bouncing from
side to side, forcing Toby to drive with two hands.

"Whatever you do," Jenna said, "don't put on the
brakes."

Toby twisted the steering wheel. "Are you kidding? I'd
feel terrible if you had to push me all the way to the strip."
The road made a large, gentle arc as it descended through
the trees, turning from north to east. As they got closer to
the drag strip, the roar of engines and the smell of tire
smoke reached out to them.

"Well, they're still racing," Toby said. "Sounds like
they're running stockers."

"Did Jude say anything about how Jim and Necie were

doing?"

"No, I don't think so. They usually stick around though, even if they get knocked out early." They broke through the foliage and into an open field. The drag strip, stretching out to the northwest on their left, was alive with activity. Loud activity. A smoky haze, tinted blue by the randomly placed pole-top lamps, hung over the entire area, gently blanketing the patchwork collection of cars, trucks, and a few trailers. The bleachers were clearly packed full, so was any other place that offered an elevated view, such as truck roofs and car hoods. Even the property's lone tree, an old maple growing near the starting line, was full of people trying to get a better view of the racing action. The tinny, nearly unintelligible voice of the announcer occasionally broke through the engine roars. Toby applied slight pressure to the brakes.

"Hang on. I'm going in this way." He turned off of the road and through a gate in the chain link fence, bouncing wildly into the pits, which was little more than a grassy, unused field.

"Whoa!" Jenna said, her hand on the dash for support.

Toby brought the truck to a jerking stop. "Whew." He slouched in his seat for a moment, then sat up and opened his door. "Okay. I'm sure someone here can spare us a little fuel. Come on." They both got out and started walking toward the racetrack. Toby reached for Jenna's hand, but she crossed her arms in front of her before he could grab it.

"It's getting chilly out here," she said, looking away."

"It certainly is… Come on, let's hurry up." He stuck his hands in his pockets and picked up the pace. On their way to the starting line, they passed through several rows of race cars: sedans, coupes, roadsters, and dragsters, all forming jagged lines through the field. Some were being worked on, some were being warmed up, and some were being loaded onto trailers. One particular car, a white Pontiac with red stripes and red rims, had about five men under its hood, all of them leaning into the engine compartment. Two more were laying underneath the car.

"See," Toby said to Jenna. He walked over to them.

"Why hello, you two," said a young woman who was sitting in the grass, leaning against a station wagon. A toddler sat on her lap. "Where have you guys been all night?"

"Hey, Necie," Toby answered. "Is Jim still running?"

Necie pursed her lips, head shaking a silent 'no'.

"Hey, Jim," Toby yelled into the crowd of guys under the hood.

"Yeah?" came a voice from beneath the car.

"What's goin' on here?"

A man in his mid twenties rolled out and sat up, switching off a flashlight. His tanned face was covered in sweaty grease smudges. "Ahh, don't ask. I think she snapped her crank."

"Oh, no." Toby lent a hand and pulled Jim up off the ground.

"Yeah, and we won last round too. We'd be going to the final. That dumb bastard Pesatski got a 'bye run, and I know we could've beat him, too."

"Hey," Necie spoke up, covering the toddler's ears. "Watch the language. Eric needs no help. Yesterday he started calling the dog a 'dumb bastard'. I wonder where he heard that…"

Toby laughed.

"Beats me," Jim said, wiping his hands on a rag. "I call that dog a son of a bitch."

"Jim…"

"What? That's what he is, isn't he?"

"Anyhow," Toby said, "I didn't miss Bell's run yet did I?"

"Naw, they're just getting ready to run the last round of gassers. I missed his last run, but I heard the crowd go crazy."

"Aren't they a little far behind? It's pretty dark down there at the top end."

"Oh, a couple'a fuel coupes got crossed up. Made a big mess. Must'a taken them an hour and a half to clean it up."

"Hmm. Alright, well, I guess I'll see you later."

"Yeah, we'll be up to the fence in a bit. And if I don't see you there, I'm sure I'll be dropping by the garage on Monday morning."

"Okay, take it easy." Toby grabbed Jenna's hand before she could pull away. "'Bye, Necie."

"See you guys later. Say 'bye, Eric." She flapped the toddler's chubby little hand.

"Buh-bye."

They continued through the pits and soon came to the asphalt staging lanes, where about a half-dozen cars sat waiting behind the announcer's tower; a white booth on stilts positioned at the starting line, in between the two lanes.

"Over there," Toby said, pointing to a very large crowd that had gathered around one of the dragsters. He pulled Jenna in that direction. Pushing through the people, he sided up next to the rail, where Gary Bell sat on the roll cage, putting on his helmet. The car was painted yellow with 'Mary Jane III' emblazoned on the side.

"Hey," Gary exclaimed, "You finally got here. Hey, Jenna. I was afraid you guys'd miss me makin' history."

Toby leaned against the massive, fully exposed engine. "Yeah, well… This rail really went 185?"

"Yep."

"Wow. That's really something." Toby spoke over a pair

of cars heading down the track.

"It don't make any difference, though," Gary yelled. "Whoever makes out the record books ain't gonna believe it anyway." He slid his goggles into place.

"How come?"

"Politics!" Gary slid down into the seat and buckled his harness up. "Okay, Frankie!" he shouted, "Ready when you are!"

Frank Hawkins, who was sitting in a pickup truck behind the dragster, began honking the horn and bellowing, "Outta the way! Everybody outta the way!"

Toby stood up straight. "Well," he said, leaning in to check Gary's safety harness, giving them a firm tug, "good luck." They shook hands.

"Luck be a lady..." Gary said, smiling.

Toby and Jenna backed away as Frank pulled up to the dragster and began pushing it away. The rail moved along silently, riding on big slicks in the rear and little bicycle tires in the front. "Come on," Toby said. "Let's go get a spot on the fence."

"Hey, there's everybody right there," Jenna said, pointing towards the left side of the track.

"Where?" Toby squinted.

Jenna motioned again, "Right there behind the fence. Dean and everybody, see?"

"Oh, yeah. Good, they saved us a spot!" They trotted across the remainder of the staging lanes and through a break in the white chain-link.

"Where the hell've you been?" Dean exclaimed, stepping aside so that Toby and Jenna had a clear view of the track. "We've been here for ten minutes."

"We ran out of gas," Jenna said. "On Ello Lane."

"Judas Priest... why'd you guys go that way?"

"Because I like the scenery," Toby quipped, leaning on the fence. "Hey, Smoosh? Can I have one of those hot dogs?"

Smoosh just laughed out loud, showing off a mouthful of ground-up meat and bun.

"That means 'no'," Jude interpreted, blowing cigarette smoke out his nose.

"Jeeze. Some pal you are, Smoosh," Toby said.

"Me?" Smoosh spoke through the food. "What *pal 'o mine* was supposed to tell me what time to be at Dean's tonight?"

"Oh. Sorry about that. You didn't miss much anyway."

"Ahh, here." Smoosh leaned in front of Dean, handing Toby a hot dog. "I'm getting a little full anyway."

"See? What a guy! I promise that the next time Dean graduates from high school, you'll be the first one at his party."

"Gee, thanks."

Toby took a bite and then pulled the wiener apart. "Here, you want some?" he asked Jenna, handing her half.

She took it carefully. "What's wrong with it?"

"Nothing is wrong with it, I just thought you might be hungry. Is that a crime?"

"I guess not..."

"There. Now what did I get for myself by doing that, huh? I can be a selfless martyr too, you know."

"Well, I guess you-"

"Here they come!" Everyone craned their necks to see down the quarter-mile, where Frank was pushing Gary towards the starting line. Frank got up to about fifty miles per hour, and then Gary popped the clutch in the dragster, causing the engine to turn over with a roar. He pulled away from the truck under his own power. No one seemed to care about the car in the other lane, Darrell Essigg's blue Strip Streaker out of Belmont; everyone's eyes were glued to Bell and Hawkins' 'Mary Jane' as it rolled by.

"This is going to be good," Dean shouted over the

cackling engines.

"You bet" Toby answered. The nitromethane fumes wafted over them, burning their eyes and noses. "Whew! Get a load'a that!" he said, soaking it in.

The two dragsters reached the starting line and turned around to face the right direction. Gary, revving his engine, waved to the crowd. A young man with a t-shirt reading 'Fire Starter' stood in the center of the track, facing the cars. He held two flags, a green one and a red one, and motioned for the dragsters to move forward. Both of the rails, with the aid of track officials, inched up to a white line painted across the track, and then were checked over for leaks or any other safety hazards. The officials seemed satisfied and stepped back. The flagman pointed his red flag first at Gary and then at Darrell. Both drivers gave thumbs up.

"Here we go!" Toby said, putting his fingers in his ears.

The starter, holding the red flag behind his back, placed the tip of the green one on the ground. He bent down for a moment, rubbed at something on his shoe, and then, suddenly, without warning, jumped up like a Jack-in-the-Box, thrusting the green flag high into the air. Both dragsters, in a deafening roar, shot off like twin rockets, sending up massive trails of billowing tire smoke behind them. They ate up the quarter-mile in a matter of seconds, hidden from the crowd's view by their own pollution. When the haze cleared, the parachutes had billowed, and the win light was flashing in Gary Bell's lane. Everyone, including Toby, cheered out and then quickly fell silent, listening for the announcer to report the speed and elapsed times.

"Gary Bell," the announcer started, "in the Bell and Hawkins' Mary Jane… with an E.T. of 8.72 seconds and a speed of 179.41 miles per hour…"

"Aww, dang it," Toby said, joining in with the rest of

the spectators' disappointment. "What happened?"

Dean pointed to the flapping flags on top of the announcer's booth. "Headwind. Oh, well. It was still a good run."

"Yeah, I guess so."

"What do we do now?" Jenna asked, looking around at all of the people beginning to file out of the stands.

"I don't know. What do we do now, Dean?"

"We can go back to my place and eat. I never got any supper."

Toby pushed away from the fence. "Or we could go over to the Grange Hall."

"To the dance?"

"Yeah, but I need to get some go-go juice for my truck first."

"Alright, well, whatever. I'll meet you there then. I want to stop at home and see if I can get my car... Uh-oh. Don't look now."

"What?" Toby said, looking around.

"Novello. Headed in this direction. See you later." Dean pulled Heidi away with him, melting into the throng.

Toby spotted Stuart Novello's smirking mug. Novello returned the glance. "Oh, no!" he exclaimed, grabbing Jenna's elbow. "Come on, let's get outta here!"

Chapter 14

Toby pulled Jenna away toward the crowded bleachers, looking over his shoulder as he went. "Do you see him?"

Jenna turned around to look.

"No, don't stop!" Toby exclaimed, pulling harder.

Jenna stumbled slightly. "Well - you - asked!"

"Careful. Don't slow down."

"What's the big deal? What are you afraid of anyway?"

They rounded the bleachers, joining a throng of people who where filing out towards the crowded parking grounds. "I'm not afraid, I'm just… uh, it looks like rain." Toby let go of Jenna and broke into a trot.

"Right…"

"Come on, I've still gotta see if I can bum some gas off of someone." They entered the pits, where cars, trucks, and trailers were beginning pull out for the night. "Hopefully Jim's left yet."

"You mean *hasn't* left?"

"That's what I said. Dang, I've gotta pee too."

"Sorry," Jenna said, "I can't help you with that." She then perked up and pointed ahead. "There goes Jim and Necie there…"

"Where?" Toby said, looking around. Then he caught sight of the Beshore's station wagon. It was moving away through the field, with Jim's white and red race car tagging along behind on a tow bar. "Dang!" He began running, waving his arms. "Hey! Jim! Wait up!" Finally, after about a hundred feet of pursuit, Jim's brake lights lit up, and Toby dropped his arms, panting heavily. Jim rolled down his window.

"What?"

"I…" Toby tried to catch his breath. "I need some gas.

Can you… spare a few drops?"

"All I've got is the stuff for the race car."

"That'll be perfect. I can… pay you back tomorrow morning at church."

"Alright… It's in a can behind the seat. In the Pontiac."

"Thanks, Jim. What a guy." Toby reached through the window and slapped him on the shoulder. He began walking toward the race car, then stopped, turned around and added, "Oh, I'm in a big hurry, so I'll bring the can back tomorrow too, okay?"

"Sure."

"Thanks, buddy. Whew. Take it easy."

"Same to you."

Reaching the Pontiac, Toby opened the door and grabbed the little red fuel can from behind the seat. He shut the door. "Thanks!" he yelled again, holding up the can. Jim waved and pulled away.

The pits were quickly clearing out, and Toby trotted across the dimly lit field as fast as his leg would allow in order to avoid any confrontations with Stuart Novello. When he reached the truck, Jenna was already sitting inside. Ignoring his throbbing thigh, he hastily screwed off the gas cap and tipped the contents of the can into the fuel tank; the truck guzzled up the liquid in seconds. Finished, Toby twisted the cap back on, threw the can in the bed, and jumped in the truck. "Okay," he said, pumping the gas pedal. "Hopefully this wor- *ahh!*" He grabbed his right thigh. "No, no, no… damn it, no!"

Jenna sat up, alarmed. "What's wrong?"

"It's locking up!" Toby said through gritted teeth. "I shouldn't have run!" He writhed, cursing as the pain pulsed up and down his leg.

"Hold still!" Jenna put one hand on Toby's thigh and one on his shoulder. "Hold still! Relax it!"

"That's… easy… for you to say! *Arrggh*… it'll go away in a minute… it'll… go away…"

Jenna tried to massage the muscles, but Toby was kicking too much. "Toby, sit still!" She put both hands on his leg, trying to hold it down.

Outside, a pair of headlights pointed their way. Toby stopped squirming long enough to identify the source. "Son of a bitch, that's Novello!" He straightened up as best as he could. "Switch seats!"

"What?"

"You drive! Switch seats!" Toby scooted towards Jenna and she climbed over his lap, plopping down behind the steering wheel. "Okay," Toby said through bared teeth. "Pump the pedal first…"

Jenna did as she was told and, crossing her fingers, turned the key. Luckily, the engine rumbled out of its parched slumber with only a few sputters.

"Now step on it!" Toby yelled. "You've gotta blow it out anyhow, so drive fast!"

Jenna shoved the shifter forward and dropped the clutch. Clods of dirt and grass spewed out from behind the rear tires as she swung the truck around and pointed its nose toward the exit gate. "Which way do you want me to go?" She yelled, speaking over the engine.

Toby hunched over his leg. "I don't care, just get away from him! Shut the lights off!"

"What?!"

"Shut the lights off and go Ello! Trust me!"

With a look of bewildered determination, Jenna steered out of the open gate and back up the gravel road, driving by patchy moonlight.

"Is he following?" Toby asked, trying to see out the back window.

Jenna glanced in the mirror. "I can't see anymore. I don't know." They reached the summit of the hill and then over, plunging once again into the eerie shadows of Ello Lane.

"You can… turn the lights back on now," Toby said. He worked his fingers into his thigh.

"Is it letting go?" Jenna asked, switching the headlights on.

"A little. It's starting to pass. Just get to the Grange as fast as you can."

"I'm already speeding."

"Speeding, shmeeding. Just get there quick." Toby leaned his head against the window and wiped the sweat from his brow.

"Why? You aren't going to be able to dance anyway. Why are you trying so hard to avoid Stuart tonight?"

Toby looked Jenna in the eye. "Jenna, he already tried to kill me once." He patted his sore leg. "And I really pissed him off this morning, so I don't think he'd just want to chat."

"Do you actually think he was trying to kill you, Toby? You still don't even know for sure it was him."

"I most certainly do. And when you jerry rig someone's throttle to stick open, it's deadly. You don't screw around with stuff like that. Even *I* don't screw around with stuff like that. And I screw around with a lot of stuff… Besides, why do you always take his side in everything?"

"I do not. All I'm saying is that when I was first met him-"

"I don't want to hear about it. I've had enough fighting for one night. Watch this corner; it's sharp." Toby rolled down his window, allowing the cool night air to whip into the cab. The earthy aroma of the swamp followed.

"You can't stand the fact that he went out with me before you did, can you?"

Toby leaned his head out the window, allowing the breeze to ripple through his hair. He didn't answer Jenna.

"Can you?"

"Can I what?"

"You heard me."

"No I didn't." Toby closed his eyes.

"Only because you don't want to. It was one time, Toby. *One* time!"

Toby opened his eyes. "Are you *trying* to make me mad?"

"No, I'm trying to figure out why you're really avoiding Stuart so much."

"Because I hate that S.O.B.'s guts! Is that a good enough reason? I'm trying to figure out how to get back at him for sabotaging the dragster *again*!"

"What?"

"Dean found a bunch of sand or some shit poured in the frame! I said I don't want to fight anymore, so will you please just shut up, okay?"

"Toby... you... fine." Jenna tightened her grip on the steering wheel.

The dark hills rolled by quickly, and, reaching Ormsby Corners again, they left Ello Lane behind, turning left onto East Riverside Drive. East Riverside's terrain was identical to West Riverside; one endless, undulating, twisting turn finding its way through an abundance of mossy rock walls. The only major difference was the lack of habitation. Not a single sign of life was seen in the mile and a half up to the Grange Hall. But once they rolled onto the gravel lot, they saw where half of the town had congregated, or at least everyone in town age eighteen and under.

"Try and park close to the door," Toby said, still massaging his leg.

"I'll try but it doesn't look like we have much of a choice."

The truck's small size allowed Jenna to squeeze into a tiny spot about thirty feet from the large white building. She shut the truck off and handed Toby the keys.

"I guess this will have to do." Toby sat still for a few minutes, resting his leg, and then grabbed his jacket and eased out of the truck. The sound of slow rock 'n roll escaped from deep within the building. He and Jenna began walking toward it.

The Grange Hall, which was situated on a steep, tree-clogged hill that overlooked most of Carson Valley, was little more than a large, retired church; white with several, bullet-shaped stained glass windows, a cross in the front lawn, and even a small steeple on it's wooden-shingled roof. A cement walkway ran alongside the building, disappearing behind a row of bushes. Toby and Jenna followed this, passing a few loitering teens along the way, and, after descending a long staircase, they found themselves stepping onto a large concrete patio surrounded by a knee-high stone wall. It was partially illuminated by light spilling from the building through a pair of open double doors, through which a crowd of slow-dancing teens could be seen. A young man, peering through thick glasses, was sitting on a chair just outside the doors. He held a small cash box on his lap.

"Hello, Toby," the young man said, adjusting his glasses.

"Hi, Coaster…"

"Two tickets?"

"Yeah." Toby said, feeling around for his wallet.

Coaster pulled out a roll of tickets and ripped two off. "That'll be a dollar."

"Yeah, I know… but I can't seem to…"

"What's wrong?" Jenna asked.

"I can't find my… oh, damn it!"

"What?"

"My wallet's in my other pants! They were wet and I… I must have…" He looked at Coaster.

"You wet your pants?" Coaster asked.

Jenna rolled her eyes. "Well what are we going to do now?"

Toby thought for a moment. "Do you have any money?"

"No… I lent Callie everything in my purse."

"Dang it…" Toby's eyes turned back to Coaster.

"Oh, no you don't!" Coaster exclaimed. "No pay, no play! No favors for anyone!"

"Ah, come on, Coaster! It's just once!"

"No! Our next big fund raiser isn't until July and the 4-H has to make enough money to last a while. We need every cent!"

"But I'll pay you back!"

"No!"

Toby clenched his jaw. "Fine." He put his arm around Jenna's waist. "Then we'll just dance out here. Nothing you can do about that."

"But…" Coaster started.

"Come on, Toby…" Jenna said, her arms hanging limply at her sides. She sighed as he pulled her away from the door.

"Come on, Toby…" he mocked, taking her hands, holding one and placing the other on his shoulder. "May I have this dance?"

"You've already taken it."

Toby pulled her close. "You know you're my favorite girlfriend in the world."

"I'm so lucky." They began to sway back and forth. "What about my Grandma?"

"She's my third favorite."

"No I mean about-"

"Oh, I love this song…" Toby interrupted as Santo and Johnny's *'Sleep Walk'* drifted out of the building. "This could be *our* song."

"What? It doesn't even have any words."

"Because there aren't any words to express your love for me," Toby said very seriously. He pulled Jenna's head onto his shoulder, and continued to dance to the dreamy mix of slide guitar and crickets. Thunder rumbled off in the distance.

Jenna glanced up at the sky. "It's going to rain."

"Yeah…" Toby sighed. "I imagine there won't be any racing tomorrow. Did I tell you I'm moving?"

"What?"

"I'm moving away from home."

"What? Oh, you mean the apartment over the garage. I was wondering when you were going to tell me. I helped your mother clean it up last week." She looked at her watch. "Dean had been staying there quite a lot it seemed…"

"And speaking of the devil," Toby said, just as Dean and Heidi stepped off of the stairs and onto the patio.

Dean stopped and stared at Toby and Jenna for moment. "What's goin' on here," he finally asked.

"Buildings are so overrated," Toby said.

"Apparently so are wallets," Jenna added.

Dean pulled a couple of wadded up dollar bills out of his pocket. "What, you need bread?"

"No, like I said," Toby cast an angry glance in Coaster's direction, "we needed the fresh air."

"Besides," Jenna said, "we're just about to leave."

"Leave?" Dean asked.

"Leave?" Toby echoed.

"My Grandmother's in the hospital. I'm staying with her tonight." Jenna tried to pull away from Toby, but he held her tight. "Come on, Toby, it's…" She looked at her watch. "It's a quarter 'till. I'm supposed to be there at eleven."

"The song's not over."

"Toby, please."

Toby sighed loudly. "Fine. Just finish the song and we'll leave, okay? I promise."

"Well," Dean said, handing Coaster a dollar, "I guess I'll see you guys later."

"Yeah, I'll be back after I drop her off." Toby turned away, burying his face in Jenna's hair. It still smelled like lilacs. She put both arms around his neck, resting her chin on his shoulder, and continued to sway slowly, in time with the Hawaiian-like music. Tiny raindrops began to spatter the concrete around them.

"I wish I could stay," she said, unconvincingly. "I'm having such an amazing time…"

"Me too."

"I'm sorry to hear that."

Toby looked up at the gently flickering clouds. "It's not your fault. Besides, there's always tomorrow night, right?"

"I guess so."

"What do you mean?"

She pulled away and looked him in the eyes. "Toby, I need to tell you something. Something important."

"What?"

"I…" She looked around. "This really isn't the place."

"What's it about?"

"You and me… and-"

"And me?" came a voice from the shadowy stairs. Toby turned around. He had been so engrossed with Jenna that he hadn't even heard Stuart Novello approach.

Toby clenched his jaw. "Son of a…"

Novello stepped out of the darkness, followed by three other men; two young and one older. He was dressed in all black, and sucking on a cigarette. "Keep going, Jenna.

Don't let me interrupt. Tell him everything…" He flicked the cigarette into the bushes. "Fraska," he said to one of the young men, "get me something to drink." Fraska disappeared into the Grange Hall.

Toby looked at Jenna, whose wide blue eyes danced back and forth between him and Novello. "What's he mean? Tell me what?"

"I… I don't know…"

"Come on, Jenna," Novello said. "Tell him. Tell him about you and me at Lexie's last week."

"What?" Toby asked, growing more edgy.

Fraska returned with a cup of punch.

Jenna spoke up. "I… that's not it. That's not what I'm talking about, Stuart…"

Novello took the punch, spiking it with something from a small metal flask. "Then what? If that's not it then tell him about the ride home. To my house."

"What the hell is going on here, Jenna?"

"And then tell him about what happened at my house." Novello looked at Toby. "Girls have certain emotional needs, LaRue. Apparently you can't fill them."

Toby turned his glaring eyes on Jenna. His face was growing red with anger. "Is this true?"

"I…" Jenna stuttered. "… no, I, I mean yes. But it's not what you think-"

Novello cut in. "It was just like the old days, huh, Jenna? Before you, LaRue." He downed the punch. "Ahh," he said, licking his lips and looking up at the sky. "As sweet and easy as…" His eyes wandered to Jenna, and then back to Toby. "Well, you know, Toby… Or maybe you don't."

Without thinking, Toby lunged at Novello, only to be suddenly stopped, grabbed from behind by someone unseen. He turned around, fists swinging at whoever it was, but came face to face with Dean. "Let go of me,

Dean!" He said, pushing away.

Novello and his cronies laughed. "Yeah," Novello said, "let him go Krindle! Let him go!"

"Shut the hell up, Novello," Dean said. "Get outta here."

"No, actually I think I'll come in out of the rain and have another drink. Come on guys." Novello pulled a wallet out of his suit coat and walked across the patio, dropping a ten dollar bill in Coaster's lap. "Keep the change." He walked into the crowd, and then looked back at Jenna and blew her a kiss. "See you a little later, sweetheart," he yelled.

Nearly shaking with rage, Toby couldn't control himself anymore. He bolted through the doors and into the building, fists clenched. Dean tried to stop him, but couldn't.

"Toby, don't!" Jenna yelled.

Toby didn't stop, making a bee-line for Novello. Young teenage dancers began to yelp and scream as Toby pushed through them. He pulled back his fist, but just before he got to Novello he was grabbed from behind again, only this time it wasn't Dean, it was Fraska, Novello's goon. Toby tried to fight him off, and one of the dance supervisors started shouting for them to break it up, but that didn't stop Fraska from whipping out a switchblade and skimming it across Toby's right thigh. Toby gasped as a six inch slit opened on his jeans; it quickly turned dark red. He elbowed Fraska in the gut, freeing himself, then peeled off his jacket and threw up his fists.

"Come on, Novello! You and me! Fair and square! Tell your punks to get the hell outta here!"

Jenna pushed in beside Toby, covering her mouth when she saw his bloody leg. "Stuart, stop!" she said.

Novello stood with his arms crossed. "Keck, Fraska; go wait in the car. Lasky, beat it."

"But, Stu-"
"Go! LaRue's right. This is between me and him…"

Chapter 15

A low chant of *'fight, fight, fight'* began to pepper the crowd as Toby stepped towards Novello with his fists raised, taking a boxer's stance. Novello stood motionless, one hand in his pocket, and the other gently swirling his cup of punch. A fresh cigarette was nestled between his fingers.

"Come on, put 'em up, pansy!" Toby said.

"Pansy? Ooo…" Novello arched an eyebrow. "Tough boy, huh?"

"You'll find out soon enough!"

Novello took a drag on his cigarette, speaking at the same time, "I'll tell you what I'm going to do for you, LaRue… I'm going to give you the chance to haul ass out of here and save that ugly face of yours. Get back, Carter!" He pointed at an advancing dance supervisor, who stopped in his tracks.

"Is that right?" Toby asked.

"Yep. You leave now and I won't think you any less of a man than I already do. Fair?"

Jenna stepped in between them. "Toby, stop. Let's go. Let's-"

"You stay outta this!" Toby said, pushing Jenna backward.

Novello narrowed his eyes. "See?" he said. "Is that any way to treat a woman? A *real* woman?"

Toby's fist drew back like a rock in a slingshot. He swung hard, but instead of getting a fistful of Novello's chin, all he got was a face full of Novello's fruit punch. Laughs sprinkled the crowd as he stumbled backward, the red liquid dribbling off of his face and onto his once white t-shirt.

A satisfied smirk grew on Novello. "Have one on me," he said.

Toby's shock quickly passed. He lunged forward, throwing a second punch, but this time, before Toby could stop him, Novello whipped his hand out of his coat pocket; his knuckles were wrapped in brass. Novello's punch found it's mark, landing squarely on Toby's jaw with a hair raising 'crack'.

Toby fell backward, hitting the wooden floor with a squeaky thud. The right side of his jaw instantly began turning purple. Groaning, he rolled over on his side and spit out a mouthful of blood, and, to his horror, part of a tooth. Jenna, Dean, and Heidi all dropped to the floor around him.

Dean helped him sit up. "I think you'd better quit while you're ahead…"

Tears streamed down Jenna's face. She scooted closer to Toby, feeling his jaw. "I'm sorry, Toby. This is all my fault. If I… I'm sorry…"

All that Toby could see was the bloody bit of molar sitting in the pool of blood. His hate-filled gaze moved from the tooth to Novello, who looked as smug as could be, laughing with the kids around him.

Dean saw Toby's fist ball up slowly. "No, Tobe, no," he spoke in a hushed tone. "Let's get outta here, come on…"

Toby wasn't listening. And Novello, who was too busy eating up praise from the other teens, never even saw the hit coming. Toby plowed him over like a bus, both of them falling into the refreshment table. Novello's head landed right in the punch bowl, and Toby's fists weren't far behind. Again and again, using both hands, he battered Novello's face, every hit strengthened by last year's endless summer of hay bailing. Fruit punch mixed with blood began to spatter everyone and everything within a six foot radius. Finger sandwiches and cookies flew off of the table in all directions. Finally, with much struggle, Dean and several other young men were able to pull Toby away from Novello, who's face now resembled a thick, moist cut of fresh beef.

"Let me… go!" Toby yelled, struggling against Dean's grip.

"Cool it! That's enough!"

Novello slid off of the table and hit the floor like a wet sandbag. After laying motionless for a few moments, he rolled onto his stomach and tried to pull himself up, groaning. His hands groped at the slippery wet table. Someone tried to help him, but they were violently shoved away.

Toby stepped back, shoulders heaving with every breath; blood still trickled out of his mouth. He spit at Novello, who finally pulled his quivering legs beneath himself.

"You…" Novello started, turning and pointing a shaky finger at Toby. "You are gonna pay." He wiped his face on his sleeve. "Mark my words…" With a deep breath, he angrily shoved himself through the crowd, exiting the building into the now steady rain.

As soon as he was gone, a cheer arose from the teens. Clapping, whistling, whooping, people slapping Toby on the back. He managed a weak version of his trademark crooked grin as someone handed him a cup of water to rinse his mouth out, which he did, and then raised the reddened liquid over his head in a toast.

"To victory," he said.

Another round of applause rippled through the throng. Toby's smile grew bigger. Bigger, that is, until his eyes locked with Jenna's. Jenna wasn't smiling. She wasn't clapping or cheering either. She was crying. Her eyes fell to Toby's bloody knuckles, and then, without a word, she turned and moved toward the exit.

Toby felt a flash of anger wash across his face. Handing the bloody water off to Dean, he took a step to follow Jenna, just as the knife cut on his leg screamed back into his consciousness.

"Ah!" he hissed, almost dropping to one knee.

"Toby…" Dean started.

"I'll be fine! Just help me to the door."

Dean walked in front of him, creating a gap in the crowd. "You are an idiot, you know that don't you?"

"Yeah, but what for this time?"

They reached the doorway.

"Here," Dean said, giving Toby his jacket and then extending a clenched fist.

"What is it?" Toby put his coat on.

Dean opened his hand, revealing the half tooth. "You'll be lucky if this is all you lose." He dropped it into Toby's open palm, and, without another word, he turned and walked back into the building.

Toby watched him disappear, and then shoved the tooth into his jeans pocket and limped out into the rain.

As he rounded the corner and began to slowly ascend the wet cement steps, Jenna was still nowhere in sight. He called for her. No answer. The rain, ice cold on his skin, smacked his face with gumball-sized drops, soaking the front of his thin white t-shirt before he had even reached the top of the stairs. He stepped onto the parking lot. A quick moving figure caught his eye; it was Jenna, walking away as fast as she could.

"Jenna!" he yelled again, his voice fringed in anger. "What are you gonna do, huh? Walk all the way home?"

Jenna turned around, her hair hanging in wet strands around her face.

Toby stopped ten feet from her. "Huh?"

"I need to go be with my Grandma."

"Screw Grandma! I need some answers."

"If you aren't going to take me then I'll find someone else."

"Like Stuart?"

"Toby…" Jenna's gaze wandered off into the darkness. "That was… it wasn't…"

"It wasn't what? What wasn't it? I don't understand, Jenna. What's been- what've you been doing behind my back?"

"Behind your back? Toby, I am *not* your possession! I don't belong to you!"

"Then who do you belong to? Novello?"

"Don't be stupid!"

"Stupid? *Stupid?* What the hell am I supposed-"

"Are you going to take me or not?

"Take you where?"

Jenna's folded arms dropped to her sides. Without a word, she turned around and began walking away again.

"What, you want a ride? Here!" Toby reached into his pocket and whipped the truck keys out. "Here!" He threw them towards Jenna; they landed at her feet in the wet gravel. "I've had it! I don't want to see you for the rest of the night!"

A look of incredulity swept across Jenna's face, lit up by a slow pulse of lightning.

Toby turned around and didn't even look back to see if she picked the keys up. "I'll come by and get my truck tomorrow!"

"Toby!"

"Goodnight!"

A strange feeling filled Toby's stomach as he walked back down the steps. A feeling of guilt. But he wasn't about to take back his words now. He'd meant everything he said.

"Girls…" he muttered to himself as he once again stepped onto the cement patio.

"Back so soon?" Coaster asked. "It's still fifty cents a ticket."

"I'll see what I can do," Toby said, walking through the door and into the crowd before Coaster could object. His eyes danced over the people.

"Hey, Toby!" came a voice from his right.

"Cal!" Toby answered, waving to the young man that approached him. Cal Rillings was about the same height as Toby, watery gray eyes, and had a grease slick for hair.

"Hey that was some show you just put on!" Cal said, adjusting his thick rimmed, Buddy Holly-esque glasses. He slapped Toby on the back.

"Thanks."

"What did it feel like?"

Toby exhaled and shook his head. "It felt really, really good."

"I'll bet!" Cal pulled a pack of cigarettes out of his shirt pocket. He put one in his mouth. "Want a cigarette?

"Sure." Toby took the Camel, which Cal lit for him. "Where's Dean?"

"Uh… I think he was back there in the corner somewhere."

"I gotta get something on this cut." Toby put pressure on the wound.

"Holy Moses!" Cal exclaimed. "What'd he use, a machete?"

"That's what it feels like. Do you know where they keep the first aid kit around here? Is Mr. Sanderson here?"

"I don't think so." Cal blew out a cloud of smoke. "If he was he'd be upstairs. The first aid kit's in the kitchen."

"Alright. Don't they keep that locked though?"

Cal pulled out a pocket knife. "Yeah, but I've got the key."

"Lead the way, Mack."

Toby received several more pats on the back before he and Cal stepped out of the auditorium and into an adjacent hallway. There, stopping in front of a plain white door, Cal pulled his knife out and made short work of the knob lock.

"Neat-o…" Toby said. "You do this often?"

Cal opened the door. "Often enough." He flipped a switch on the wall, shedding light on the pristine-looking kitchen. He started rummaging through the cupboards. "I'm not sure where I saw it…"

Toby stepped into the kitchen, shutting the door behind him. He followed Cal's lead and began searching the cupboards. "What's it look like?"

"Like a first aid kit. Ah! Here it is…" Cal produced a white metal tin. He sat it on one of the kitchen's two, eight-foot island counters and began to examine its contents. "Okay… Band-Aids, gauze… tape, alcohol… Look's like everything you'll want."

Toby pulled the kit toward him."I'm gettin' pretty sick go these damn things today…"

"You need help?"

"No, I don't need help! I gotta pull my pants down! Jesus… What are you, some kind of a sick pervert or something?"

"I don't know. That's what my girlfriends keep telling me."

"Girl*friends*?"

"Sure. I keep a few backups in my address book."

"Well, if you want to help, send one of *them* in."

"Ha. If you need anything, call your mother." Cal opened the door.

"I'll be out in a minute… jeeze," Toby said, sitting on the edge of the counter. After Cal shut the door, Toby smashed out his cigarette and began rummaging through the kit. "Hmm…" He sat the Band Aid tin aside; they were too small to help in this situation. The rolls of gauze and tape came out, along with a bottle of hydrogen peroxide. With a glance at the door, he unbuttoned his pants and pulled them down just far enough to get to the wound, which, under closer examination, didn't look nearly as bad as it felt. It was the fact that the cut ran right through his pink, hairless burn scars that worried Toby.

"Fraska, you son of a bitch…" he muttered. He continued to dig through the tin, looking for something to apply the peroxide with. When nothing suitable was found, he stood up, shuffling across the room with his pants around his knees, and grabbed a clean dishcloth off of the counter. "Perfect," he said, moving back to the island. He soaked the cloth and began to clean off the blood. With that done, he reached for the gauze.

"Need some help?" came a soft, female voice from the door.

Toby jumped, reaching for his pants in vain, at the same time knocking over the bottle of peroxide. His head whipped toward the door, where a woman now stood, her pretty face peeking into the kitchen. "Wh-what do you want? Who are you?"

The girl, whose brilliant blue eyes stood out against her short black hair, looked over her shoulder, making sure that no one saw her, and then entered the room, pulling the door shut behind her.

"I saw you and Cal Rillings come in here," she said.

"Who are you?" Toby repeated, finally grasping a belt loop on his pants and pulling them most of the way up.

"My name is Settie… Settie Edwards. I live over in Parkberry."

"Oh… well," Toby cleared his throat, righting the bottle of hydrogen peroxide. "What- what do you want?"

"Well… I saw you get cut up pretty badly out there,"

she nodded in the direction of the auditorium, clasping her hands behind her back, "and I thought maybe you could use some help… I'm a volunteer at Blossom County Medical," she added quickly, biting her lip.

"Uh, no, no I'm- I've got it all under control. It's really just a scratch anyway."

Settie moved closer. "Are you sure?" She looked older up close, at least twenty. "You left a pretty big trail of blood behind you." Her white satin skirt rustled as she sat next to him on the island counter.

"Umm… Oh, that-that was mostly from my mouth. Yeah, I- he knocked out a tooth… and, I, uh… yeah, I broke a tooth."

"Oh. Well, do you mind if I at least have a look at the cut? Something that big could get infected very easily." Her eyes sparkled like the Caribbean. She bit her lip again.

"Uh-uh," Toby stuttered, gripping his pants tighter. "I-I don't think I'll be affected- *infected*, I mean. It's just a scratch, really."

"Come on, don't be a baby…" She put her hand on his, tugging it away from his jeans.

Toby watched dumbfounded as she pushed his pant leg down, revealing the ragged knife cut. He'd had to ward off girls before, but none had never been this persistent. Or pretty. And they'd never been older than him. She looked like one of the Gil Elvgren pinups that were hanging in his room. If Jenna, or anyone who even *knew* Jenna walked in, he would be sunk. Settie's warm fingers probed at the wound, brushing out a few denim fibers with the dishcloth. Then she began wrapping his leg with the gauze.

"You're Toby LaRue, right? You know, I've seen you race before. At Stardust."

"…Oh, yeah?"

"I was there when you got in that terrible crash."

"Really?"

"Mm-hmm. What happened that time?"

"Our-our car was, uh… sabotaged."

"Wow. By who?"

"A competitor."

"Hmm. And, uh, don't you… don't you have a girlfriend?"

There it was. Toby stood up. "I, uh… thanks. That's good enough." He jerked his jeans up and fastened them, and then started walking toward the door.

"I saw you two arguing."

Toby stopped and slowly turned around. "You were eavesdropping on us?"

"I couldn't help it. I was out in the parking lot when you…"

"We had a disagreement, that was all."

"You threw something at her."

Toby turned back around and put his hand on the door knob. "Yeah, well… people do stupid things when they're mad."

Settie stood up and cat walked slowly toward Toby. She put her hand around the back of his neck. "Maybe she deserved it."

A pulse of electricity shot up and down Toby's spine as Settie whispered. When she pulled him closer and kissed his ear, his hand began to shake, rattling the doorknob. "Uh, listen, I gotta go, uh," he said quickly. "It was nice meeting you."

Settie smiled a mischievous smile, arching one eyebrow. "Don't you want to stay for a while?" Her finger tips brushed over the purple knuckle marks on his jaw.

"Uh, uh , n-no… Sorry but I-I have to be somewhere." Her hands felt good. Smooth, like a feather duster. But there was something about her that made him uneasy. Toby turned the doorknob and opened the door.

"Cheshire-27099."

Toby's step wavered. "Huh?"

"My phone number. Cheshire-27099." Settie's eyes softened as she cocked her head to one side. She leaned in and kissed him, grabbing a belt loop to pull him closer. He felt the tip of her tongue slither past his lips. He wanted to stop her, push her back, but at the same time it felt good, feeling her body pressed up against him. When she finally pulled away, she gently bit his lower lip, tugging on it with her teeth until it slapped back into place.

"Call me."

"Uh…" He stood with his mouth hanging open, stunned. "I'll… Okay, maybe…"

Regaining his senses, Toby left the kitchen door open, getting away as fast as he could. He broke out of the short hallway and into the crowd.

"Dean!" He motioned to his friend, yelling over Elvis Presley.

Dean turned away from Heidi, with whom he was dancing. "What?" he mouthed.

Toby made his way toward Dean, snaking between the slow dancing teens, bumping a few shoulders. He glanced back in the direction of the kitchen, where Settie Edwards was leaning on the hallway door frame, watching him intently. "Are, uh… Are you leaving anytime soon?"

"In a little bit," Dean answered. "Why?"

"Well, I let Jenna take my truck, and now I'm stranded."

Heidi, whose head was resting on Dean's shoulder, piped in without opening her eyes. "That wasn't very smart of you, now was it?"

"Yeah, well, I didn't plan on being attacked by Bettie Page either."

"Huh?" Dean asked.

"In the doorway over there…"

Dean peered over Toby's shoulder, where Settie was standing, now smoking a cigarette. "Judas H. Priest. *She's* after *you*? What, is she blind or something?"

"What? Come on, it's not that unbelievable!"

"Since when do Esquire girls chase *you*?"

Toby rolled his eyes. "Can you give me a ride or not?"

"Depends on where you want to go."

"I don't care. Wherever you guys are going."

Heidi opened her eyes for the first time and raised a brow.

"Within reason," Toby added.

"We don't really know what we're going to do next," she said, "Any suggestions?"

"Well… what time is it?"

"Going on midnight."

"Already? There's not much left to do then." Toby thought for a moment. "What about going down to The Strawberry? It's Saturday night, they don't close for awhile."

"That's where Jude and Arvel went. Are you hungry again?" Dean asked.

"I'm always hungry."

"I don't know…" Heidi said, sounding tired. "Maybe we could just go to the pool hall or something."

"I don't care." Toby was becoming impatient. "Just make up your minds. I'll be waiting for you guys outside, okay?"

Dean sighed. "Fine, we'll be out in a minute."

Outside, the rain hadn't subsided at all, causing Toby to blink rapidly as he stepped from the building, shoulders hunched and his hands in his jacket pockets. A blanket of cold raindrops pecked incessantly at the concrete steps beneath his quick moving feet. A bright, pole-mounted light at the top of the steps illuminated his accent, and, when he crested the top, a loving couple huddled underneath an awning to his right. They were startled mid-kiss.

"Jeeze, Toby!" It was Cal. "Can't a guy get any privacy around here?"

"Yeah... Try the kitchen."

"Good idea. Hey, this is Gina. Gina, this is my good friend Toby LaRue."

"Hello."

"Hi."

"What, are you leaving?" Cal asked.

"Yeah, it's past my bedtime."

"Alright. Well, I'll - hey, where are you racing tomorrow? Blossom or Stardust?"

"Probably just Blossom, if it dries out by then. Why?"

"Just wondered. I guess I'll see you around."

"Yeah, take it easy." Toby left the lovebirds to their own devices and continued onward, out into the parking lot, where, after a few soaking minutes of searching, he finally found Dean's yellow '57 Chevrolet. He opened the passenger's side door. A pile of at least fifty Dum-Dum pops sat on the seat. "Good grief," he said, pushing them out of the way. "Boy, I wish I was your dentist..."

Chapter 16

The unceasing rain pounded the roof of Dean's car like a hopper full of marbles, then trickled down the windows to fracture Toby's view. It didn't take long for the glass to fog over. With the outside world fully obscured, all he could do was sit and watch as headlights from exiting cars washed over the windows, briefly illuminating the interior of the Chevy. He picked at the rip in his jeans. His leg throbbed. He kept catching whiffs of Settie's perfume. Finally, after what seemed to him like days, the shadowy silhouettes of Dean and Heidi appeared.

"It's about time…" Toby said as Dean opened the driver's side door. "You guys get lost?"

Heidi slid across the seat toward him. "We were hoping you'd get tired of waiting and find someone else to babysit you."

"Ha."

Dean scooted in after Heidi. "What-? Toby!"

"What?"

"What'd you do, just knock all my suckers on the floor? Jesus!"

Toby looked at Heidi. "And *I'm* the one who needs a babysitter?"

"Those aren't free, you know." Dean started the engine and backed out of the line of cars, after wiping the condensation off the windshield. "Jeeze…"

"So what are we doing?" Toby asked.

"Well," Dean said, "thanks to you I'm still starving, so…"

"What do you mean 'thanks to me'? Just because I knocked your Dum-Dums on the floor?"

"No, because you knocked all the food on the floor.

When you and Novello plowed into the table back there."

"Oh… Yeah, that was a good one with his head landing in the punch…"

"So I was thinking we could go to Lexie's or something, then call it a night. I've been up since five-thirty." He stopped at the road, waiting for Toby's answer. "Well?"

"Lexie's? I guess that'd be alright."

"Just alright?"

"No, that's fine. It's just that… never mind. Lexie's it is."

"Okay." Dean turned right, pointing the car toward Willowgrove.

The five mile stretch of road that led into town was dark and wet, reflecting light sources like a black mirror. Traffic was sparse. Dean turned the radio on, catching the tail end of The Flamingos' 'I Only Have Eyes For You', which was followed by one of Dion's many hits. Toby, tenderly rubbing his jaw, leaned his head back and closed his eyes.

"I'm so pissed off at Jenna right now, I should've went out with that girl back there," he said. "She seemed a lot more affectionate than Jenna's been lately."

"Who was she?" Heidi asked.

"I don't know. I've never seen her before."

"What was her name?"

"Settie. Edwards."

Callie paused. "Are you serious?"

Toby opened his eyes. "Yeah, why?"

"You're not joking?"

"Why would I joke? I've never seen her before and her name is Settie Edwards. What is there to joke about?"

Heidi turned to Dean. "Have you ever heard of her?"

Dean didn't answer.

"Toby," Heidi continued, "Settie Edwards is a… a…

you know… a lady of the-"

Toby sat up straight. "No, you're kidding me! She's a… hooker?"

"And a stripper. She works at The Doll Den in Catalpa."

"You're pulling my leg, right?"

"No, Toby. My brother lives in the apartment over the strip club. I've seen her name in the window. 'Sizzlin' Settie Eddy' they call her."

"You mean she's not really a nurse?"

"Well, she may dress up like one, but…"

"Good Lord! I've been kissed by a stripping hooker! Wait'll I tell the guys…"

Heidi looked puzzled. "You're happy about this?"

"I guess it's a good thing I didn't go out with her then, huh?"

"I'd say so."

"'Cause I left my wallet at home…"

"You're disgusting, Toby."

They crested a hill and the dappled lights of residential Willowgrove shone out before them, spilling off of a tall, mostly wooded ridge that ran from north to south as far as the eye could see. This ridge, several miles wide, was ample enough to give roots to the largest part of Willowgrove, including the entirety of downtown, which was casting a dull, yellow glow into the rainy night sky. Dean downshifted as they began the climb into town.

"What time is it? Toby asked.

Heidi glanced at her watch. "Quarter after twelve. Why? You have somewhere better to be?"

"No, I just wondered. Jeeze… Why's everybody always so cranky?"

"You'll get over it."

Dean cleared his throat. "Hey, Toby, did you tell your dad or Ace that we're out of transmission fluid?"

"Uh… no, it must've *slipped* my mind… heh. I'll tell him tomorrow, though."

"Toby, I told you on Wednesday that we needed it. How am I supposed to do Denham's Merc on Monday? Now it won't come until Tuesday."

"I'm so glad you know the days of the week…"

"Come on, man. You gotta pull some weight around that place. You know, your dad won't pay you for doing nothing."

"Ha. What do you think he's been doing for the past five years?"

Dean just sighed and continued weaving the car through the west side's somewhat convolutedly tiered, brick paved streets. Most of the homes that they passed were dark and silent, with the exception of several that were still hosting late-running graduation parties. The rain had increased somewhat, streaming down the sides of the street in miniature torrents, and forcing Dean to flip the windshield wipers to high. His car, like Toby's truck, was wearing essentially bald racing slicks on its rear wheels, so he had some difficulty coaxing it over the last slippery brick hill before breaking onto downtown Willowgrove's flat, well-maintained concrete streets. They passed through a few blocks made up of both large buildings and small businesses, and then, finally, a relatively bustling town square panned out around them.

"Hopefully we can get a spot…" Dean said, pointing the car down Holbrook Avenue towards Lexie's. Unfortunately, all of the parking places in front of the red brick, two story building were filled, forcing Dean to park in the narrow alley that separated Lexie's from Holbrook Avenue Hotel. "I guess this'll have to do." He turned the car off.

"I wish this rain would let up," Toby said, opening his door. "It's putting a damper on my celebration. Oh, just great…" A splashing cascade of water was falling right outside his door, pouring from a malfunctioning gutter high above. "Just had to park here, didn't you."

"Just for you." Dean slammed his door shut.

Their shoes slapped against the wet blacktop as they walked through the alley, shoulders hunched and trying their best to avoid all of the puddles that spotted the ground. Thankfully, after reaching the sidewalk, most of the way was shielded from the drenching rain by a green and white overhang that ran the entire front of the building, right up to the black glass entrance door. A small sign announced that no one under eighteen would be served alcohol. Toby grabbed the brass handle and opened the door for Dean and Heidi.

"Such a gentleman," Heidi said, feigning surprised.

"Yes, yes, I'd rather keep that a hidden quality. Now, go. Get out of my way."

A cloud of cigarette and cigar smoke hit them as they stepped through the breezeway and into the long, narrow interior of Lexie's. Besides the oval bar, the crowded building was furnished with a pair of pool tables and about a dozen or so circular tables with bench seating, all of which were occupied. Smooth, melancholy jazz wafted from the black-clad quartet at the end of the somewhat humid room. Toby's attire was more akin to those at the bar, so he found a vacant stool and sat down. Dean and Heidi were forced to sit a few seats away.

The bartender, sliding a beer to Toby's neighbor, spoke up in a husky voice. "What'll it be, pal?"

"Umm," Toby thought for a second. "just a Bud and some pretzels."

Without a word, the bartender filled the order.

Toby picked up the crystal mug and sipped at the golden froth.

"You sure that's a good idea?" Dean asked, leaning forward from his spot at the bar.

"I'll be fine. What are you having?"

"Fish sandwich."

Toby put his mug down. "Damn it."

"Huh?" Dean asked, looking puzzled.

"I forgot I don't have my wallet."

Dean rolled his eyes. "I've got it. Hey, Lenny…"

The bartender turned around. "Yeah?"

"Put the little boy's bill on mine." He pointed at Toby.

"I'll pay you back," Toby said.

"I got it, don't worry about it."

Toby smiled. "In that case…"

"And, Lenny, don't give him any more alcohol. He's allergic to it."

"I am not," Toby said defensively.

"You are too. It makes you drunk."

Toby tried for a moment to think up a good argument to Dean's statement, but finally resigned himself to rubbing the salt off of the pretzels. He tried to eat a few, but his throbbing jaw wouldn't allow it, so he began building a log cabin. When that got boring, he reached in his pocket and pulled out the broken tooth. The mostly drunk man next to him took notice.

"What ya got there, p-partner?"

Toby rolled the molar between his index finger and thumb. "This…? A blue ribbon."

"Hmm… Kinda s-s-small idn't it?" The red-nosed man squinted.

"Believe me, it doesn't feel small."

The man held out his sweaty palm. "Lemme s-see it, b-buddy…"

Toby hesitated for a moment, then placed the tooth in

the drunk's hand.

"How'd you w-win it?" the man asked, studying it at nose length.

"In a war."

"Ohh… I w-was in a w-war once, didn't get nothin' like this though… What were you f-fightin' for?"

"The right to my own girlfriend." Toby took another sip of beer. The man, handing the tooth back, did likewise.

"Oh! Heh, heh… I had a g-girlfriend once… Problem was I had a wife too! Heh, heh…"

"Hmm. Where's she now? Your wife, I mean."

The mans face fell, and he seemed to sober up a little. He sat his empty mug on the bar and slowly pushed it away from himself. "She left me… should'a took better care of 'er…"

"She was a good one, huh?"

"Oh, yes sir. Sh-she put up with me for l-long time. Problem with people like that, you don't know how much they mean to you 'til they're g-g-gone…" He hiccuped and then fell silent.

Toby tried not to connect the dots of the old drunk's story to his relationship with Jenna. He slipped the tooth back into his pocket and watched as Dean applied half a bottle of mayonnaise to his sandwich. "What are you trying to do, drown the poor fish?"

"Yeah."

"Jeeze…" His eyes wandered to the clock on the wall. Barely visible through the haze, it read a little past twelve-thirty. He turned back toward Dean. "Hey, where do you want to-"

He was interrupted by a loud ruckus coming from the doorway. The door swung open violently, and the soaking, staggering form of Stuart Novello entered the room.

"Shhhhit…" Toby moaned to himself.

Novello stumbled up to the opposite side of the bar. His

hair had fallen from its usual pompadour and lay flat and wet, its black strands plastered against his forehead. A smudge of dirt streaked his right cheek. Toby couldn't hear the order, but he saw the bartender bring two shots of something. Novello's quivering hand reached for the glasses, downing one. Toby had never seen him this visibly shaken before. He glanced at Dean and Heidi, who had stopped eating to watch. Novello was about to throw back the second shot, but just as he brought the glass to his lips, he caught sight of Toby.

His eyes widened and he dropped the whiskey. Without a word, or even an acknowledgment of the alcohol that was running down the front of his wrinkled coat, he stood and barreled out of the building, knocking over several bar stools in the process.

Toby and Dean turned toward each other.

"What the heck was that all about?" Toby asked.

"Beats the hell outta me…"

"Must've hit him harder than I thought. Weird." Toby knocked over his pretzel log cabin.

"Didn't your mom ever tell you not to play with your food?" Dean asked.

"Are you almost done?"

"Yeah. In a hurry?"

"I'm…" Toby yawned, "…getting tired." The bartender took Toby's empty mug.

"Anything else for you tonight?"

"Uh… no, I don't think so," Toby answered, but then thought of something. "Wait, yeah, there is something. You know that guy who just came in here? Stuart Novello?"

"Who don't? He's the mayor's brat, uh… *son*, I mean."

"Yeah, right. Did you, uh, happen to see him in here with Ed Gibson's daughter last week sometime?"

"Which daughter?"

"Jenna. She's my girl."

"Well, look at you… Nice work, kid. Yeah, they was here. But they didn't come together. The other Gibson girl came with her."

"Oh… Really?"

"Yeah. The other one.. uh… uh…" Lenny swirled his hand around, trying to pull something back into his memory.

"Callie."

"Right. She left with some punk and, uh, Jenna was here by herself. Then she said something about not being able to find her keys."

"Oh… But Novello…?"

"He offered her a ride. She didn't really want to go, but, well… you know how slick an asshole is when it's doin' what it does best. She left with him. Don't know what happened after that."

"Oh… Thanks…. Thanks a lot."

"You bet."

It took Toby several minutes to digest this new bit of information. "Shhhh…" he said, sliding off of the bar stool. "I'm ready to go, Dean."

"Yeah, well…" Dean swallowed his last bite of sandwich. "Since I'm the one with the wheels, we'll leave when I'm ready." He wiped his mouth. "You ready Heidi?"

"Umm… I guess we-"

"That means 'yes'," Toby interrupted, moving away.

"Hold your horses! Jesus…" Dean said, pulling his wallet out. He threw two dollars on the counter. "Thanks, Lenny."

"Sure thing, Deano."

Toby was the first one to the door, but never got to open it. An out of breath Cal Rillings burst into the room, panting heavily.

"What the... Cal?"

"T... Toby. Thank God!" Cal's expression was a grave one. He swallowed heavily. "I wasn't sure if you were... I've... I've been looking everywhere for you!"

"Why? What's wrong?"

"There's... There's been an accident..."

Chapter 17

"What… What do you mean? Who? What kind of…"

Cal put his hand on Toby's shoulder. "Just come with me."

"But…" Toby was pulled out of the building. Dean and Heidi were right behind him. Cal's car sat on the sidewalk, engine running and it's headlights casting yellow, rain-filled beams directly into their eyes.

"What kind of accident?" Dean asked. "Where?"

"*Who?*" Toby nearly yelled, pulling away from Cal.

Cal stopped and put both hands firmly on Toby's shoulders. "It's Jenna. Somehow she went off the road over on Riverside and the truck…"

A steel trap snapped shut on Toby's stomach. Thousands of tiny pinpricks washed over his body.

"She was-"

"Oh, no… Riverside…?"

"She-"

"No, no…" Toby's face went blank. He began to collapse, but Cal held him up.

"Listen! She went over the edge about a mile from the Grange Hall and the truck got wedged between a couple'a trees about fifty feet down. The medics are there-"

Toby began breathing heavy. He felt as if someone were pounding on his chest with a sledgehammer.

"The medics- your brother is there, Toby." Cal began walking Toby to the passenger's side of his car and opened the door. "But we have to hurry, there may not be much time…"

"I'm right behind you," Dean yelled over his shoulder, as he and Heidi ran into the alley.

Toby sunk into the passenger's seat. Cal slammed the

door. Images of twisted metal and shattered glass flashed though Toby's mind like the splintered frames of a high speed motion picture, accompanied by a shrill ringing that was slowly filling his ears. His stomach felt as if it were trying to climb up his throat. Cal got in and put the car in gear. He drove off of the sidewalk and pointed the car westward, quickly accelerating to and well past the twenty-five mile per hour speed limit.

"Is she...?" Toby asked in a wavering voice, clasping his trembling hands together.

"I don't know, Toby." Cal increased his speed as they reached the residential area. "All I could see was a lot of lights. I was on my way home and the police and medics were just getting there. I tried to get out and look, but a cop stopped me. The last thing I saw before I came looking for you was your brother pulling a bunch of rope out of an ambulance."

Toby could barely hear Cal over his heartbeat. Trees and houses flew by outside, but they weren't flying fast enough for him. "He didn't say how she... if she...?"

"I didn't even talk to him. He-" Two pairs of flashing red lights filled their mirrors. "Oh, great..." Cal slowed down and pulled over to the side of the street, but the police cars didn't stop; they sped by at full speed, sirens blaring. "They must be going over there too..." Cal said, pulling away from the curb.

Soon Willowgrove was left behind, and the dark, winding line that was Courier Lane stretched out before them, disappearing into the unceasing downpour. In a matter of minutes, Cal was steering the car onto East Riverside. Any fatigue that Toby had felt before was now long gone; he was perched on the edge of his seat, eyes wide and alert, waiting. Waiting for flashing lights. They continued higher into the hills. The Grange Hall, it's parking lot nearly empty now, passed by on their left.

"We're almost there…" Cal said.

The first thing Toby saw was the pulsing red glow of emergency lights, muted through a filter of rain and trees. His breathing deepened. They rounded a corner and were halted by a line of waiting cars that stretched for about a hundred feet. In front of that, at the top of an incline, a fire truck and several police cars were blocking the road and the view. Cal eased the car to a stop.

"Maybe they-"

Toby didn't wait to hear Cal. He threw the door open and jumped out, and as he began running past the cars, a few people that he knew yelled after him, but the slap of his shoes on the wet blacktop didn't waver. It wasn't until he neared the end of the line that the raincoat-clad policeman standing guard took notice.

He stepped in front of Toby. "Whoa, whoa, whoa. Hold it, kid."

Toby plowed into the policeman, nearly knocking him over.

"I said hold it!" The cop said, wrapping his arms around Toby. "Nobody's allowed past here!"

"Let go!" Toby writhed in the man's grip.

"Now simmer down, or I'll have to use force!"

Cal caught up to Toby. "Toby! Officer, this is Toby LaRue! It's his truck that went over!"

The policeman thought for a moment, and then loosened his grasp. Toby broke free and ran around the fire truck. His eyes were immediately drawn to the long, wavering skid marks that cut across the road, ran beneath the broken guard rail, and disappeared over the lip of the ravine. A group of men with ropes stood at the edge, and a steel cable, stemming from a tow truck's winch, was being lowered down the precipice. Toby began walking slowly across the road. The drenched rescue workers didn't seem to notice as he stepped over the twisted guardrail and stood beside them. The gaping ravine, its sides bristling with all manner of trees and bushes, opened before him, bottoming out several hundred yards below. His gaze followed the ropes and cables. As Cal had said, about fifty feet down, the truck had been jammed nose first into a four foot gap between a pair of oak trees. The still-shining taillights illuminated the medics who were standing on the tailgate. Beyond them, Toby could see that the back window had been broken out of the cab, and there was another medic inside. He didn't see Jenna.

"Who are you?"

Toby turned into the beam of a fireman's flashlight. He squinted at the glare. "Huh?"

The fireman lowered the flashlight. "What is your name?"

Toby turned back toward the wreck. "Is… is Jenna alright?" he choked.

"Who?"

"That's my truck. Jenna Gibson was driving it."

"That's your truck? Are you Toby LaRue?"

Toby's eyes remained fixed on the medic in the cab. "Yes."

"Then come with me."

Toby looked at him. "What?"

The fireman motioned with his hand. "Come with me."

"But, I…" Toby pointed to the truck.

"She isn't there, son."

"What?"

"Come on." The man began to walk away.

"But what are they…" Toby pointed to the truck again.

The fireman stopped and turned around. He hesitated for a moment. "She hit someone. A young man by the name of Ronald Fraska. He's… dead." He motioned in the medics' direction. "They're just picking up the pieces."

As the fireman guided Toby to a police cruiser, an entirely new wave of emotions began rising in him. He fought off the urge to throw up. The scene of what might have happened where he was standing flashed through his already reeling mind, made believable by the shattered glass crunching beneath his feet. "Where's Jenna?" he asked again, nearly tripping over an empty shoe sitting in the middle of the road. He shuddered.

The fireman walked up to the police officer sitting in the cruiser. He spoke through the open window. "Lieutenant Marshall, this is Mr. LaRue. Toby, the lieutenant will have a few questions for you."

"Mr. LaRue..." Lieutenant Marshall said, pulling out a pad of paper.

"Where's Jenna?"

The Lieutenant raised an eyebrow. "She's been taken to Blossom County Medical Center, and you will be escorted there shortly as well, per your brother's request. I owed him a favor. But first-"

"How was she?" Toby asked impatiently.

Lieutenant Marshall cleared his throat, and, seeming slightly aggravated, closed his notepad. He sighed. "Get in."

Toby didn't hesitate or ask questions. He ran around to the other side of the police car and got in. Lieutenant Marshall, after starting the car, switched on the headlights.

The ride into Catalpa, Blossom County's largest city, was long, and, for the most part, silent. The merciless rain continued to pummel the windshield.

"H-how was she?" Toby finally asked.

"All I can tell you is that her condition was critical. I

don't know anything else."

"You talked to Jack?"

"Your brother? Yes. But he didn't tell me about her, he just said that if you showed up to make sure you got to the hospital as soon as possible."

"Oh…" Toby shivered, partly because of his rain drenched clothes, and partly from distress. He pulled at his transparent, once white t-shirt, which clung to him like a second skin. He zipped up his jacket.

"Here," Lieutenant Marshall said, turning on the heater.

"Thanks."

The land west of Whitefeather Lake was much flatter than anywhere else in the county, and the glowing, staggered outline of Catalpa came into view long before they had passed through its limits. Stardust Drag Strip, one of Toby and Dean's favorite weekend haunts, flew by on their left, shrouded, like everything else, by the soggy, rain slicked darkness. Finally, with the police scanner babbling and the incessant squeaking of the windshield wipers, they passed through the suburbs and into the city. Fifteen and twenty story buildings grew out of the dark, mostly vacant sidewalks, towering over them as they continued north on Guild Street. After a few seemingly endless miles, the sprawling form of Blossom County Medical Center appeared on their left. Lieutenant Marshall pulled up to the emergency room entrance.

"Good luck, kid. I hope she's alright. I'll have some questions for you later."

"Thank you, officer," Toby said, meaning it for the first time in his life. He jumped out of the cruiser and sprinted toward the doors, but before he got there, a voice called after him. He turned to see his brother Jack jogging up the walkway.

"Wait!" Jack panted.

"Why? I can't…"

"Just…" Jack coughed, coming between Toby and the door. "Just let them take care of some things before you rush in there."

"But is she…?"

"I don't know, Toby. She… she's not fully conscious, and…"

"And what? What, Jack?"

"We think her back is broken."

"What?" It was like a bad dream; a reeling, thrashing tornado of a dream. It didn't even seem real to Toby. He tried to digest this new bit of information, but it kept regurgitating into the section of his brain that was usually reserved for hellish nightmares. It was like he was trying to run from something monstrous or deadly, but his legs just wouldn't move. This couldn't really be happening.

He woke up to someone gently shaking his shoulder. "Toby?"

His eyes cracked open to see the bleary outline of a woman.

"Honey?" It was the voice of his mother. It took him a few seconds to remember where he was and why the foul taste of bile lay in his mouth. Facts began to settle in his mind like flies on a dead animal, turning his stomach on end.

"Honey, wake up."

As the last few pieces of information fell into place, Toby hit his feet. "Where is she?" he exclaimed.

His mother tried to calm him down, but the tears in her eyes made him all the more frantic. "Toby, sit down! Sit down!"

Toby's eyes darted to the swinging doorway that led deeper into the hospital, desperately searching for something, looking for a doctor, a nurse, anything.

Anything that would slow the tempo of his painfully rapid heartbeat. Elaine pushed him back into a sitting position, and he realized that his father was there too, helping her. Everything seemed so unreal, like he was trapped underwater.

"I have to see her! Let me go!"

His mother tried to hold him in the seat. He barely felt the back of his father's hand, but it was enough to get his attention. "Settle yourself!"

Toby shut his eyes and forced himself to breathe deep, slow breaths, trying to focus his mind on something. Again, his mother's voice echoed in his ears.

"Are you listening? Toby?"

Toby managed a shaky nod. He opened his eyes. Elaine took her hands off of his shoulders and eased into the chair beside him; his father remained standing. Toby, swallowing hard, realized for the first time that Dean, Heidi and Cal were sitting across from him, all on the edges of their seats. Dean was smoking.

"I want to see Jenna."

"Sweetheart," Elaine began softly, blinking at her tears, "honey… she's in a coma. The Gibson's are in there now. The doctor… well, he… he doesn't think she has much time.

Toby's greatest fear was being realized before his eyes. In a way completely unlike any he had ever imagined, Jenna was leaving him. He tried to form a question, but all that came out was a jumble of unintelligent, wavering mumbling, whispered from a painfully dry mouth. He didn't even attempt to still his quivering limbs.

"I'm so sorry, sweetheart," Elaine managed. She reached for Toby's hand. He let her pull him close. "I'm so sorry…"

Toby's shock didn't allow for tears, instead turning his world into a dark, engulfing abyss of mortified disbelief.

Something was dying inside of him. He sat silent, unable to move or even think, cemented in place by his growing detachment from reality, not feeling his mother's arms, hearing nothing but the blood rushing through his ears as it made its way back to his throbbing heart.

"This can't be happening," he finally croaked. Turning his glassy eyes to the swinging double doors, he waited.

Chapter 18

The large wall mounted clock's painfully slow hour hand fell to the three. Toby, still glued to his chair, remained silent as more friends and family trickled into the emergency room; he ignored any attempt at conversation. Elaine left to make a phone call. His father sat alone in the corner, smoking. In the past hour, Toby's world had slowly turned from one of carefree freedom into a blurry watercolor of exhaustion and denial, tension and dread. His tooth throbbed, his leg was on fire, his knuckles ached, but, strangely, the pain was fuzzy, detached, and nothing in comparison to what he was feeling in his heart.

Three-thirty came and went. Every now and then he would spot a doctor or a nurse through the tiny door windows and his pulse would quicken, but they always stayed behind the doors, offering no word. At a quarter 'till four, a man and an obviously pregnant woman rushed in and where whisked away to the delivery room, followed soon after by a mother and her small, pajama-clad son, who appeared to have fallen out of bed and cut his forehead open

Several minutes passed, and then he heard someone else enter the room. He closed his eyes and leaned forward, bowing his head, trying to send a clear message that, whoever it was, he didn't want to talk to them. Sweet-smelling perfume washed over him and he heard a rustle of clothing as the person approached. A gentle, almost hesitant touch settled on his shoulder. He didn't move. Neither did the hand. The chair next to him creaked slightly and the hand turned into an arm, sliding across his shoulders, pulling him close.

"I'm so sorry, Toby," Shelly whispered.

Toby, ridged with pain and confusion, didn't respond, nor did he allow himself to be drawn into her arms.

"Toby…" Shelly didn't push him, instead laying her head on his shoulder. She rubbed her hand up and down his still-wet back, trying to comfort him. "I'm so sorry…"

Toby ignored her. His thoughts, coming faster than he could process them, rampaged through his head. Thoughts of 'why?' and 'what if?' and 'how could this happen?', all of them accompanied by an image of his keys at Jenna's feet. He shifted uncomfortably. His own experiences in this hospital, nearly all of them frightening, couldn't compare to how scared and helpless he felt now, as his mother's words about Jenna not having much time continued to echo in his mind. For him, having been in both positions, it was much easier to be the one on the stretcher than the one in the waiting room. An uncontrollable shudder ran though his body. Shelly's hand stopped for a moment and then lifted, as did her head from his shoulder. The warmth that she'd been transmitting to him quickly left his body.

Finally, of all things it was Toby's bladder that forced him out of his semi-conscious state. He stood slowly, drawing more than one glance.

"Sweetheart?" Elaine said, leaning forward.

Toby, his voice hoarse, said slowly "I just need to use the restroom.

Dean stood up. "Me too."

Together they left the waiting room behind, pushing through the doors and into the long, brightly lit hallway. Their footsteps echoed off of the pale green walls as they passed dozens of shadowy rooms, some empty, some occupied and a few whose residents were clearly awake, listening to radios or talking to a nurse.

Soon they came to an intersection and as they were passing through, Toby made the mistake of glancing down the crossing hallway, where, about fifty feet away, he saw Jenna's sister Callie standing with her head against the wall, arms crossed. Toby's step faltered. Callie must have heard him because she glanced up, directly into his eyes. Even from this distance he could see the florescent lights reflecting off the tears on her cheeks. She held his gaze until Dean pulled him away by the elbow.

A sign on the wall announced that the cafeteria and restrooms were dead ahead, and, though serving hours were long over, the modest-sized, glass-walled room that opened on their left was still basking in the glow of its humming white lights. Toby and Dean walked through the doorway. The furnishings were sparse and simple: tables, chairs, a water fountain, and a long counter with its serving window closed. The men's room door was in the far right corner, hidden by a jutting, white block wall.

"I'll wait for you," Dean said, pulling out a chair and sitting down.

Toby slowed. "But I thought you had to…"

"I must've walked it off."

Toby shrugged slightly and walked around the wall and into the restroom. It had recently been cleaned, apparent by sparkling chrome, glistening white porcelain and the biting smell of bleach that hung heavy in the air. Toby quickly did his business and then walked over to the sink. He looked in the mirror. The face that stared back was almost unrecognizable; dark, haggard, slightly swollen on one side, but most of all it looked lost. And alone. For years, Toby had thrived on the praise and accolades of his friends and family, lapped up the attention that was heaped upon him, soaked in the respect of his peers. But now none of that mattered. Nothing mattered. Not a single thing he could think of made a dent in his despair. Dragsters, pin-ups, The Strawberry. Worthless. He would trade them all for Jenna Gibson. He wanted nothing more than to see her right now, to hold her hand and feel her warm skin, but he was also afraid. Afraid to see what he had done to her. He stared deep into his own eyes and watched as a single tear snaked down his cheek, wondering how often Jenna had cried because of him. At least twice today. He turned on the faucet and splashed the tear away in anger. He had no right to cry. He deserved this.

Even before he rounded the wall, he could hear Dean talking to someone. He walked back into the room. A man with a long white coat slung over his arm stood next to Dean, sipping on a mug of coffee.

"Hello, Toby."

"Hey, Mr. Krindle." Toby managed a weak, less-than-half-hearted wave.

Dr. Fred Krindle was tall, dark haired, and fit-looking. It was obvious to anyone that he was Dean's father. "Dean here was just telling me about everything that's happened tonight. I'm sorry."

Toby nodded silently.

"Is there anything I can do or any questions I can answer? I haven't seen Jenna myself, but Dr. Everhardt is a very competent physician, I assure you."

Toby nodded again.

"If there's anything I can do…" Dr. Krindle's eyes dropped to the blood stained rip in Toby's jeans. He looked at his watch. "If you'll excuse us, Dean. Follow me, Toby."

"I'll be in the waiting room, Tobe," Dean said, turning away.

Dr. Krindle led Toby down a short corridor to an unoccupied examination room, switching on the lights and shutting the door behind them. "Let's have a look," he said, slapping the table.

Toby took off his jacket and pulled his pants down to his knees. He wasn't capable of argument at the moment. "I cleaned it out once," he said, clearing his throat.

"Mmm-hmm…" Dr. Krindle cut off the bandage that Settie had wrapped around Toby's leg. "I was unaware that you were studying medicine…"

Toby cracked a weak smile. "Only on my days off."

"Have a seat." Toby sat and Dr. Krindle pulled the rest of the bandage off. "You cleaned it out, hmm?" The cut had opened up and was bleeding slightly. "How?"

"I don't get many days off, really."

"Well, if this is how you clean out a cut, I'd hate to see you remove someone's tonsils." Dr. Krindle began cleaning the wound. "My God, Toby," he exclaimed softly. "What happened?"

"I…"A vision of Ron Fraska filled Toby's mind, first wielding a knife, then standing in a pair of headlights. "It doesn't matter.."

Dr. Krindle didn't probe for further information, just continued cleaning. "If I didn't know you as well as I do, I'd have this stitched up right away."

"I'd rather you not."

"I know. I'm going to put a bandage on, but you aren't going to be able to get it wet, understood?"

Toby nodded. When he was finished cleaning the cut, Dr. Krindle went to a cupboard and pulled out some gauze and tape. He worked quickly, applying a few layers of bandage, and then the adhesive.. "Here, press the wound together… That's right." He snipped off the excess tape. "Okay, Toby. I think you'll live."

"Thanks, Mr. Krindle," Toby said, trying to sound like

living meant something to him right now.

"As long as you don't get it wet you can take it off in a few days."

Toby pulled his pants up. "Okay."

Dr. Krindle began washing his hands in the sink. "I see that your burns have healed up very well"

"Mm-hmm."

"Ever have any problems with your leg?"

Toby slipped back into his jacket. "Sometimes."

"Like what?"

"It cramps up if I run or walk too fast."

"Hmm, well, just keep it exercised. Drink plenty of milk. Sometimes muscle cramps can be caused by a lack of calcium." He towel-dried his hands.

"Okay."

Dr. Krindle opened the door. "Come on, I'll walk you to the waiting room."

Toby walked with his head down, overcome by the waves of despair that kept rolling over him. He realized for the first time that his truck was gone, not that it mattered at the moment, but it was just one more blow. Again, he held back tears. He wasn't trying to be strong, he was punishing himself. Being strong didn't mean a thing to him right now. In fact, he wasn't even sure if he knew how to be strong.

Dr. Krindle cleared his throat and slowed down.

Toby looked up to see why. Right into Callie's eyes.

"Toby…" she started. "Sh-she's asking for you…"

His entire being froze. The expression on his face must have been one of bewilderment, because Callie said it again.

"Jenna wants to see you."

"But…" Toby stuttered. "I…"

"The doctor said he doesn't know how long she'll remain conscious, so you need to hurry."

"Go, Toby," Dr. Krindle said, putting a hand on his shoulder. "Hurry."

"Follow me." Callie turned and started into a brisk walk.

Toby hesitated for a second. Fear began to fill his veins.

"Go, Toby," Dr. Krindle repeated, more stern this time. "Every second counts."

Toby forced himself to take a step. Then another. Soon his feet were pounding the floor, echoing his heartbeat. He caught up to Callie, slowing next to her. "Jack said she was…"

"She's fading in and out of consciousness," Callie said. "But she keeps saying your name."

"Can she… what- what do they say her chances…"

Callie sniffed, fighting off tears. "She has a lot of internal bleeding. Her ribs are all broken." Her voice quivered and she began weeping softly. "They don't expect her to make it through the night."

Normally, Toby would have offered a beautiful girl like Callie a shoulder to cry on or a comforting embrace, but he had no comfort to share. He felt spent, empty, unable to hold on to or conjure up any sort of hope. He was losing the only thing worthwhile in his life and it felt like he was dying right along with it.

"It's right up here." Callie said as they rounded a corner. She wiped the tears from her eyes.

Toby could see a small group of people huddled around one of the doorways; Mrs. Gibson, his parents, Dean and Heidi. They all turned his direction as he and Callie approached. Mrs. Gibson, tears streaming down her cheeks, greeted Toby with open arms.

"I'm so sorry, Toby."

Toby didn't say anything. Couldn't say anything. He just let Mrs. Gibson wrap her arms around him.

"I know this must be awful for you…" she said, her

voice shaky.

Toby couldn't even look her in the eye. In his mind, she was trying to comfort the one who had caused all of this.

"I'm sorry we didn't call you earlier, but Ed's… he's having a very hard time with this." She stepped back and took his hand. "This way."

He couldn't move.

"It's okay, honey. Come on." She tugged harder.

Toby allowed himself to be pulled to the doorway. At this point, he could not keep track of the emotions swirling violently inside him; fear, sadness, anger, guilt. They canceled out any self-consciousness within him. "I-I can't… I don't…"

His mother came up behind him. "It's okay, Toby." She put her hands on his back and gave him a gentle push.

The relative comfort of the hallway was left behind, replaced with a dim, unfeeling hospital room. His vision was uncontrollably drawn to the bed, where the hunched figure of Ed Gibson hid Jenna from view.

Mrs. Gibson came up beside him and spoke softly, "Eddie?"

Mr. Gibson turned around. His gaze locked onto Toby for a split second, and then darted away in what appeared to be anger or hurt. He didn't speak, just stood up and left the room.

Toby's eyes fixed onto Jenna. The first thing he saw was her chest gently rising and falling. Her eyes were closed, her arms lay beside her on top of the bed sheets, and her hair had been pulled away from her face, forming a silky brown pillow beneath her head. She looked peaceful. As he took one slow, shuffling step toward her, the door closed behind him. The only sound he heard was the patter of rain against the window. And then a voice so faint that it almost sounded like a kitten's mew.

"Toby…" Her eyes cracked open slightly.

Toby's voice had to fight the lump in his throat. "I-I'm here…" He took another step.

"I'm sorry," she whispered.

As he got closer, he could see that her face and arms were covered in hundreds of tiny, and some not so tiny, cuts and scratches. A large, reddening bandage covered one side of her forehead. "You… you didn't do anything wrong, Jenna." Just saying her name sent a wave of goose bumps over his skin.

She inhaled sharply. "I… want you to know…"

Toby eased himself onto the edge of the bed.

"I'm sorry that I hurt you…" she continued.

"Jenna… you've never hurt me." He took her hand in his. It was cold. Tears began to well up in his eyes and this time he didn't try and stop it. "I'm the one who hurt you. All the time…"

"I can't remember… any of it…" Her voice was so weak that he had to lean over her to hear. "I love you so much…"

"I'm a jackass, Jenna," Toby cried, his tears falling onto her face. "I took you for granted, I didn't care if I hurt you, and now…"

"…don't remember…"

"I'm sorry, Jenna. Forgive me…"

"I love you… Toby…"

"Please, Jenna. I… can't live without you."

Jenna's eyes opened wider. "You won't…"

"Forgive me, Jenna."

"Toby, you taught me…" She spoke through another sharp pain that visibly racked her whole body. "How to really love someone. Unconditionally."

He looked deep into her eyes. They were growing darker by the second. "I'll never love anyone like I love you right now," he sobbed.

"I… Yes, you will… Right now you're just learning how to."

"Here," Toby said, pulling off his school ring. "I was afraid you'd loose this…" He put it in her hand. "It's my ring." He thought he saw a faint smile play across her lips.

"Thank you… Toby. But you'll… probably need it for someone else…"

He was bawling at this point. "I don't want anyone else. I want you." He kissed her gently. "I want to get old with you, I want to live with you and love you forever. There isn't anyone else on earth who can take your place. You can't do this…"

"Please, Toby… Promise me you'll be okay."

"Don't leave me! Lovers never say goodbye! You can't say goodbye!"

"…promise me…"

Toby wiped his running nose on his wrist. "Okay, I promise. But you promise that this isn't goodbye."

"I'll always be…" She was fading fast. "I love you, Toby LaRue."

The door opened. Toby spun around, standing and wiping his face. Two orderlies and a kindly looking, middle-aged doctor walked in. The orderlies began preparing the bed for movement.

"Mr. LaRue?"

Toby nodded, drying his eyes on his shirt sleeve.

"I'm Dr. Everhardt. Gentlemen, take Miss Gibson to the operating room. Dr. Hutchinson is preparing for her." The men started wheeling the bed out.

"Wait," Toby said. He picked up Jenna's hand and kissed it.

This time Jenna did smile. "…Toby…" She said his name with such a gentle sweetness that it was hard for Toby to smile back.

"I love you, Jenna Gibson." He let go of her hand and

watched as the men wheeled her out. As he did, something in the hallway caught his eye; his mother stood with her face buried in his father's chest, shoulders heaving. At the sound of the orderlies pulling the bed out, she turned and glanced into the room. Her eyes were flooded with tears. She looked at Toby for a moment and then turned back around as Dr. Everhardt shut the door.

"Where are they taking her?"

"Toby, isn't it?"

Toby sniffed. "Yes, sir."

Dr. Everhardt motioned to one of the chairs. "Have a seat, son." When Toby didn't sit, Dr. Everhardt shrugged slightly and took the chair himself. He leaned forward, resting his elbows on his knees. "I don't think I'd be wrong in pegging you Miss Gibson's, ah… beau. Would I?"

"No, sir. Where are they taking her?"

"She's…" Dr. Everhardt hesitated. "How long have you known her?" He removed his glasses and put them in his jacket pocket.

"Since second grade."

"I will rephrase the question; how long have you been courting her?"

"Two years."

"Hmm. And did you have any further plans together? Marriage perhaps?"

Toby was becoming uncomfortable. "I… don't know. We talked about it like everyone else. Why?"

Dr. Everhardt sighed and looked away. "Toby, my job is to help people get well, not impose moral judgment. So I'm going to say this as objectively as I can." He turned his gaze back on Toby. "Jenna was… pregnant."

Toby staggered. Those three words hit him like a shotgun blast to the chest. "Oh…" His stomach dropped out from under him. "Oh, my… oh, my God…"

"Is it possible that you were the father?"

The room began to swirl. "Oh, my God… Oh… *Shit*." The room dimmed and the floor rushed toward him.

Dr. Everhardt struggled to get Toby up and into the chair. Toby remained limp, in a daze.

"This isn't real…"

"I'm afraid it is, Toby. Here." He poured a cup of water from the pitcher on the end table and offered it, but Toby just stared straight ahead.

"This is…" Toby stood suddenly. "I have to go."

Dr. Everhardt's brow furrowed. "What? Wait, Toby…"

Toby didn't answer. He walked to the door and, with a wildly trembling hand, slowly opened it. The cool air of the hallway hit him in the face. Everyone still stood there, waiting, with the exception of Mr. and Mrs. Gibson. He walked past them all. Their voices echoed in his head, as if they were standing far away, but he didn't stop to answer them. His walk became a jog, and his jog became a sprint, and, as he burst through the hospital exit, his sprint became a flat out run.

Chapter 19

It didn't take long for the rain to penetrate every piece of clothing that Toby was wearing, and if it wasn't for the fact that he was running as fast as he could, it would have chilled him to the bone. His only destination was 'away'. Away from Blossom County Medical Center, away from his family, away from the mind numbing pain, both physical and mental, that was trying to engulf him. He ran across the four empty lanes of Guild Street. With every footfall, Dr. Everhardt's words reverberated in his ears, cutting away at his mind. Jenna was pregnant. There was no doubt in his heart that he was the one responsible. How could he have been so stupid, so careless? What had possessed him do what he had done? And now Jenna was paying for his mistake, taking the fall for him.

"It's my fault!" he screamed, face to the leaden sky, tears flowing freely. "*My fault!*"

The streets were dark, save for the few lampposts that cast their meager yellow glow on the puddle-flooded sidewalks, through which Toby's slapping feet splashed. He ran for what must have been miles, past buildings and shops, past homes and cars. He couldn't feel a thing. His legs pumped effortlessly, fueled by an uncontrollable hurricane of emotions that was tearing its way through his insides. Questions and answers filled his head. Curses flew from his lips, mostly aimed at himself. He could offer no excuse for his actions. He was the one that should die, he thought, it was his bones that should be broken, his blood that should be spattered on the windshield. Compared to him, Jenna was an angel. She had loved him in spite of his selfish, self-centered view of their relationship, and had ungrudgingly put up with his domineering attitude towards her. He had horribly taken that love for granted on so many occasions, both when they were alone and, worse, when they were among friends. Time after time he had casually brushed her desires aside, not caring, not thinking, not even considering the fact that she could have left him any day of the week if she had wanted. Sure, he joked to her about breaking up, but he never really meant it, he just used it to make her feel obligated to do something. Like satisfying his passions on a frosty night back in February.

As the thought of that encounter entered his mind, an uneven sidewalk slab sent him sprawling across the wet cement, where he rolled to a stop in a patch of tall weeds growing next to a set of railroad tracks. Fatigue instantly swept over him, pinning him to the ground. He had been running for what seemed like hours. It didn't take long for his body to succumb to its lack of sleep, and, as he lay there, the dark sky soaking him like a mammoth watering can, he drifted away on a wave of dream-riddled exhaustion…

    … *"I'm named Toby. What's yours?"*

"Jennalyn."

"Jennalyn? What kind of a name is that?"

"It's my name… Everyone calls me Jenna, though."

"What class are you in?"

"Mrs. Hawley's."

"Oh. I'm in Mr. Spiker's class. He's mean."

"My sister is in his class. She never said that."

"Really? What's her name?"

"Callabria."

"What? Callabria? What kinda parents do you have anyway?"

"She goes by Callie."

"Ohh, you mean Callie Gibson. She's... nice. I suppose."

"My first grade teacher was Mr. Burgess."

"Mine was Miss Elout. Where do you live?"

"Willowgrove. My father owns Gibson's Fine Fashions downtown."

"I live in Carson Creek. My Dad owns a... garage."

"Hmm..."

"It's a nice garage, though... It's not-"

"Oh! There's the bell! It was nice talking to you... um..."

"Toby."

"Yes, it was nice talking to you, Toby."

"Well... wait! Where are, uh... meet you here tomorrow?"

"...okay..."

...Toby exhaled and rang the doorbell.

He could hear voices inside. Excited voices. And then high-heeled footsteps approaching from within. A second later a woman in a black dress opened the door.

"Why, hello!" she said, trying to sound surprised. "You must be Toby!"

"Yes, ma'am."

"Well, it's nice to finally meet you! I'm Mrs. Gibson. Jenna has told me so much about you. Come in, come in! She'll be right down..."

Toby stepped over the threshold and into a huge, maple paneled foyer. Mrs. Gibson showed him to a small, gold colored loveseat.

"Have a seat, sweetheart. She'll be down any minute."

Toby sat down, barely. His eyes darted from his shoes to the gardenia in his hands to the staircase. A thousand questions buzzed in his mind. Was his hair combed right? Had he brushed his teeth? Could he pin the flower on

Jenna without stabbing her to death? He was on the edge of his seat with worry when he heard a rustle on the stairs. Almost afraid, he turned to see Jenna descending.

"Hello, Toby."

She looked more beautiful than he had ever seen her, in her white satin dress, mink stole, and diamond earrings. Her hair was pulled back into a curled ponytail and her eyelashes were accented with mascara. It was the first time he'd ever seen her with makeup on.

"Toby?"

"Oh! Hello, uh… Jenna," he stuttered, jumping to his feet. "Uh, here." He held up the gardenia. "This is for you."

"Why, thank you." She came closer. "But with the stole…"

Toby could have kicked himself. She had said something about wearing her new mink stole. "Oh…"

"Never mind," Jenna said, slipping the mink off. "There." She stepped up to him, so that he could pin the flower on her dress.

He hesitated. Then, with somewhat quivering hands, he tried his best to affix the gardenia to the satin. "Ow!" he said, pricking his finger. "Uh… maybe you'd better…"

Without judgment, Jenna took the flower and straight pin and did the job herself. "There."

"Yeah, that looks good."

"Okay… are we ready?"

"Uh, yeah. I think so. I hope you don't mind, but all I could get tonight was my Dad's truck…"

"That's fine, Toby."

He liked the way she said his name. "Okay, well… I guess we can go then…"

"Wait!" came Mrs. Gibson's voice. A moment later she entered the foyer with a camera. "You can't leave without having your picture taken! Now, stand together… that's right." She snapped a few shots. "Oh, you two look so good together! I guarantee, you'll be the most handsome couple at the prom!"

"Okay, mama… Can we go now?"

"Okay, sweetheart. You two have yourselves a good time. It was nice meeting you, Toby."

"You too, Mrs. Gibson…"

…Toby slipped his helmet on, cinching the neck strap tight.

"Toby, wait!"

He turned to see Jenna jogging toward him, alone, with a look of mild concern on her face. One of the drag strip officials tried to stop her but Toby waved him off. "What's up?" he asked as she walked up to him.

"I just wanted to… be careful, okay?"

Toby paused for a second, ready to pull his goggles down. "Okay."

"No, I mean it. I mean say it like you really mean it." She bit her lip.

"Okay…" Toby allowed his bewilderment to show. "I'll be careful. I'm always careful."

"No you're not.

"What?"

"You always say-" Her voice was drowned out by a pair of dragsters leaving the starting line.

"Huh?" Just then, Dean came over.

"Okay, Tobe. We're up for the push start."

"Alright." Toby walked over to the dragster and slipped down into its cramped cockpit. Dean began belting him in. "I'll be fine, Jenna, don't worry. This isn't the first time I've done this."

Jenna stood wringing her hands. "I know, I just…"

"Okay, all set," Dean said, stepping away.

Toby did his best to turn in Jenna's direction. "See you

in a few seconds, sweetheart."

Dean got into the push car.

"Wait," Jenna said, walking up to the dragster. She leaned in and planted her lips right on Toby's. It was their first kiss.

"Be careful, because I love you..."

"...Toby..."

"Hmm?"

"What are you doing?"

"Keeping my hands warm."

"Stop it."

"What? I... just..."

"We can't do this."

"Why not? Everybody does..."

"Who's everybody?"

"Everybody."

"That doesn't make it right. This is supposed to be special, Toby. Something worth waiting for..."

"Come on, Jenna... don't be such a square."

"I'm not... I just... think we should wait."

"For what? For us to break up?"

"...What?"

"I take this relationship seriously, Jenna. If you don't... then maybe it's time to move on..."

"Toby, what are you saying?"

"Do you think of this as a real relationship?"

"...Yes..."

"Do you love me?"

"Yes..."

The sound of tires splashing through a mud puddle brought Toby back to life. It took him a second to remember where he was and why he was there, and when he did, he wished he hadn't. Above him, the sky had brightened and the rain had ceased, giving way to dawn's first glowing ribbon of light. His heart was sick. So was his stomach. He rolled over and vomited in the grass, then eased himself into a sitting position, groaning. He watched for a few minutes as a sparse array of cars passed by. Finally, brushing some of the dirt and grass off of his jacket, he stood and examined his surroundings. A car rolled to a stop in front of him.

"You okay, son?"

Toby turned his attention to the middle aged man in the car.

"You alright?"

Toby thought for a second. If he was anything, it was not alright. "No."

The man's eyes wandered over Toby's soaked and tattered clothing. "Anything I can do? You need a lift somewhere?"

"No, thanks." Toby turned and began walking alongside the railroad tracks.

The man yelled after him. "Wait! You sure?"

Toby kept walking. He wasn't sure of anything.

At first, he walked beside the tracks, and then between them. Walk, that is, if that's what you could call Toby's limp. All of the running had taken a toll on his already sore legs, and he had a hard time not tripping over the railroad ties. He didn't think about anything. There was nothing left to think about. The rising sun began to break through the trees, warming the air slightly, but not enough to still the vapor streaming from Toby's mouth. He no longer wept, just kept his eyes to the ground.

The tracks wound their way through town, between

buildings, through parking lots, under the freeway. After a few miles, Toby found himself in the warehouse district, on the outskirts of the city. He looked ahead. A couple of hundred yards away, the ground dropped off into a deep ravine, with the railroad tracks suspended over the gorge on a high trestle. He kept walking. With every step, his pulse quickened. Maybe this was the answer. He had nothing else to live for, did he? An image of his family flashed into his mind, but he quickly suppressed it, telling himself that they'd be better without him. With Jenna gone, he had no future, no direction. Except down.

The gorge opened up before him. He wasn't sure how deep it was, but the bottom was far enough away to look hazy, and a shallow, rock-filled river snaked its way through the canyon floor. He took several steps onto the trestle. The ground fell away beneath him, causing him to feel dizzy and unbalanced. He shook his head and continued onward. The farther he walked, the faster the earth seemed to disappear, leaving nothing between him and the rocks below but thin air. A thought crossed his mind of a train barreling down the tracks toward him, but he didn't care. It would save him from losing his nerve. After fifty yards or so, he reached the middle. He was now at the furthest point possible from the bottom. Staring down, the last twenty four hours of his life flooded into his mind. So much had happened. So much had changed. But he just couldn't make himself believe that any of it mattered anymore. Jenna was everything to him, but he hadn't seen it until it was too late. He took a step toward the edge. He couldn't live without her.

"Promise me that you'll be okay...Promise..."

"I'm sorry, Jenna," he whispered, taking another step.

A familiar rumble caught his ear, followed by the sound of crunching gravel. He turned to see Dean's yellow Chevy pull up to the edge of the ravine, parking right on the tracks. Dean shut the engine off and got out, walking around to the passenger's side. He didn't come across the trestle, though, instead he just leaned up against the car's front fender and crossed his arms.

Toby wavered. If he was going to do this he had to do it now. He kept telling himself he had nothing to live for, no future. Nothing in his life could ever be the same again. He had destroyed everything that had ever had any meaning to him.

"Promise…"

Something lurched in his stomach. He was losing. He tried to take the last step, but something held him back.

"…I love you, Toby LaRue…"

He lost. Unable to hold himself up any longer, he sat down, legs hanging over the edge. Tears filled his already red eyes, but these tears were different. They felt clean, pure.

The sound of boots against the wooden railroad ties reached his ears. A few seconds later, Dean was standing beside him.

"What're you doing?"

Toby sniffed. "Waiting for a train."

"Oh… well then I'd better go move my car, huh?"

Toby allowed an amused sound to escape through his nose. Dean didn't crack many jokes.

"Ah…" Dean sighed, easing himself down next to Toby. He pulled a pack of cigarettes out of his shirt pocket and tossed them into the ravine. "Long night?"

"Yeah."

"Me too." Dean cleared his throat. "For a while there, I thought I was gonna lose *two* friends. I'm glad I didn't."

"Really?"

"Yeah. Who else is gonna drive the Jolly Roger?"

Toby lowered his head. "I… I don't know if I'll ever go back to driving, Dean."

"Hmm. Well… I know a lot of people that would be glad to hear that."

"Like who?"

"Well, your mother, for one."

"Yeah… I guess you're right."

"She… uh, she wanted whoever found you first to tell you that she, uh…" Dean cleared his throat again, "That she loves you no matter what happened."

"What do you mean 'whoever found me first'?"

"Oh, we've all been out looking for you the past few hours. Me, Cal, my Dad, your parents… They were worried sick about you, Toby. Thought you were gonna do something real dumb. Like jump off a bridge or something."

"Really?"

"Yeah, can you believe that?" He got serious. "I've never seen your Pop that scared before, Toby. All of the time that I've worked with him."

Toby didn't say anything.

They sat in silence for awhile, and watched as the sun slowly rose over the landscape, its warm, orange light soaking into their tired frames.

Finally, Dean looked at his watch. "Well… It's seven o' clock." He stood up, offering Toby a hand. "What do you say we get outta here?"

Toby looked down into the ravine one last time. "Yeah… let's go home."

Chapter 20

McDermott and Trask Funeral Home was located on the outskirts of Willowgrove, perched on the side of a gently sloping hill that overlooked Carson Valley. It was surrounded in part by a thick grove of trees that cast their shade on the large building, and in part by the cemetery that stretched from behind the funeral home, around the side, and spilled over the hill. The sun, nearing its peak, shone brilliantly out of the crystal blue, cloudless sky, glinting off the tops of the varying headstones. Birdsong filled the warm summer air, as if they weren't aware of the sadness that hung over the area.

Toby tugged at his necktie. From inside Dean's car, he had full view of the wooden double doors, where a group of black-clad mourners were filing into the building. Some of them he knew, others were complete strangers, but whoever they were, he didn't want to follow them. Going through those doors was the last thing he wanted to do right now. But he had to. He opened the door and stepped out.

He had only taken a few steps before a voice called after him.

" LaRue! Wait!"

He turned to see a haggard looking Bernie Keck coming up the hill toward him. He hadn't seen Keck since Saturday night at the Grange Hall dance, right before he and Stuart Novello's little brawl. Keck was one of Novello's goons. Toby continued walking.

"Wait up!"

"What do you want, Bernie?" he yelled over his

shoulder.

Keck picked up his pace, making up the distance between him and Toby. "I just wanted to say... I'm sorry. About everything that's happened. I-I was the one who called the police."

"And?"

"I'm sorry. Novello was waiting for you up on that hill, not Jenna. When she came around that corner in your truck... she just..."

"I don't want to talk about it, Bernie."

"I know I just... I'm sorry, okay?"

Toby stopped and looked at Keck. He could see the sincerity in his eyes. "Forget about it. It's over."

Keck nodded. "Thanks."

Toby turned and took a few steps, then stopped. "And Bernie," he said without turning around.

"Yeah?"

"Thanks for doing what you could. Calling the cops."

"Sure thing, Toby... I'll see you around."

"Yeah."

The building loomed over Toby's head as he approached the front doors, almost daring him to turn and run. It would have been easy. He saw himself just taking off through the cemetery, hiding until this was all over. He could walk home if he had to. But instead, he stepped through the doors. It took a moment for his eyes to adjust to the dim interior of the funeral home, and when they did, it seemed to Toby that every eye in the building had turned toward him. Several hushed whispers were exchanged. Toby forced himself to take a step toward the front of the room, where, on a pedestal, the glossy black coffin rested, its lid propped open. He eked out another step, then another. Each one seemed to pound against the oak floor, making him even more uncomfortable and self aware. He searched the crowd. The only friendly faces he could find were Dean, Smoosh, and Cal's. And Mr. Gibson's. At the sight of those watery blue eyes, Toby's step faltered. But he took a deep breath, quickly composed himself, and continued onward, focusing straight ahead. A couple stood in front of the casket, viewing the body, forcing Toby to wait his turn. He didn't want them to step aside, though. He had tried for the last two days not to think on what he was about to do, tried to convince himself that it wasn't worth worrying over. As the seconds passed, his heart began to beat through his chest. He licked his lips nervously. And then the couple stepped aside, leaving nothing between him and the coffin but his apprehension. He had been very blessed in his life, not having been to many funerals, and right now he wished he could bolt back down the aisle way and keep that number the same. Somewhere in the room a person cleared their throat. Toby took the last step.

The wax-like figure of Ronald Fraska came into view. The ghostly pale face and neck were all that was visible; the rest of the body was covered by a white satin sheet. The features were sunken slightly. Toby put a hand on the casket and then drew it back quickly, unconsciously wiping it on his suit jacket.

"Sorry, Ron..." he whispered. "That was a bad way for anyone to go." He turned to where Mr. and Mrs. Fraska were sitting. Walking over to them, he took the weeping Mrs. Fraska's hand. "I'm sorry, ma'am. Ronald was a good... classmate."

"Thank you, honey..." Mrs. Fraska sniffled.

Toby, glad that the worst part of the day was over, walked back to his empty chair between Dean and Smoosh, sighing quietly as he sat.

Dean leaned over. "I was wondering if you were ever going to come in."

"I'm here." Toby wiped his brow with his sleeve.

"In body anyway." Smoosh pitched in, and then blinked, realizing what he said.

"What's that supposed to mean?" Toby whispered.

"You left your heart in Room 316. How late did they let you stay last night?"

"I left at eleven. Shh."

The priest stepped up to the podium and began his monologue. "Dear friends, we are gathered here today to remember the life of young Ronald Ward Fraska…"

The service passed swiftly, and Toby soon found himself filing down the aisle behind his friends. A hand landed on his shoulder.

"Toby?"

He turned to look Ed Gibson directly in the eye. His pulse quickened. He had successfully avoided conversation with Mr. Gibson for the past three days, not because he was mad, but because he was afraid.

"Are you going back to the hospital right now?"

"Yes, sir…"

"Will you ride with me? We need to talk."

Toby's heart sank. "Okay…"

Outside, the sun still beat down, refracting off of all the chrome bumpers and windshields in the parking lot, and helping to keep the air at a balmy 85 degrees. Chattering locusts filled the trees. Dean, Smoosh, and Cal all went their own separate ways, leaving Toby, nervously loosening his tie, to trail behind Mr. Gibson, who's car must have been further from the funeral home than anyone else's because it seemed to take forever to get there. Ed had driven the Corvette, and upon reaching it, he unlocked and opened the passenger side door for Toby. Toby reluctantly sunk into the red leather seat.

"Hopefully," Mr. Gibson said, getting in and starting the engine, "we can get out of here without much hassle…" He put the car in gear and pointed its nose to the exit. "You can roll your window down if you like."

Toby did so.

Ed navigated through the crowded parking lot and turned right onto Wilson Avenue. "There… that wasn't so bad. Radio?"

"Uh… if you like."

Ed tuned in a pop station and Connie Francis filled the speakers. They rode without speaking through three whole songs, and then, finally, Ed cleared his throat. "Uh, Toby, what I wanted to-"

"Mr. Gibson," Toby cut him off, "before you say whatever you need to say, I… I just want to tell you that I'm sorry for everything that happened. Beyond sorry. I took advantage of your trust and… I wouldn't blame you if you told me that I was never allowed to see Jenna again." He coughed. "I… I acted immaturely and I don't know how I could ever make it up to you. I'm really, really sorry… I should have told you sooner, but I was scared. If I could ever make it up to you and Mrs. Gibson…"

Ed was silent for a moment. He turned down the radio. "Um… well, I… accept your apology, Toby. I wasn't prepared for it, but I accept it."

"Thank you, sir." Toby relaxed, feeling a weight lift off his shoulders.

"We all make mistakes, Toby. You aren't the only one. I just want you to know that not fixing and running from those mistakes only makes everything worse." He paused, almost hesitant. "That's why I wanted you to ride with me… I wanted to tell you something. Something that I've never told anyone."

Toby's relaxed feeling began to fade.

"It… it somewhat parallels your situation." Ed took a deep breath. "Back during the war, I was stationed in France. And one weekend, a few pals and I went up to Paris. We had a few days reprieve, not really enough to go far, so we went to Paris. The first night I was there, I met a girl. Her name was Marianne. She wasn't French, she was Lithuanian… but anyhow, we met in a little bar by the river and we talked for awhile, and then I asked her if she'd like to meet me for lunch the next day. She said she would. So…" He took another deep breath. "So… we met, ate lunch, walked around the city for hours. Our conversation… uh, our conversation eventually led to… other things. I left the next morning. Five months later I get a letter. At this point, the war's over, I'm back here and have been married for three weeks, so I didn't even open it. I burned it. I was afraid of whatever it might have said. I try and push it out of my mind and go on with life. But… a few months after that, I get a telegram. All it says is: 'It's a boy'."

Toby's eyes widened.

"I… burnt that too. I was bound and determined that I was going to erase this 'mistake' from my past. I must have thought that if I closed my eyes to it long enough, it would all go away…" He trailed off.

"What happened?" Toby prompted.

"Well, after a few years, the letters and telegrams stopped. I was free and had all but pushed it from my mind. And why not? I had two daughters, a beautiful wife… life was good. Then… one terrible winter day, I got one last letter. It was from Marianne's brother, whom I had never met. In it…" Ed tried to keep his voice even. "In it he said that… Marianne and… my *son*… had drowned when her car went off a bridge." Tears began to trickle down Ed's cheeks. "All he wanted was some money for the funeral bills."

"Wow…"

"I put some money in an envelope, but… I never got around to sending it." Ed wiped his eyes dry and cleared his throat. "If you make a mistake, do your best to make it right, Toby. Don't do what I did… That's why I wanted you to hear this. If you don't do anything and just hope it all goes away, it'll kill you…"

Toby didn't know what to say.

"I don't want you to stop seeing Jenna, Toby. In fact, I want you to stay with her. She's going to need a lot of looking after. Dr. Hutchinson said that her full recovery could take months, even years, that it was a miracle she'd even survived the operation."

Toby's head dropped. "I talked to him. Thanks to me, she'll never have kids."

"You've been given a great opportunity, Toby. The chance to fix this. I was given the same opportunity, only I never took the chance and will regret it for the rest of my life. Trust me, it's not something that you want to live with."

"What do you want me to do?"

"I want you to do whatever you have to in order to right your wrong."

"But…"

"Things will never be the same, Toby. Every mistake has some permanency, there are casualties in every war, but do what you can do. Fix what you can fix." He looked at Toby. "Can I count on you?"

Toby thought for a moment. He wasn't sure if now was the time or place, but he asked anyway. "Mr. Gibson… I know that I haven't always been… the ideal candidate, and I don't know if this will answer your question or not, but I- I'd like your permission to… to ask Jenna to marry me. I know that I have a long, long way to go, but I love her. More than anything else in this world. And I can promise you now, after everything that's happened, that I'll never take her for granted again, and that I love her more than anyone else in the world. I really don't deserve her, I know that… but I love her."

Ed didn't reply for a mile and a half. Toby, not knowing if he had done the right thing or not, sat silent as well, able to hear his own heartbeat. Finally, very calmly, Ed spoke. "Is this something that you've thought through?"

"Yes, sir."

"Have you talked to Jenna about it?"

"Yes, sir. Sometimes it was all she ever wanted to talk about."

"So you think she'd say yes."

"I think so. I hope so."

Another long, deafeningly silent stretch of road passed by, and Toby, trying to remain calm, wiped his sweaty palms on his dress pants. He forced himself not to count the seconds and minutes that seemed to ooze along. Outside, Stardust Drag Strip blew by, marking their entrance to Catalpa's outskirts. The hospital was only a few miles away.

"And do you really think you're ready for the responsibilities associated with being married? Being a husband?" Mr. Gibson finally asked.

Toby continued to stare out the window. He thought about his own parents and the adversities that they faced on a regular basis, how they acted and reacted to certain things, and then he forced himself to be honest. "No, sir… I guess not. But I'm willing to learn."

"I appreciate your truthfulness, son. You…" He sighed deeply. "You have my permission."

"What?" Toby turned and blurted, caught off guard.

"Marriage is like swimming, Toby. You can read all you want about it, think you know what it'll be like, but until you jump in the water... that's when you really start learning. Being willing to learn is all that matters. Are you sure you are?"

"Yes, sir!" Toby exclaimed, hardly able to contain himself.

"Good. Just keep in mind everything that I've told you, alright? Live life one step at a time, think before you act, use good judgment. God didn't give us common sense just because He couldn't think of anything better to do. You don't have to learn everything the hard way unless you choose to, like I did. Okay?"

"Yes, sir!"

"Okay. I'm holding you to your promise." Ed held out his hand. Toby shook it eagerly, smiling from ear to ear.

Soon afterward, Blossom County Medical Center came up on their left. Mr. Gibson drove the Corvette up to the visitor's entrance, stopping in front of the rotating doors.

"I'll see you after awhile, Toby," he said, not making any motions to get out of the car.

"But..." Toby asked, confused. "You aren't coming up?"

"I'll be up in a bit. I don't think you'd want me there when you ask her..."

"Ask her what? Oh! Right!"

Ed smiled and shook his head. "Good luck, son. You may need it."

"Thanks, Mr. Gibson. For everything." Toby opened his door and stepped out onto the sidewalk.

"If you ever need me, you know where to find me."

"Yes, sir. Thank you." He waved as the 'Vette pulled away from the curb, and then he turned and pushed through the doors.

He didn't waste his time waiting for the elevator.

Instead, six flights of stairs flew by faster than they ever had in his life. He burst through the door and into a sixth floor hallway, beaming with joy and almost knocking over a pair of nurses.

"Sorry!" he yelled over his shoulder, continuing on toward Room 316. As he reached the '300' corridor, he slowed his pace, trying to calm himself. Room 310… 312… 314…

"Toby!" came a voice from the side.

Toby looked in its direction. He'd been so engrossed in reading the room numbers that he hadn't even seen his Aunt Shelly, make-up free and clad in very non-movie star attire, quickly walking toward him.

"Aunt Shelly…" He hadn't seen her since Saturday night, in the emergency room.

"Hello," she said, her face set off by a wide smile.

"What are you- I thought you'd left for the airport."

"I did. Dad's waiting in the car for me. But I just had to stop and see you two before I left." She wrapped her arms around him. "How are you doing?"

"I'm doing great. How's Jenna?"

"She's tired." Shelly stepped back. "I can't tell you how happy I am. Happy that… they were able to save her. That sounds so direct, but I don't know how else to put it. This has changed me, Toby, changed my views. I'm sure not as much as it's changed yours, but, nevertheless, it has changed me."

"Really?"

Shelly thought for a moment. "I was… about to lose someone in my life. Forever. Someone very dear to me. But this has reminded me more than anything that people are worth fighting for. Love is worth fighting for. Remember that, Toby, okay?"

Toby smiled. "Okay, Reverend."

Shelly laughed, and embraced him once more.

"Goodbye, sweetheart. Good luck. If you ever need anything, I'm only a phone call away." She stepped back.

"Thanks, Aunt Shelly."

"Now I'm sure you want to get in there…" Shelly nodded down the hallway.

Toby took a deep breath. "…Yeah. I do."

Room 316's door was slightly ajar, and a sliver of sunbeam, filtered somewhat through the room's large tinted windows, escaped out into the hallway. Toby took another deep breath and pushed the door open. Jenna was laying peacefully on the sunlit bed, propped up slightly. She appeared to be asleep, but her face was toward the window. Toby stepped into the room and she turned toward him.

"Hey," she said, sounding sleepy.

"Hey." Toby walked over to her. "How're you feeling?"

"I've been better. How are you?"

Toby pulled a chair up and sat down next to the bed. He noticed that his high school ring sat on her chest, strung around her neck with a small silver chain. "I've been worse…"

"How was the funeral?"

"It was a funeral. You didn't miss much." He brushed a few locks of hair away from her face. The bandage on her forehead had been replaced with a smaller one.

"Hmm." Jenna smiled at him.

"I, uh, rode up here with your father."

"You did?"

"Yeah."

"Wow…"

"Yeah, wow, I know. He, uh… we had a good talk."

"Yeah? What about?"

"Different things. Important things. Life, decisions… and, uh…"

"What?"

"I, umm… Jenna… I…" Toby cleared his throat, taking her hand in both of his. He looked deep into her bright, glistening blue eyes, beautifully full with life. "I have a question for you…"

Epilogue

Dean Krindle remained Toby's closest friend, working with him at A&L Automotive and serving as the brains of their racing operation. He later married Heidi and moved to Willowgrove. They had three children: Pamela, Becky and Thomas.

Toby's Aunt Shelly returned to Hollywood and began the heavy task of mending her marriage. She continued working as a successful actress until 1967, when she decided to pack up her things and come home, along with her husband James. They moved into a house on Whitefeather Lake.

Stuart Novello was killed in April of 1962 when he ran a red light and his car collided with a bus.

Eddie 'Smoosh' Vinsen got a job with Goodyear Tire and Rubber in Akron, working as a marketing specialist. In the mid-60's, he was able to procure Toby and Dean a modest sponsorship for their racing endeavors.

Cal Rillings eventually settled down and married. He became a successful drag racing showman and daredevil, touring the East Coast in his many crowd-pleasing jet cars, wheelstanders and V8-powered motorcycles.

Jack LaRue was diagnosed with cancer in the fall of 1972, and he and Elaine moved into town. Jack, no longer able to work at A&L, willed his half of the business to Toby, who had already taken much of the responsibility.

He passed away in 1974.

Toby's older brother, Jack Jr., continued to drive an ambulance until 1966, when he was drafted into the Vietnam War as a combat medic.

In 1967, Tracy LaRue graduated at the top of her class. She moved to the city with her parents and later married a baker.

Ed Gibson continued to run Gibson's Fine Fashions in downtown Willowgrove, and later opened a department store in Catalpa.

Callie Gibson moved to New York, where she effectively pursued a career as a fashion model and later married a millionaire executive, becoming Callie Hollander. She eventually gave birth to two children: Jonathan and Michael.

Ace Axemberg survived a heart attack in 1966, and sold his half of A&L Automotive to Toby. He and his wife Mary moved to Florida in late '68.

In July of 1967, Gary 'The Lone Wolf' Bell was killed when an engine explosion in his top fuel dragster caused him to lose control and careen violently into a spectator parking area.

In the weeks and months that followed the accident, Jenna grew increasingly stronger. She was released from the hospital at the end of June, and returned home to live with her parents as she continued on to a near full recovery. She accepted Toby's marriage proposal and they were wed the following spring, in 1962. The apartment over A&L Automotive, where Toby began working full time, became their home. He and Dean continued to terrorize every drag strip they visited, successfully campaigning top fuel dragsters through the 1960's, and then switching to nitro funny cars in the early 70's. Later, when his father and mother moved into town, Toby and Jenna took up residence in his childhood home on Briggle Avenue. With Jenna unable to give birth, they never had children.

Sneak Peek of

The Ballad of Carson Creek
-The Lone Wolf-

Coming Soon!

Cottonmouth

June, 1959

Gary flipped through the wad of bills for what must have been the tenth time. Seven hundred dollars. Every cent he owned and a few he didn't.

"You know, Bell," Frank said with a smile, "if you're having second thoughts, it's not too late to let *me* buy it."

Gary raised a brow. "I don't have second thoughts, Frank. Waste of time." He gestured to an intersection coming up. "Turn right up here."

Frank began downshifting. "For that price, he should throw in his daughter."

"His daughter's eight."

"She could wash the dishes."

"A bit too young for me."

"I didn't know there was such a thing as too young for you. You go the other way easily enough." Frank turned onto the dusty, pasture-lined side road.

"Will you shut up about that? It was *one* time."

"She was thirty."

"She looked twenty-five."

"Yeah, but you were only *seventeen*."

"And if it hadn't been for her husband... It was really somethin', the way she..." Gary trailed off with a smile.

Frank waited with anticipation for Gary to continue. A few moments passed. "Well?"

"Well what?"

"The way she what? What happened?"

"You wish."

"You bastard... Still, seven hundred bucks is a helluva lotta bread for a car."

"Trust me, this one's worth it. The place is right up here,

by that big oak."

A huge white farmhouse, nestled between a cluster of barns and smaller enclosures, came up on their left. Frank pulled the truck onto the wide gravel driveway, and a pack of mismatched, wildly barking dogs came bounding around the side of the house.

"Don't worry about them," Gary said. "Most of 'em don't have any teeth left."

"I'm not a dog person."

"Ah, don't be a baby, baby. They're old, they can't hurt you."

"I can wait here, no big deal."

Gary groaned and rolled his eyes. "Suit yourself, Hawkins." He opened his door and got out.

The side door of the house swung open before he had a chance to knock. A man, mid-thirties and wearing thick-rimmed glasses, greeted him with a vigorous handshake.

"Good to see you again, Mr. Bell," the man said, smiling.

"You too, Mr. Winston." Gary held up the wad of bills. "But you'll be happier to see this."

Mr. Winston's smile widened. "You'd be correct, sir. This way," he motioned. "The car's in the barn."

Mr. Winston dragged the creaking, squeaking barn door across its rusty track and stepped inside. Sunlight streamed into the otherwise darkened building, cutting bright yellow ribbons through a dust that seemed to hang in the air like smoke. He led Gary to an automobile-shaped canvas tarp.

"The last I knew, it had plenty of gas in it," he said, grabbing the cloth and pulling it off. "And I had the wife wash it up good..."

Gary's eyes twinkled at the sight. He'd seen it before, but now it was different, now it belonged to him; a wicked-looking, gleaming little hot rod, a '32 Ford, dripping with the most important word in his vocabulary: speed. He gently ran his hand across it's glossy black body.

"It's been a pleasure doing business with you, Mr. Winston."

"I'm just glad to be rid of it. Not too many people in the market for a widow maker."

"I love a car with history," Gary said, opening the door. "Especially if it's infamous."

"Well, you certainly got yourself that. Keys are in the ignition. Title's in the door pouch."

Gary slid in behind the steering wheel, his head nearly brushing the chop-top ceiling, and felt out the key. He turned it. The engine coughed to life, helped along by a few revs from Gary's right foot.

"We're gonna have to do something about these mufflers," he said.

"What's wrong with them?"

"Too quiet!" Gary cracked a smile, putting the car in gear and easing her out of the barn. He steered across the gravel and up to Frank's car. "Well?" he asked, getting out.

Frank was speechless for a moment. "It's gorgeous!" he finally exclaimed.

Gary pulled a small toolbox out of Frank's backseat. "I told you."

"But what's with the grille?"

"Hmm?"

"Why isn't it painted?"

Gary slid the toolbox across the '32's seat. "It'll get painted."

"But why isn't it already?"

"It had to be replaced. In fact, everything in front of the firewall's brand new." He lit a cigarette and puffed on it for a moment. "This was Hank Mitchellson's car."

Frank's jaw dropped again, further this time. Just then, Mr. Winston walked up.

"Everything to your liking?" he asked.

"Yes, sir," Gary replied, shaking hands with the man. "Like I said, pleasure doing business with you."

"Anytime, Mr. Bell. You fellas have yourselves a pleasant day." He waved, then disappeared into the house.

"Hank Mitchellson?!" Frank blurted. "The same poor bastard who got it in that Beach City chicken match? The same poor bastard who went through the windshield and ended up in the other guy's car?"

"Only half of him went through the windshield."

"Jesus Christ, Gary! What the hell are you doing buying a $700.00 coffin on wheels?"

"She's fast, Frank. A demon. Some fella up in Catalpa put her back together again, just like she was."

"Yeah, well, who put Hank Mitchellson back together again?"

"C'mon, Frankie! This is me we're talkin' about! Give me a steering wheel, a few tires and I'm in like Flynn. This little honey is fast. I had her up to an easy 100 the other day when I took her for a test drive, and I'm still in one piece. What are you so worried about?"

Frank sighed and shook his head, slowly. "Nothing, I guess. You want me to follow you home?"

"Nah. A guy in Belle Vista owes me money. I gotta go collect it." He rubbed his knuckles and then hunkered down into the hot rod.

Frank shook his head again. "Alright, then. I guess I'll see you tonight."

"If you're lucky." Gary flashed a smile, bringing the RPMs up a bit. "See you around, pal."

The landscape outside was blowing by in a blur. With one hand firmly planted on top of the steering wheel, the other on the shifter and both feet working the pedals, Gary was having the time of his life. The speedometer's needle was bouncing between 80 and 90 miles per hour, hardly Gary's fastest, but probably faster than anyone else had ever dared on the winding, packed dirt road that was twisting and falling beneath his wheels. The car felt alive, breathing, like a wild horse. He was guiding her, but at the same time had a strange sensation that he wasn't entirely in control. It was exhilarating. The road eventually turned to blacktop and took its course beside Whitefeather, hugging the western edge of the lake, and Gary decided that one of the many lakeside clearings would be as good a place as any to lose the mufflers. He found a suitable spot and pulled off.

After waiting for the exhaust to cool down somewhat,

Gary grabbed the toolkit and squeezed himself beneath the car, thankful for the two large, flat rocks he'd found to raise the front end up slightly. He went to work, unbolting everything from the headers back. The engine was still quite hot, as was the summer air, and he squinted at the sweat that was dripping into his eyes. A curse escaped as the wrench slipped, sending his knuckles into the drive shaft. While he was sucking on the fresh wound, he heard it; a faint rustle in the grass above his head. He froze, slowly craning his neck to see what its source was, and came face-to-snout with the ugliest snake he'd ever seen, a mere two inches from his face. His stomach dropped out from under him. The snake's tongue flickered, smelling him. Without thinking, Gary let his arm fly, flailing almost blindly at the serpent. The space beneath the car was too cramped; the snake obviously had the advantage. In a flurry of motion, while he was trying to cave its skull in with a wrench, it latched onto his arm, sinking its two, inch-long fangs into his flesh. It all seemed to happen in slow motion. The pain came a second later, and he frantically rolled out from beneath the car, grabbing the snake by the head, ripping it away from his forearm and squeezing as hard as he could. He felt bones snapping, but the snake was still writhing in his grasp, so he took it by the tail and planted its head into the side of the car with all of his might. After several swings that would've made Babe Ruth proud, and just as many new dents in the car door, the snake finally went limp. He glanced down at his arm; blood was trailing from the two, reddening puncture wounds.

"Son of a bitch..." he said through clenched teeth, as the pain began to mount. He moved his fingers, but could barely feel them, just a buzzing, intense numbness that was pulsing up and down his arm and shoulder. He needed a doctor, and fast. Not even bothering to pick up his tools or the disassembled exhaust pipes and mufflers, he flung the dead snake on the passenger's side of the car seat and brought the engine to life.

He wasn't sure if it was his speed or his vision or both,

but the road between him and Blossom County Medical passed by in a haze. His right arm sat lifelessly on the shifter; he could feel only pain. He'd ripped off his sleeve and tied it right above the wound, hoping to keep the venom from spreading, but it certainly didn't feel like his plan was working. The extra noise coming from the open headers was turning his already aching brain to mush. Finally, he arrived at the hospital. With his good arm, he swung the car to a crooked halt in front of the emergency room doors, grabbed the snake by the tail and went to stand. His legs buckled wildly beneath him, nearly sending him to the ground. He did his best to stagger toward the building. It took him a few moments, but he finally made it to the doors, stumbling through like a drunken sailor, right in front of a group of nurses who all gasped at the sight of the snake dangling from his hand.

"It's..." he tried forming a sentence, but his somewhat swollen tongue wasn't cooperating. "I... need to see a..."

One of the nurses, an older woman, stepped forward and took Gary by the elbow. "Right this way..." She turned back to a young, dark-haired nurse. "Susan, get Dr. Scott right away."

Gary awoke to his brow being patted with a cool, damp washcloth. It took him several moments to recall where he was and why, and when he did, he became acutely aware of the dull throbbing sensation on his entire right side.

"Good morning, Mr. Bell." The washcloth was apparently connected to a pleasant-sounding young woman.

Gary slowly opened his eyes, squinting at the sharp daylight that was coming in through his hospital room window. He wondered how long he'd been sleeping, but his vision was too blurry to read the wall clock. "What time is it?" Thankfully, his tongue had returned to its normal size.

"Seven-thirty. How are you feeling?"

He finally focused in on the nurse, a dark-haired, blue-eyed woman, probably just a year or two older than him.

She was gorgeous, in a girl-next-door kind of way. "I'll let you know as soon as I find out."

"Well, my name is Susan. If you need anything, let me or one of the other nurses know, okay?"

"Okay... Am I gonna live?"

"According to Dr. Scott, yes. That was smart of you, bringing the snake in to be identified."

"It was a cottonmouth, wasn't it?" Gary tried to move his legs slightly, wincing at their stiffness.

"I don't know. You'd better get some rest, though. The nurses' station is just outside your door if you need anything."

"Thanks... uh..." his brow furrowed.

"Susan."

"Susan." He made a mental note to get her phone number.

Two Weeks Later...

"Nope, nope, nope..." Gary said, shaking his head, squinting in the setting sunlight. "I don't race for pinks. Ten bucks."

"Aww, come on, man!" Bernie Keck whined, slapping the hood of his Mercury. He was quite obviously drunk. "Whatsamatter? Don't think you can beat me?"

Gary snorted. "Are you kiddin' me?" He looked around at the large group of cars gathered in the cemetery. "I could beat all'a you creeps blindfolded... with both arms tied behind my back."

"Well, then prove it, hotshot."

"Ten bucks is my final offer, Mack. Take it or leave it." Gary lit a cigarette, and then added, "For two reasons: one, I don't want that piece of shit car of yours in the first place, and two-"

"Hey..." Keck began to protest, stepping back to look at his car.

"Two, you never know what'll happen; I'm hard on this old girl," he patted the '32's door, right on the dents left by the cottonmouth's head. "and you just never know when something's gonna break. I'm not willing to risk her on that. This'll be her first race, too, so you should feel lucky I'm even gonna let you lose to me."

"Well..." Keck kicked at the dirt. "Twenty bucks, then."

"Ten."

"Fifteen."

Gary took a long drag on the Lucky Strike. He thought for a moment, running his fingers through his hair. "Fifteen...? Yeah, okay. Fifteen."

"Alright, deal! Let's go!" Keck ran around and hopped in his car.

"Now, wait a second, hold on... Who's gonna start us?" Gary's eyes roamed over the crowd of people, coming to rest on a sandy-haired young man about sixteen years old. "Toby LaRue?"

Toby's eyes widened, looking around to make sure he was the only Toby LaRue there. "Yeah?"

"Does your pop know you're out here?"

"Uh... Well, kinda..."

"C'mere," Gary waved him over. He reached through the car window and pulled out a flashlight. "You think you can handle this?" he asked, grabbing the cigarette that dangled from Toby's lips and flicking it away.

Toby took the flashlight. "You bet I can, Gary!"

"Alright." He turned to Keck, who already had his car started. "Let's go."

"Yeah!"

Gary opened the '32's door and settled in. "Okay, baby doll..." he whispered to the car, knocking on the dashboard. "Time to wake up." He started the engine and pulled out of the cemetery onto Ello Lane, lining up to the right of Keck's Mercury. He watched as a group of cars and trucks, all loaded with spectators, pulled out after him and took off for the finish line, roughly a quarter of a mile down the tree-lined road. Toby walked out to stand in between the two cars. He gave both Gary and Keck a thumbs up. Gary revved the engine, one hand gripping the steering wheel, the other hand firmly planted on the shifter. He sure hoped that whoever put this car back together knew what they were doing... because he didn't have fifteen bucks. He didn't even have ten. His eyes focused on the end of the flashlight. "C'mon, kid, let's get this-" Toby flipped the light on and Gary instantly dropped the clutch, sending a hail of gravel and dust out from under the car's rear tires. Keck was about even with him on the start, which caught him by surprise, given the young man's lack of sobriety. Second gear. He began to gain some traction and felt himself being pressed into the seat. Keck was right there with him. That piece of junk must be more than meets the eye, he thought. He grit his teeth and power shifted into third, not letting off the gas, silently praying that the transmission wouldn't blow apart, and finally began pulling ahead of the Mercury, but only slightly. He pressed down on the accelerator as hard as he could, the engine screaming through the open headers. Up ahead, the finish line was getting close; he could see people standing around, pumping their fists in the air. He allowed a quick look to the left. Keck's front bumper was about even with his door. "Come on, baby, don't blow..." He glanced at the tachometer, and then wished he hadn't; the needle was well past the redline, closing in on 6500 RPMs. "Jesus..." he muttered. Almost there. About a hundred feet to go. The Merc was holding steady at his side, not falling behind at all. Fifty feet. He was only going to win this one by inches, and that was if everything held together. *Twenty... Ten... Finish line.* He immediately shoved in the clutch pedal and threw the shifter into neutral. "*Whew...* Damn, that was close." He let out all the breath he'd been holding. "First thing I'm doing when we get home is tearing you apart. You gotta be quicker than that around here, Cottonmouth..."

About the Author

James Russell was born in 1985 and grew up in the small, rural town of East Sparta, Ohio, to a family of drag racers, mechanics and (a few) hoodlams. More than anything, he loves a warm day at the races surrounded by friends and fast cars, but also enjoys an evening at home in the garage, where most of his writing takes place, under the watchful eyes of his feline companion Lila.

www.ingramcontent.com/pod-product-compliance
Lightning Source LLC
Chambersburg PA
CBHW020053180626
46812CB00006B/2315